PENGUIN BOOKS

# DAYS OF AWE

A. M. Homes is the author of the memoir *The Mistress's Daughter* and the novels *This Book Will Save Your Life*, *Music for Torching*, *The End of Alice*, *In a Country of Mothers*, and *Jack*, as well as the story collections *The Safety of Objects* and *Things You Should Know*. She lives in New York City.

## Praise for *Days of Awe*

"A. M. Homes skillfully circles and tugs at the question of what it means to live in flawed, fragile, hungry human bodies. . . . *Days of Awe* is sliced through with Homes's dark humor. . . . One wants to read passages of a Homes story aloud because they are so fine. . . . *Days of Awe* feels like the part of the day when the sun is about to go down and the light is brighter while the shadows are darker. Everything has a sharp edge, is strikingly beautiful and suddenly also a little menacing."
—Ramona Ausubel, *The New York Times Book Review*

"Exuberantly transgressive." —*O, the Oprah Magazine*

"[Homes] has shown a unique penchant for cracking open the dark heart of human nature—with irreverent wit, devastating empathy, and haunting shocks . . . *Days of Awe* [is] a memorable assortment of new tales about family, love, death, and an unqualified man who somehow stumbles into becoming a populist political candidate." —Mary Elizabeth Williams, *Salon*

"Homes's keen ear for speech—surreal as her characters' conversations often are—lends itself to varying degrees of self-aware misunderstanding, highlighting the complexity of language and the challenges . . . The impossibility of knowing another person completely is one of life's painful truths, and [this] collection remind us of that—but [it] also shows that there are, at least, tools available to help us try." —*Vanity Fair*

"Fascinating . . . I consumed these stories exactly like a spectator of a good fight or a neighbor peering through the hedge, and I felt sharply observed in turn. Homes, with her fierce sharp wit, reveals her characters' deep flaws. No one gets away with anything and the spectacle is delightful."
—Molly Livingston, *The Paris Review Daily*

"With dark humor and sharp dialogue, Homes plumbs the depths of everyday American anxieties through stories about unexpected situations."  —*Time*

"In the title story, a Holocaust survivor taps into a theme of the collection when he describes the way people hold the history of previous generations inside them. 'We carry it with us, not just in our grandmother's silver,' he says, 'but in our bodies, the cells of our hearts.'"  —*The Wall Street Journal*

"Versatile and imaginative, Homes brings her literary daring and prowess . . . to short stories. . . . In her third provocative story collection, she displays her command of the viciously realistic and the pointedly surreal, the comic and the tragic. A master of honed dialogue—play-like in their momentum, many of these tales have an Edward Albee aura—Homes is also potently visual and acknowledges artists who inspire her. . . . [It] is the searing precision of her language and her profound and thorny concerns that infuse these unpredictable tales with their unnerving power. . . . Virtuoso Homes, aligned with Grace Paley, Joy Williams, and Lydia Millet, is fierce, witty, defining, and compassionate."  —*Booklist* (starred review)

"With her signature humor and compassion, A. M. Homes exposes the heart of an uneasy America in her new collection—exploring our attachments to each other through characters who aren't quite who they hoped to become, though there is no one else they can be."  —*Chicago Review of Books*

## Also by A.M. Homes

# Days of Awe

A.M. Homes

PENGUIN BOOKS

PENGUIN BOOKS
An imprint of Penguin Random House LLC
penguinrandomhouse.com

First published in the United States of America by Viking Penguin,
an imprint of Penguin Random House LLC, 2018
Published in Penguin Books 2019

"Brother on Sunday" first appeared in *The New Yorker*; "Whose Story Is It and Why Is
It Always on Her Mind?" in *The National Media Museum*; "Days of Awe" in *Granta*;
"Hello Everybody" in *Electric Literature*; "All Is Good Except for the Rain" in *The Guardian*;
"Your Mother Was a Fish" in *Ghaha Amer*, Gagosian Gallery; "The Last Good Time" in
*Insomnia and the Greenhouse*, Koen van den Broek, Hatje Cantz Germany; "Be Mine" in
*The Guardian* and *East Magazine*; "A Prize for Every Player" in *Bill Owens Collected Works*,
Damiani Editore, Italy; "The Omega Point, or Happy Birthday Baby" in *One Story*
and *Petah Coyne: Everything That Rises Must Converge*, MASS MoCA;
"She Got Away" in *Playboy*.

ISBN 9780143133261 (paperback)

THE LIBRARY OF CONGRESS HAS CATALOGED THE HARDCOVER EDITION AS FOLLOWS:
Names: Homes, A. M., author.
Title: Days of awe / A.M. Homes.
Description: New York, New York : Viking, [2018] |
Identifiers: LCCN 2018013217 (print) | LCCN 2018026667 (ebook) |
ISBN 9780525558934 (ebook) | ISBN 9780670025497 (hardback)
Subjects: | BISAC: FICTION / Family Life. | FICTION / Short Stories
(single author). | FICTION / Literary. | GSAFD: Short stories.
Classification: LCC PS3558.O448 (ebook) | LCC PS3558.O448 A6 2018 (print) |
DDC 813/.54—dc23
LC record available at https://lccn.loc.gov/2018013217

Printed in the United States of America
1  3  5  7  9  10  8  6  4  2

Set in Garamond Pro
Designed by Cassandra Garruzzo

*For Katherine*

# Contents

# Days of Awe

# Brother on Sunday

She is on the phone. He can see her reflection in the bathroom mirror, the headset wrapped around her ear as if she were an air-traffic controller or a Secret Service agent. "Are you sure?" she whispers. "I can't believe it. I don't want to believe it. If it's true, it's horrible. . . . Of course I don't know anything! If I knew something, I'd tell you. . . . No, he doesn't know anything either. If he knew, he'd tell me. We vowed we wouldn't keep secrets." She pauses, listening for a moment. "Yes, of course, not a word."

"Tom," she calls. "Tom, are you ready?"

"In a minute," he says.

He examines himself in her makeup mirror. He raises his eyebrows, bares his teeth, smiles. And then he smiles again, harder, showing gum. He tilts his head, left and right, checking where the shadows fall. He turns on the light and flips the mirror to the magnifying side. A thin silver needle enters the reflection; there's a close-up of skin, the glistening tip of the needle, surrounded by a halo of light. He blinks. The needle goes into the skin; his hand is steady on the syringe. He injects a little here, a little there; it's just a touch-up, a filler-up. Later, when someone says, "You look great," he'll smile and his face will bend gently, but no lines will appear. "Doctor's orders," he'll say. He recaps the syringe, tucks it into his shirt pocket, flips the toilet seat up, and pees.

When he comes out of the bathroom, his wife, Sandy, is there, in the bedroom, waiting. "Who was that on the phone?" he asks.

"Sara," she says.

He waits, knowing that silence will prompt her to say more.

"Susie called Sara to say that she's worried Scott is having an affair."

He says, quite honestly, "Of all people, Scott isn't someone I'd think would be having an affair."

"She doesn't know that he's having an affair—she just suspects." Sandy puts her cover-up into a tote bag and hands him his camera. "Can't leave without this," she says.

"Thanks," he says. "Are you ready to go?"

"Check my back," she says. "I felt something." She turns, lifting her blouse.

"You have a tick," he says, plucking it off her.

Somewhere in the summer house, a loud buzzer goes off. "The towels are done," she says. "Should we take wine?" he asks.

"I packed a bottle of champagne and some orange juice. It is Sunday, after all."

"My brother is coming after all," he says. His brother, Roger, visits the beach once a year, like a tropical storm that changes everything.

"It's a beautiful day," she says. And she's right.

Tom sits in a low chair, facing the water, his feet buried in the sand. Just in front of him, hanging from the lifeguard stand, an American flag softly flutters. His sunglasses are his shield, his thick white lotion a kind of futuristic body armor that lets him imagine he is invisible. He believes that on the beach you are allowed to stare, as though you were looking not at the person but through the person, past the person at the water, past the water to the horizon, past the horizon into infinity.

He is seeing things that he would otherwise not allow himself to see. He is staring. He is in awe, mesmerized by the body, by the grace and lack of grace. He takes pictures—"studies," he calls them. It's his habit, his hobby. What is he looking for? What is he thinking while he does this? This is something he asks himself, noting that he often thinks of himself in the third person—a dispassionate observer.

The beach fills up, towels are unrolled, umbrellas unfurl like party decorations, and as the heat builds, bodies are slowly unwrapped. He, of all people, knows what's real and what's not. There are those who have starved the flesh off their bones and those who have had it surgically removed or relocated. Each person wears it differently—the dimpling on the thighs, the love handles, the inevitable sag. He can't help noticing.

Around him his friends talk. He's not listening carefully enough to register exactly who is saying what—just the general impression, the flow. "Did you have the fish last night? I made a fish. We bought a fish. His brother loves to fish. I bought a necklace. We bought a house. I bought another watch. He's thinking of getting a new car. Didn't you just get one last year? I want to renovate. Your house is so beautiful. His wife used to be so beautiful. Do you remember her? Could never forget. Tom went out with her once."

"Just once?"

"He doesn't have the best social skills," his wife says.

Now they are talking about him. He knows he should defend himself. He lowers the camera and turns toward them.

"Why do you always say that?"

"Because it's true," Sandy says.

"It may be, but that's not why I only went out with her once."

"Why didn't you date her again?" she wants to know.

"Because I met you," he says, raising the camera as if inserting a punctuation mark.

The intensity of the sunlight is such that he has to squint in order to see, and at times he can't see at all—there is a blinding abundance of light and reflection. He thinks of a blind girl who lived in his neighborhood when he was growing up: Audra Stevenson. She was smart and very pretty. She wore dark glasses and tapped her way down the sidewalk with her cane, a thick white bulb on the end of it. He used to watch her go down the street and wonder if she wore her glasses at home. He wondered what her eyes looked like. Perhaps they were very sensitive; perhaps she oversaw—that's how he thought of it. Maybe she wasn't blind in the sense of everything's being black but blind in that there was too much light, so that everything was overexposed and turned a milky white with only spots of color punching through—a red shirt, a brown branch, the grayish shadows of people. He asked her out once. He stopped her on the street and introduced himself.

"I know who you are," she said. "You're the boy who watches me go home."

"How do you know that?" he asked.

"I'm blind," she said, "not dumb."

He picked her up at her house, hooked his elbow through hers, and led her to the movie theater. During the film he whispered in her ear, an ongoing narration of the action, until finally she said, "Sh-h-h. I can't hear what they're saying if you keep talking to me."

After the date, Roger, who was two years older, made fun of him for being too shy to ask a "regular girl" out and, no doubt, for going on a date long before Roger himself ever would. No girl was good enough for Roger: eyebrows were too thick, Grace's chin too long,

Molly's eyes too wide, Ruthie's laugh too high-pitched. Every girl was just one twist of the genetic helix away from having a syndrome of some sort. Roger mocked "Tom the younger," as he liked to call him, loudly, as Audra was walking away, and Tom was so mortified, so sure that Audra had heard every word, that he never spoke to her again.

Behind him they are still talking. "Arctic char, orata, Chilean sea bass, swordfish, ahi tuna. Mole sauce, ancho chili, a rub, a marinade, a pesto, a ragout, a teriyaki reduction." They love to talk about food and exercise—running, biking, tennis, Pilates, trainers, workouts, cleansing diets. The one thing they don't talk much about anymore is sex; the ones who are having it can't imagine not having it, and the ones who aren't having it remember all too well when they were the ones having it and saying they couldn't imagine not having it. So it has become off-limits. Also not discussed is the fact that some of them are having sex with one another's spouses— i.e., hiding in plain sight.

He is only half listening, thinking about how life changes. If he met these people now, he's not sure he would be their friend, not sure he would have dinner with them every Saturday night, play tennis with them every Sunday, vacation with them twice a year, see the movies they see, eat at the places they eat at, do whatever it is that they all do together just because they're a kind of club—all while worrying about what will happen if he strays, if he does something other than what they expect of him, and he doesn't mean sex, he means something more. He looks at his friends; their wives all wear the same watches, like tribal decorations, symbols of their status. The gold glints in the sun.

He is looking at them as they absently sift sand with their hands and imagining them as children in cotton hats, pouring sand from one bucket to another as their parents talk over and around them.

He is thinking of their parents, now either dead or single in their eighties or attended by new "companions" they met in physical therapy or on Elderhostel vacations. He looks at his friends and wonders what they will be like if they make it to eighty. The men seem oblivious to the inevitability of aging, oblivious to the fact that they are no longer thirty, to the fact that they are not superheroes with special powers. He thinks of the night, a year ago, when they were all at a local restaurant and one of them went to grab something from the car. He ran across the road as though he thought he glowed in the dark. But he didn't. The driver of an oncoming car didn't see him. He flew up and over it. And when someone came into the restaurant to call the police, Tom went out, not because he was thinking of his friend but because he was curious, always curious. Once outside, realizing what had happened, he ran to his friend and tried to help, but there was nothing to be done. The next day, driving by the spot, he saw one of his friend's shoes—they had each bought a pair of the same kind the summer before—suspended from a tree.

"What time is Roger coming?" someone asks.

"Not sure," he says.

A friend's wife leans over and shows him a red dot, buried between her breasts. "What do you think this is?"

"Bug bite," he says.

"Not skin cancer?"

"Not cancer," he says.

"Not infected?"

"Bug bite," he says.

"And what about this?" She shows him something else, as though hoping for bonus points. This spot is on what his father jokingly used to call "the tenderloin," her inner thigh.

"Isn't it funny that your father was a butcher and you're in the business of dealing with human meat?" another of the friends asks.

"It's all flesh and blood," he says, pressing the spot with his finger. "Pimple."

"Are you sure?"

"Yes."

"Not skin cancer."

"Does it look infected?"

"If you leave it alone, it'll be fine," he says.

He is forever being asked to step into the spare bedroom, the bathroom, the kitchen, even the walk-in closet, because someone wants to show him something. It's as though they were pulling him aside to make a confession. Mostly the answer is easy. Mostly whatever it is is nothing. But every now and then, he's surprised; they show him something that catches him off guard. "How'd you get that?" he asks.

"You don't want to know," they say.

But of course in the end they tell him more than he wants to know.

"Was your father really a butcher?" the visiting sister of one of the friends asks.

"Yep. And he really talked about women's bodies like they were cuts of meat. 'Boy, she's got good veal cheeks! That girl would make one hell of a rib roast, trussed, bound, and stuffed.' And then he'd laugh in a weird way. My mother thought of herself as an artist. She signed up for a life-drawing class when I was eleven, and she took me with her, because she thought I'd appreciate it. I just sat there, not knowing where to look. Finally, the instructor said, 'Draw with us?' I'd never seen a bare breast before—drawing it was like touching it. I drew that breast again and again. And then I glanced at my mother's easel and saw that she'd drawn everything but the woman. She'd drawn the table with the vase, the flowers, the window in the background, the drapes, but not the model. The instructor asked her, 'Where's the girl?' 'I prefer a still life,' my mother said. 'But my son, on the other hand, look how beautiful he thinks she is!'"

"Was she being mean?"

He shrugs.

"She shouldn't have taken you to the class," Sandy says. "She was teasing you."

"I thought maybe I'd take Roger out on the boat this afternoon," one of the friends says. "Sound like fun?"

"Only if you capsize," he says cryptically. The friend laughs, knowing that he isn't kidding.


Ahead of him on the beach, a boy is spreading lotion on an older woman. He imagines the viscous feel of lotion warm from the sun, gliding over her skin—friction. He imagines the boy painting the woman with lotion and then using his fingernail to write his initials on her back. He thinks of a time in St. Barts, when Sandy was lying nude on the beach while he painted, and he picked up his brush and began making swirls on her skin. He painted her body, and then he photographed her walking away from him into the water. In the sea the paint ran down her skin in beautiful color. Later, one of the friends, the one with the boat, confessed, "I got hard just watching."

"You should try it sometime," he said. "With your wife."

"Oh, we did, that night, but I didn't have any paint. All I could find was a ballpoint pen. It wasn't the same."

"Drink?" Sandy asks, snapping him back into the moment.

"Sure," he says. She pours a combination of orange juice and champagne into a plastic cup and leans toward him. He can smell her, her perfume, the salty beach. As he takes the drink, it splashes up out of the cup and onto his arm. He licks it, his tongue tickled by the carbonation, the flavor of citrus, of wine, mixed with salt and sweat. He thinks that it's strange he can't remember ever having tasted himself before. His tongue rakes the fur on his forearm and picks up a tinge of blood from a scrape this morning. The flavor is good, full of life.

"Is Roger still with that woman?" one of the wives asks.

"His hygienist?" he asks.

"Is that who it was?" the friend asks.

"Yep, he left his wife to fuck the hygienist."

"And he's still with her," Sandy says.

"She must rinse and spit. I assume she doesn't swallow," he says.

"Stop, you're being crude."

He wonders when Roger is coming. On the one hand, he's dreading his brother's arrival; on the other, he's starting to think it's rude that Roger's not there yet and hasn't called to say he's running late. Tom closes his eyes. The sun is high. He feels it baking him, and then, suddenly, a shadow, like a cloud, crosses over him. He shivers. One of the women, Terri, is standing in front of him, holding out a plate of muffins. "High-protein, high-fiber. Take one." She had breast cancer a year ago—a mastectomy—and six weeks later they were all on their annual St. Barts adventure. When everyone went to the beach, she stayed in the house. They all talked about her behind her back, worrying that they were doing something that made her uncomfortable. Then, on the third day, just before lunch, she walked out onto the beach and stood before them. He took a picture. She unbuttoned her blouse. He took another picture. Her husband started to get up, to stop her, but one of the women grabbed his arm, holding him back. Terri unbuttoned her blouse and opened it, revealing the remaining breast and the red rope of a scar. Click, click, click. He shot her again and again. In the end what was amazing about the images was not the scar but her expression—terrified, defiant, vulnerable, her face in a dance of emotion, frame by frame. He gave her a set of prints—it was one of the rare times that he was the one to take someone aside, into his study. When she opened the package, she wept. "For a million reasons," she said. "For what was lost, for what remains, for how you saw what no one else did—they were all too busy looking at my boob."

"A meal in a muffin," he says, biting it. "It's perfect."

In front of them, a woman is stepping out of her shorts. One side of her bathing suit is unceremoniously wedged in the crack of her ass; she pulls it out with a loud snap. Her rear end is what Sandy calls "coagulated," a cottage cheese of cellulite, and, below it, spider veins explode down her legs like fireworks.

"Do you ever look at something like that and think about how you could fix it?" Terri asks.

"The interesting thing is that the woman doesn't seem bothered by it. The people who come to me are bothered by their bodies. They don't go to the beach and disrobe in public. They come into my office with a list of what they want fixed—like it's a scratch-and-dent shop."

"Maybe she doesn't realize how bad it looks?"

"Maybe," he says. "And maybe that's okay." He thinks about Botox and Restylane and lasering spider veins and resurfacing a face, and sometimes he feels like a conservator, like the guy he once sat next to at a dinner who worked at the Met, touching up artworks when they chipped or when the ceiling leaked on them.

He thinks about the time he volunteered to go on a mission

with a group of doctors who were heading to an impoverished spot to do good for five days—a kind of spiritual recompense for the fortune that modern elective cosmetic procedures had brought them. He fixed cleft palates, treated skin rashes, gave routine immunizations. "I've heard of it," his mother said. "What's it called again, Doctors Without Licenses? Maybe next time you could take Roger—he's an excellent dentist. Everyone needs a good dentist, rich or poor. It would be nice if the two of you did something together."

"Do you think he'd rather play tennis?" the friend asks. "Would it be more fun for Roger to play a round-robin or go out on the boat?"

"I have no idea," he says. "I'm not Roger."

"He always gets like this when his brother comes," Sandy says.

"Since I was five, Roger has been stealing my friends."

"Your friends are nice to him because he's your brother. Roger can't steal them."

"Roger thinks they're his friends. He tells everyone that he was the favorite, that I was an afterthought, an accident."

"Were you?" someone asks.

"All you have to do is get through it," Sandy says. "It'll be over soon."

"Not soon enough," he says.

"You have nice friends. Who wouldn't want them?" the visiting sister says. As she rolls over, her top drops off. His eyes are reflexively drawn in—her nipples are large and brown, more beautiful than he would have imagined.

"Hey, there." A booming voice goes off like a bomb in his head—Roger. "I thought I'd find all you flabby asses here. If it's Sunday, they must be at the beach." Roger smiles, his hundred-thousand-dollar smile. Click. Tom catches the poppy seeds at the gum line.

Click. He's got Roger's pink shorts with embroidered martini glasses. Click. Roger is wearing crocodile tassel loafers. "Tommy, can you put the fucking camera down and actually say hello?"

"Hello. Are you on your own? We thought maybe you'd bring what's-her-name, your hygienist? We were just talking about her."

"She's got her kids this weekend. Twins."

"Roger, come sit next to me." Sandy gives her chair to Roger and pours him a drink.

"Breakfast of champions," Roger says, sipping the mimosa.

"We were wondering when you'd get here," Tom says.

"I stopped to hit a bucket of balls. Oh, God," Roger says, "isn't that Blarney Stone?"

"Who is Blarney Stone?" the visiting sister asks.

"That rock star—is that his real name?" someone says.

"Yeah, I think it is," he says, and now they're all squinting and staring at an exceptionally pale, skinny figure in a form-fitting swimsuit.

"That suit must have been made for him," Terri says.

"As skinny as he is, he's still got a little paunch," Roger says. "Do you remember how Dad used to do a thousand sit-ups every morning in his underwear?"

"It wasn't a thousand, more like a hundred."

"Whatever. He thought of himself as a perfect specimen."

"Yes. And Mom used to say, 'Your father is a beautiful man.' It gave me the creeps." Tom puts his camera back in the bag.

"What do you make of that guy?" Roger points to someone farther along the beach.

"Don't point," Tom says, horrified.

"Poliosis," Roger says.

"Actually, that's piebaldism—dark and light patches on the skin. Poliosis is the white forelock."

"Like Susan Sontag," the friend's sister says.

"Roger, what appeals—boat or tennis?" the friend asks.

"I don't know. Tom-Tom, what do you think?"

"Boat," Tom says.

"If brother says boat, I go with tennis. A word to the wise: Never do what brother says." Roger laughs alone.

Tom stands. "I've got a headache. I need to go home. Go on the boat—the water looks rough, it'll be exciting—and I'll see you later."

"Should I come home with you?" Sandy asks. "Are you okay?"

"It's just a headache from the champagne. I don't usually drink at breakfast."

"I'll come with you," Sandy says.

"Don't," he says firmly, hating her because he knows she doubts that the headache is legitimate. "I'll see you later. We're all set for dinner?"

"All set," Roger says. "I made the reservation myself."

Later Tom and Sandy argue about it.

"Of course I knew your headache was real. I offered to leave with you."

"You offered to leave because it was the thing to do in front of the others, but you didn't mean it."

"I'm not doing this," Sandy says. "I can't prove that I meant what I said. You should take me at my word."

"You think I'm faking a headache because Roger is here, but you're the one who brought champagne to the beach. Who does that? Who pours people drinks at eleven in the morning when everyone is just sitting there baking in the sun?"

"Now you're blaming me for your headache," Sandy says. "Next you'll say that I tried to poison you."

Roger knocks on their bedroom door. "Excuse me," he says,

knowing all too well that his timing is lousy. "I forgot my floss. Can you imagine that, a dentist forgetting his floss? Have you got some I could use?"

"No," Tom says.

Sandy goes into the bathroom and returns with floss.

"Thanks, sweetie," Roger says.

"No problem," she says. Roger leaves the room. "Can we just stop for now? Let's just get ready for dinner."

"Nice that Roger picked the best place in town. Is he paying?"

"I have no idea," Sandy says.

"Do me a favor and don't do that thing where you order two appetizers and then I get stuck paying the same as if you'd ordered a rack of lamb."

"Am I supposed to order something I don't want?"

"In this case yes. Order something special, treat yourself. Have the fish."

"Why don't you just order two main courses? Instead of getting a starter, why don't you just leap right in and have a fish and a steak?"

"Because people would notice. They'd say, 'Oh, you should pay more, you ate double.' They never notice when you eat less."

"This is the least of your problems," she says, spraying herself with perfume.

Tom sits on the other side of the table, leaving Roger to the friends. When the waiter offers them the wine list, Roger takes it, studying carefully.

"See something appealing?" Sandy asks.

"The wine list is mediocre at best," Roger says, "but I'll find something. That's the true test, finding quality where there is none."

At the table next to them, an old couple are having dinner with their adult child; the couple are in their eighties and refer to each other as Mommy and Daddy.

"Daddy, what are you going to have?"

"I don't know, Mommy. How about you?"

"I'll have the snapper," the son, who must be sixty, says.

"I'll go with the sole, as long as it's not soaking in butter—it's not soaking, is it?" Mommy asks the waiter.

"It's perfect for you," the waiter says.

After the first course, Tom gets up to go to the men's room; one of his friends follows him. Here we go again, he thinks, imagining that the friend is going to show him something—a fungus between his toes, a ditzel on his chest. He doesn't turn around.

When they are side by side at the urinals, the friend says, "I'm leaving Terri."

"What are you talking about?" Tom says, genuinely shocked.

"I can't stand it anymore. I'm miserable."

"Is it because of the cancer?"

The friend shakes his head no. "Everyone will think that's why, but it has nothing to do with it. I was going to leave last year, before she got sick."

"Did you meet someone?"

"Yes, but that's not why."

"It's always why. Men don't leave unless they've met someone."

He shrugs. "Terri doesn't know."

"About the other woman?"

"About anything. I'm telling you first. I don't know what to say to her. We've been married for twenty-six years."

"That's a long time."

"She'll be fine," he says, "once she gets over the initial shock."

At the sink Tom checks his face in the mirror. "When are you going to tell her?" he asks, watching himself talking.

"I don't know," the friend says. "Please don't tell Sandy. The girls can't keep a secret."

"Not a word."

And they go back to the table.

"Everything okay?" Sandy asks.

"Wonderful," he says, reaching for the wine.

"If you have a headache, maybe you shouldn't drink," she says.

"Trust me, I need a drink."

At the end of the meal, at the table next to them, Daddy is asleep. He has basically fallen asleep in his scallops, a dot of sour cream on his tie.

"Daddy," his wife says, waking him. "Do you want some dessert?"

His head lifts, as if he had only been looking for his napkin under the table. "Do they have vanilla ice cream?" he asks.

"We do," the waiter says.

"And what do they get for that?" Daddy asks.

"Six-fifty," Mommy says, looking at her menu.

"I'll have it at home," Daddy says.

And the son says to the waiter, "We'll take the check."

Roger pays for dinner, and they all thank him.

"You didn't have to," Sandy says.

"I know I didn't."

"You can buy them dinner, but you can't buy their friendship," Tom hisses into Roger's ear.

"Shall I drive?" Sandy asks.

"I'll drive," Tom says.

"You drank," she says.

"Not so much."

"Enough," she says, taking the keys.

Back at the house, Tom and Roger are having a drink in the living room, a nightcap and a cigar. Sandy excuses herself for a moment, and when she comes back, the brothers are on the sofa, pummeling each other.

"What happened?" she asks.

Neither says a word.

What happened was that Roger said something like, "Really too bad about Sandy. She used to be such a looker."

And, not sure that he was hearing it right, Tom said, "What do you mean?"

And Roger said, "Well, you know, she's let herself go, and I imagine that for someone like you it must be depressing. I never was all about a great figure or a pretty face. As you know, for me it's the smile—they've got to have the smile."

"I think you should leave," Tom says.

"Well, that would be awkward, wouldn't it?" Roger says.

"Not really."

"If I leave, I'm not coming back—ever," Roger says.

Tom is giddy with the idea but says nothing.

"When Mom hears about this, she's going to be very angry," Roger says.

"You're fifty-three years old and still threatening to tell Mom?" Tom says.

"Fine, you little fucker, how about I call your friend Bobby and tell him I can't go on the boat tomorrow because you kicked me out of the house? And I'll call your other friend and tell him you were staring at his wife's one boob."

And, with that, Sandy says, "Get him," and Tom punches Roger. "You ungrateful little son of a . . ."

"Butcher and an artist," Roger says.

# Whose Story Is It, and
# Why Is It Always on Her Mind?

She is seeing the doctor now; it was a condition of her release.

"The thorns?" he asks.

"Yes," she says. Having plucked them from rose stems, she drove the thorns deep into her skin, pressing them like shark's teeth, in a line up and down her arms. She pressed the thorns into her skin until the skin gave way and buried the thorn. And then she took off her shoes and pushed the thorns into her feet and walked from park to park, carefully collecting more thorns—"specimens," she called them. Her wounds became infected, the infection spread into her blood.

"We almost lost you," her mother said.

"I was right here the whole time, hiding in plain sight."

"I see you are walking with a limp," the doctor says.

"I am treading lightly."

"Why thorns?"

"It runs in the family."

She glances over her shoulder to see if the doctor is listening and catches him off guard.

Their eyes meet, and she looks away.

———————

"Continue," the doctor says.

She lies back; her fingers stroke the deep blue fabric on the doctor's couch.

"My mother rearranges the furniture constantly. She is trying to re-create something that she remembers, but I'm not sure it ever really happened. She says she is getting closer. She is no longer young, but she gathers the energy to push the sofa around the room. And when she is done, she cries. It will never be the same again. It is always almost there, but not quite. She can't put her finger on it—the light, the silence? Every day she tries a new combination, hoping the pieces will fall into place like the pin tumblers of a lock, hoping that there will be an opening and something will be revealed or recovered. 'Where are you going with that?' I ask as she moves a lamp from this table to that. 'I am going back to where I came from,' she says. 'But it does not exist,' I say. She makes still lifes, tableaux of how she wishes it were. 'Is it the same sofa—the one from before?' she asks me, now confused. 'That's what you've always told me.' 'I don't know anymore,' she says. 'Maybe it came after the fact.' She calls the war 'the fact.' My mother's sofa is also blue."

Finished for today, she gets up carefully.


The next time she visits the doctor, she notices a hair. She sees it as she is approaching the doctor's couch, a blond hair like a golden thread, glinting in the light. She doesn't know what to do—pick it up, stretch it between her fingers and pluck it like a harp string? She imagines winding it round and round a finger until the finger turns blue, pressing it against her neck like a fine gold wire. What to do? She pretends not to see it. She lies down on it—the blond hair beneath her own brown hair, the blond hair becoming for the time a part of her. But she can't bear it. Whose hair is it? Does the doctor have sex on the sofa?

"My mother was born the day before the war ended. She was a girl without a father, a miracle. For a long time, she believed that—we all did. The fact is, during the war my grandmother was left at a Catholic boarding school. Her parents brought her there in the middle of the night, turned their backs and left. As she screamed for them, the nuns held their hands over her mouth. The way the story goes—he appeared in the garden behind the school. She pretended not to know what happened—but it's possible she really didn't know. It was a war. She was terrified they would die. The only thing that kept her sane was that the roses went on blooming. That's where they found her—entangled in the rosebushes, pinned by the spindly arms of the prickly vines. He came into the garden, bent to smell the roses, and saw her. He pushed her into the roses. When he was gone, she remained trapped. She lay in the garden all night. She watched the sky grow dark, the stars come out. She looked up into the blue, the eternal, the unending, and the unnamable. She was asleep when they found her. Grandmother woke up, but only partially, it was as if she were under a spell, in a fog. We thought she would come out from under, but mostly she seemed baffled, like it all just didn't make sense. As a child my mother knew that her mother hated her, but she didn't know why or what she had done wrong. My mother kept herself hidden, in boxes or under the table, inside closets. She would pretend she was invisible. Later she would hide in the woods, behind trees, or in piles of leaves. She would play chameleon and practice shifting her skin to match the environment. When other children came to play, my mother would hide, and only after they left would she rush to the window, press her face to the glass, and look at them leaving. My mother found out when she was about thirteen; she doesn't remember how, but she said it explained a lot. When she found out, she went on a nighttime rampage through all the parks of London and cut the roses. She brought back hundreds of roses. She filled my grandmother's house with roses from bud to bloom to past their prime—cabbage rose, common rose, tea rose—each with delicate petals like human flesh, each with a perfume, a beautiful scent turned putrid. The theft of roses was a crime; the roses belonged to the city, to the people, and they were not for the benefit of just one. The story of the theft made all the papers. Her mother was horrified and threatened to turn her daughter over to the authorities. 'I can't have this. It is too much. You are doing it to me again. You are just like your father. You are the proof that you can't escape your history.' And together they cut the roses and their long, thorny stems into tiny little pieces and boiled them down." She pauses. "Does anyone have a life of their own?" she asks the doctor.

He doesn't answer.

Her third visit is different; there is something on the sofa—like a doily, or a napkin covering the little pillow. Is the hair still beneath it? Is it being hidden, kept safe? She lies back and says nothing. She looks at the room, the light through the windows, a lamp, part of a painting, an extra chair, and a table with a plant. She is thinking of her mother moving furniture, of her grandmother trapped in the roses. She stares at the plant—a beautiful white-and-purple orchid—and wonders, did the doctor buy it or receive it as a gift?

"Is it real?" she asks.

"Does it look real?" the doctor answers.

When the session is over, she sits up. The room spins, a kaleidoscope, blurring. She falls back on the sofa.

"Your time is up for today," the doctor says. But she cannot get up. The doctor seems flummoxed—this has not happened before. He goes to his desk, rummages through the drawer, and finds a tin of hard candy. He offers her one; it is red and the shape of a rose. She sucks the candy and the succor works wonders. She dreams she is walking on water and it is raining rose petals.

# Days of Awe

He is the War Correspondent, she is the Transgressive Novelist. They have been flown in for the summit on Genocide(S). She spots him at the airport baggage claim and nods in the direction of a student holding up a legal pad with his name written on it in heavy black marker—misspelled.

"Want to share my ride?" he asks.

Caught off guard, she shakes her head no.

She doesn't want anyone picking her up, doesn't want the obligation to entertain the young student/fan/retired teacher/part-time real-estate broker for the forty-five minutes it takes to get where they're going.

Every time she says yes to these things—conferences, readings, guest lectures—it's because she hasn't learned to say no. And she has the misguided fantasy that time away from home will allow her to think, to get something done. She has brought work with her: the short story she can't crack, the novel she's supposed to finish, the friend's book that needs a blurb, last Sunday's newspaper. . . .

"Nice to see you," the man at the car-rental place says, even though they've never met. He gives her the keys to a car with New Hampshire plates, LIVE FREE OR DIE. She drives north toward the small college town where experts in torture politics and murder, along with neuroscientists, academics, survivors, and a few "special guests," will convene in what's become an ongoing attempt to make sense of it all, as though such a thing were possible.

It is September, and despite her having been out of school for decades, the academic calendar still exerts its pull; she's filled with the desire for new beginnings. It is the season of bounty; the apple trees are heavy with fruit, the wild grass along the highway is high. Wind sweeps through the trees. Everything breathes deeply, nature's end-of-summer sigh. In a couple of hours, a late-afternoon thunderstorm will sweep through, rinsing the air clean.

The town has climbed out of a depression by branding itself "America's Hometown." Flags fly from the lampposts. Signs announce the autumn harvest celebration, a film festival, and a chamber-music series at the Presbyterian church.

She parks behind the conference center and slips in through the employee entrance and down the long hall to a door marked THIS WAY TO LOBBY.

On the wall is a full-length mirror with a handwritten message on the glass: "Check your smile and ask yourself, Am I ready to serve?"

The War Correspondent comes through the hotel's front door at the same time as she slides in through the unmarked door by the registration desk.

"Funny seeing you here," he says.

"Is it?"

He stands at the reception desk. The thick curls that he long ago kept short are receding; in compensation they're longer and more unruly.

He makes her uncomfortable, uncharacteristically shy.

She wonders how he looks so good. She glances down. Her linen blouse is heavily wrinkled, while his shirt is barely creased.

The receptionist hands him an important-looking envelope from FedEx.

She's given a heavily taped brown box and a copy of the conference schedule.

"What did you get?" she asks as he's opening the FedEx.

"Galleys of a magazine piece," he says. "You?"

She shakes the box. "Cracker Jacks?"

He laughs. She glances down at the schedule. "We're back-to-back at the opening ceremonies."

"What time is the first event?"

"Twelve-thirty." She thinks of these things as marathons; pacing is everything. "You've got an hour."

"I was hoping to take a shower," he says.

"Your room's not quite ready," the receptionist tells him.

"Did you fly in from a war zone?" she asks.

"Washington," he says. "There was a Press Club dinner last night, and I was in Geneva the day before, and before that the war."

"Quite a slide from there to here," she says.

"Not really," he says. "No matter how nice the china, it's still a rubber chicken."

The receptionist clicks the keys until she locates a room that's ready. "I found you a lovely room. You'll be very happy." She hands him the key card. "You're both on the executive floor."

"Dibs on the cheese cubes," he says.

She knew him long ago before either of them had become

anyone. They were part of a group, fresh out of college, working in publishing, that met regularly at a bar. He was deeply serious, a permanently furrowed brow, and he was married—that was the funny thing, and they all talked about it behind his back. Who was married at twenty-three? No one ever saw the wife—that's what they called her, the wife. Even now she doesn't know the woman's name.

An older man approaches the War Correspondent. "Very big fan," the man says, resting his hand on the Correspondent's shoulder. "I have a story for you about a trip my wife and I went on." He pauses, clears his throat. "We were in Germany and decided to visit the camps. When we got to our hotel, I asked, 'How do we get there?' They tell us take a train and then a bus, and when you arrive, there will be someone there to lead you. We go, it's terrifying; all I can think of as the train goes clackety-clack is that these are the same rails that took my family away. We get to the camp, there's a café and a bookstore selling postcards—we don't know what to think. And when we get back to the hotel, the young German girl at the front desk looks at us with a big smile and says, 'Did you enjoy your visit to Dachau?' Do we laugh or cry?" The man pauses. "So what do you think?"

The War Correspondent nods. "It's hard to know, isn't it?"

"We did both," the man says. "We laughed, we cried, and we're never going back."

The Correspondent catches her eye and smiles. There are delightful creases by his eyes that weren't there years ago.

She's annoyed. Why is his smile so quick, so perfect?

As she moves toward the elevator, a conference volunteer catches her arm. "Don't forget your welcome bag." The volunteer hands her a canvas tote, laden with genocide swag.

She goes straight to her room, puts the Do Not Disturb sign on the door, and locks it. What is his room like? Is it the same size, one window overlooking the parking lot? Or is it bigger? Is it a suite with an ocean view? They're hundreds of miles from the sea. Is there a hierarchy to Genocide(S) housing?

"Do you ever go off duty?" she hears her therapist's voice asking.

Not really.

She unpacks the welcome bag: a coffee mug from the local college, a notepad and pen from a famous card company—"When You Can't Find Words, Let Us Speak for You"—and a huge bar of chocolate from a pharmaceutical company that makes a popular antidepressant. The wrapper reads *"Sometimes Getting Happy Should Be Simple."*

She thinks of her therapist. She has the opposite of transference—she never wishes the therapist were her mother or her lover. She thinks of the therapist and is relieved not to be married or related to her. A decision as small as trying to decide where to go for dinner or what to eat would take hours of negotiation and processing. Eventually she would cave in and do whatever she had to to make it stop. She secretly thinks the therapist is a passive-aggressive bully and perhaps should have been a lawyer.

"You wrote an exceptionally strong book illustrating the multi-generational effects of Holocaust trauma. You knew there would be questions." She hears the therapist's voice loud and clear in her head.

"It's a novel. I made it up."

"You created the characters, but the emotional truths are very real. There are different kinds of knowing."

Silence.

"You spent years inhabiting the experience on every level—remember when you starved yourself? When you drank tainted water? When you didn't bathe for thirty days?"

"Yes, but I was not in the Holocaust. I am an impostor—the critics made that quite clear."

The therapist clucks and shakes her head.

The Novelist wonders, aren't therapists trained not to cluck?

"Critics aren't the same as readers, and your readers felt you gave language and illumination to a very difficult aspect of their experience. And you won an international award." The therapist pauses. "I find it interesting that you have to do this."

"Do what?"

"Undermine yourself."

"Because I'm better at it than anyone?" She glances up, smiling.

The therapist has the sad face on.

"At least I'm honest," she says.

Still the sad face.

"Really?" she asks.

"Really," the therapist says.

She said yes to the Genocide(S) conference after having made a pact with herself to say no to everything, a move toward getting back to work on a new book. She'd spent the better part of a year on book tour, traveling the world giving readings, doing interviews, answering questions that felt like interrogations. It was as if the journalists thought that by asking often enough and in enough languages, eventually something would fall out, some admission, some other story—but in fact there was nothing more. She'd put it all in the book.

In the hotel-room mirror, she takes a look at herself. "Check your smile and ask yourself, Am I ready to serve?"

She blushes. She was thinking about him—the War Correspondent.

Her phone rings.

"Are you there yet?" Lisa asks. "I wanted to make sure you arrived safely."

"I'm fine," she says.

"Did you get the box?"

"I think so," she says.

"Did you open it?"

"No."

"Well, go ahead."

She doesn't open the box, just the note on top: *Sorry we fought. Here's making it up to you. . . .*

"But we didn't fight," she says.

"I know, but we usually do, and I had to order it ten days in advance," Lisa says.

"You could have tried a little harder," she says.

"What do you mean?" Lisa says. "I planned the whole thing weeks ago."

"I mean you could have at least picked the fight if you knew you'd already sent a makeup gift," she says.

"I don't get you," Lisa says. "I really don't."

"I'm joking. You're taking it way too literally."

"Now you're criticizing me?"

"Never mind," she says. "Thank you. You know I love chocolate."

"Indeed I do," Lisa says, not realizing that she hasn't even opened the box.

She knows Lisa well enough to know exactly what's in the box. Instead she opens the chocolate bar sponsored by the antidepressant manufacturer and takes a big bite. The thick sound of chocolate being chewed fills air.

"That's more like it," Lisa says.

"I have to go," she says. "I'm just getting to the check-in desk." She looks at herself in the mirror; can Lisa tell when she's lying?

"What is going on with you?" Lisa says. "I can't read you."

"Ignore me," she says. "I'm lost in thought."

"I'll find you later," Lisa says, hanging up.


The welcome lunch is served: cold salads like the sisterhood lunch after a bar mitzvah, a trio of scoops, egg salad, tuna salad, potato salad, a roll and butter, coffee or tea.

She is seated at the head table among the academics with university appointments in the fields of trauma and tragedy. The War Correspondent is two seats down.

The man she wants to meet, Otto Hauser, the ephemerologist, is missing. His seat is empty. His plate is marked "vegan."

"Has anyone seen Otto Hauser?" she asks repeatedly. She has been obsessed with Otto Hauser for years, having read the only two interviews he's ever given and seen a glimpse of him in a documentary. She heard later that he asked to have himself taken out of the picture.

Finally someone tells her that Otto has been delayed; there was a fire in his warehouse near Munich.

The conference leader, himself the victim of a violent attack that left him with only half a tongue, calls the room to order. It is difficult to understand what he's saying. She finds herself looking for clues from the deaf interpreter on the far side of the stage.

"This year's program, From Genocide(S) to Generosity: Toward a New Understanding, brings together diverse communities, including but not limited to Cambodia, East Timor, Rwanda, the Sudan, the former Yugoslavia, the Holocaust of World War II, the history of colonial genocides, and the early response to the AIDS epidemic. And this weekend we ask the important question: Why? Why do Genocide(S) continue to happen?"

He goes on to thank their sponsors, an airline, two global search engines, an insurance firm, the already mentioned antidepressant manufacturer, and a family-owned ice cream company.

Before turning the microphone over to a fellow board member, he says, "The cash bar in the Broadway Suite will be open until midnight and serving complimentary fresh juices donated by Be My Squeeze, and this year we have a spiritual recharge room for meditation or prayer with the bonus of a free chair massage brought to us by Watch Your Back."

Following the conference leader's welcome, the chair of the local English department does the honors, introducing her. The chair's words are passionate and strange, a simultaneous celebration and denigration of her, both personally and professionally. All in the same breath, the chair mentions the author's being known for her lusciously thick dark hair, that she won France's Nyssen Prize for International Literature, and what a shock it was to her that the book had sold so many copies.

The War Correspondent leans across and whispers loudly over heads, "I think she wants to fuck you."

"I feel like she just did," she whispers back before standing and taking the microphone briefly. "Thank you, Professor," she says, intentionally calling the woman "Professor" rather than "Chair." "You clearly know more about me than I know about myself."

There is laughter in the house.

The War Correspondent is introduced by the college's football coach. "*When Dirt and Blood Mix* is Eric Bitterberg's very personal story of being on the front lines with his best friend from high school, a U.S. Army sergeant."

"Is it Biter-berg or Bitter-berg?" she whispers loudly in his direction.

"Depends on my mood," he says.


The afternoon session immediately follows lunch. While others go off to sessions such as Australia's Stolen Generations and The Killing Fields Revisited, she heads toward the Americas Suite for her first panel, Where I'm Calling From: Modern Germany and Related His/Her Stories.

Her fellow panelists include a young German scholar, who despite being fluent in English insists on speaking in German, and Gerda Hoff, an elderly local woman who survived the camps and more recently cancer and has now written a memoir, called *Living to Live.*

"You look different from the photo on your book," the moderator says as she sits down—it's not a compliment.

And then, without a beat, the moderator begins, "Germany and family history—where was your family during the Holocaust?"

The German panelist says that his grandparents were in the food business and struggled.

"They were butchers," the moderator says; it's not a question but a statement.

"Yes," the German confirms, and declines to say more.

The survivor says her father was a teacher and her mother was a woman known for her beautiful voice. She and her siblings watched as her parents were shot in the back and fell into large open graves. She is the only one still alive; her sisters died in the camps, and two years ago her brother jumped in front of a train.

"And you?"

The Novelist would like to buy a vowel. She'd like to pass, to simply evaporate, or at least have someone explain that clearly there was an error in putting these panels together, because she doesn't belong here.

She draws a breath and allows for the weight of the air to settle before she explains: Her family wasn't from Germany but rather Latvia. They arrived in America before the war, and were dairy farmers in New England.

It's like she's on a quiz show with points awarded for the most authentic answer. She's plainly the loser.

She scans the audience. There are no young people. It reminds her of the classical concerts her parents used to take her to; no matter how old she got, she was always the youngest one.

The moderator carries on. At some point, while her mind is elsewhere, the conversation turns back to her, with the question, "Is there such a thing as Holocaust fiction? Are there experiences where the facts of history are already so challenged that we dare not fictionalize them?"

She takes a moment, then leans forward in her chair, drawing the microphone close, unnecessary considering the size of the room. This is the question asked around the world, the moment they've all been waiting for.

"Yes," she says definitively, and then pauses. "Yes, there is such a thing as Holocaust fiction. It's not something I invented. There are many novels that are set during or relate to the Holocaust, including books by Elie Wiesel, Thomas Keneally, Bernhard Schlink, and so on. With regard to the question 'Are some subjects so historically sensitive that we shouldn't touch them in fiction?' I'd say the purpose of fiction is to illustrate and illuminate. We see ourselves more clearly through the stories we tell."

"But what is your relation to the Holocaust?" the moderator drills down.

"I am a Jew, my grandfather's brothers died in the camps."

"What does it mean to you to be a transgressive woman who writes books that are intentionally shocking?"

"'Transgressive' is a word you use to describe me; it's what you label me to make me other than you. The very history we are here to discuss reminds us of the danger of labels and separating people into categories."

Throughout the audience there are murmurs of approval. Despite the fact that these panels are supposed to be conversations, they are actually competitions, judged by the audience. "As for the question regarding an intention to shock, I have written nothing that didn't first appear in the morning paper," she says, aware that she's got a week-old paper in her bag right now. "What is truly shocking is how little we do to prevent these things from happening again and—"

"Fiction is a luxury our families didn't have," Gerda Hoff cuts her off. "We didn't pack our summer reading and go off to the camps, happy, happy. This isn't even your story. What right do you have to be telling it? It is insulting. I am one little old lady, but I am here representing six million Jews who cannot speak for themselves."

The audience applauds. Score for Gerda Hoff!

She's tempted to quote her mother's frequent comment—"Well, you're entitled to your opinion"—but she doesn't. Instead she says, "And that is exactly why I wrote my book: to describe the impact of those six million lives on the subsequent generations. I wrote this book so that those of us who weren't there, those of us who were not yet born, would better understand the experience of those who were present. And," she says, "and prevent it from happening again. Never Again."

"So it's all a big lie?" the old woman says.

"You show no love for Germany," the German scholar says, clearly feeling left out of the debate.

"My novel is not about Germany. It is the story of four generations of a family struggling to claim their history and their identity."

The panel ends, and even though the members of the audience don't hold up scorecards, she can tell that Gerda came in first, she was second, and the German a distant third.

Never again, she tells herself. Never say yes when you mean to say no.

After the panel she sits at a small table signing books and answering questions.

"Are you a gay?" an old woman whispers, in the same voice her mother would ask, Are they Jewish? "I think you're a gay? My son, I think he's also a gay. He doesn't tell me, but a mother knows."

When the line is gone, she buys a copy of her own book and gives it to Gerda Hoff as Gerda is leaving.

"I don't want it," Gerda says.

"It's a gift. I think you might find it interesting."

"I'm eighty-three years old. I watched my parents shot in the back. I buried my own children, and now I'm dying of cancer. I didn't live this long to be polite about a piece of dreck that you think I might 'like.'"

"I'm sorry," she says.

Gerda leans toward her, "You want to know what I like? Chocolate ice cream. That's something to live for. Your book, *a shaynem dank dir im pupik*. I lived it, I don't have to read it," she says, and then toddles off down the hall.

She finds the War Correspondent by the elevator—waiting. "How'd it go?" he asks.

"Eviscerated," she says.

"I wouldn't take it so personally." They step in, and he hits the button for the fourth floor.

"They may be senior citizens, but they're pugilists," she says. "They're not just taking Zumba, they're also boxing, and they know where to punch. What about you?"

She looks at him; the top two buttons of his shirt are open, dark hair spinning out from between the buttons. She has the urge to pluck a hair from his chest like it was a magical whisker.

"Apart from the heckler who called me a pussy, it was okay."

The elevator opens on the executive floor. "So I'll see you at the cocktails?" she says, stepping out.

"Not for me. I'm on deadline." He pauses. "I don't think I've seen you in years except at the book awards. Congratulations, by the way. Your book is the kind of thing I could never do," he says as he starts down the hall.

"In what way?" she calls after him.

"Fiction," he says, turning back toward her. "I could never make it up. I have no imagination."

She smiles. "I'm not quite sure what you mean, but for now I'll take that as a compliment."

"Drink later?"

She nods. "In my head I keep calling you the War Correspondent. Years ago I used to call you Erike, but somehow that no longer fits."

"You called me Erike because that's what my mother used to call me."

"You were married. We were all impressed; it seemed very grown-up. We talked about you behind your back."

"That's funny," he says.

"Why?"

"I was miserable."

"Oh," she says.

"I thought I was so smart, had it all figured out." He shrugs.

"And why did we hang out there, at the Cedar Bar?" she asks. "Who did we think we were? Painters?"

"Up and coming," he says. "We thought we were going someplace."

"And here we are."

There's an awkward beat. "So what are you going to do now? I remember that you used to ride your bike everywhere. You never went on the subway."

"Yes," she says. "I used to ride my bike everywhere—until I blew out my knee."

"Do you remember that I got you to go on the subway?"

"I do," she says, smiling. "It was January."

"The seventeenth of January, 1991, the night the bombing started in Baghdad."

She nods, surprised he remembers.

"I made you take the subway all the way uptown."

"It was a big night," she says.

"Yep," he says, and then seems lost in thought. There's a silence, longer than feels comfortable. "All right, then," he says, and abruptly heads down the hall, leaving her to wonder—did something happen?

She goes to her room and sits to meditate. Her meditation is punctuated by thinking about him. She keeps bringing herself back to her body, to the breathing and counting, until she falls deeply asleep. She has horrible dreams and wakes up forty minutes later, sweaty and confused as if roused from general anesthesia. She has no idea where she is and is trying to process whether anything in the dream was real.

The antidote—calling her mother.

"What are you doing?" her mother asks, her tone an instant reality check.

"I just took a nap. It was awful, nightmares," she says. "I'm away at the conference."

"What is this one about?"

"Genocide(S). I accepted the invitation thinking of you."

"Why me? I wasn't killed in a genocide."

"Because of the Holocaust, because of Pop-Pop's brothers."

"Oh, that was very nice of you," her mother says.

"It's not about being nice," she says, "it's about remembering."

"It's good you remember," her mother says. "I completely forgot you were going away. When are you coming home?"

"Sunday night?"

"And when are you coming to see me?"

"Maybe next weekend."

"Next weekend isn't good. I have theater tickets."

"Okay, then maybe the following."

"It would be nice if you could come sooner. Come during the week. I'm not so busy then."

"I work during the week."

"Is that what you call creative writing—work?"

"Yes."

"When my friends say they love what you do, I say they're entitled to their opinion."

"Thanks, Ma, I'm glad that I work so hard only to have it embarrass you." She takes out her computer, puts her mother on speaker.

"Are you typing now while you're talking to me?"

"Yes."

"I hope you're not writing down what I'm saying."

"No, Mom, I'm looking up synagogues and texting one of the conference organizers to ask if tonight's dinner is seated."

"I'm a private person. I don't need the world to know so much about me."

"But Mom, the book isn't about you."

"That's what you say, but I know better. So when are you coming to visit me?"

"I have to go, Ma. I love you. I'll call you tomorrow."


The agitation of talking with her mother has prompted her to get up, wash her face, unzip her suitcase, and contemplate what to wear. There's a full-length mirror mounted to the wall. She looks different than she remembers, shorter, rounder. It's happening already—the shrinking?

Lisa texts, "Are you dead? It's unlike you not to call or write."

What's the problem? she asks herself. Is the problem Lisa? Or is it something else?

"We talked just two hours ago. Meanwhile, I had the pink one," she writes back. It started as a joke when they were newly a couple and has become a recurring theme. "I sucked it. The chocolate melted in my mouth," she texts.

"Lol, not on your hands," Lisa writes.

She dresses for temple, simple black pants and a shirt. On her way out of the building, she passes the "gathering." They don't call it a cocktail party because that sounds too festive, and between those who don't drink for religious reasons, those who are in AA, and those whose blood thinners or pain medications interact badly, the "Freedom and Unity" mocktail is doing a brisk business.

One of the organizers spots her and insists she mingle. Mingling, she searches for Otto Hauser, who has still not arrived. She's introduced to Dorit Berwin, a Brit, who rescued hundreds of children from certain death in Sudan. Dorit personally adopted fifty-four children and would have taken more, but her biological children made a show of distancing themselves from her with a public campaign titled "They're Kids, Not Kittens."

She finds it odd that it is Friday night and none of the conferees at the gathering seem to notice that it's Shabbat.

Around the world it is her habit to go to temple; she's the only one in her family who practices.

"What do you mean, practices?" her mother says. "We're Jewish, what are we practicing for? Haven't we been through enough?"

"It makes me feel I'm part of history."

As she drives over the hills on a two-lane country road, the sun is dropping low on the horizon. There are cows making their way

home across fields and self-serve farm stands with fresh eggs, to-
matoes, cut flowers, and free zucchini with every purchase. The
sky is a glorious and deepening blue.

It's just past sunset when she pulls in to the tiny town. The raised
wooden Star of David and the mezuzah are the only outward markers on the old narrow building. She knocks three times on the heavy
wooden door, like a character in an Edgar Allan Poe story. She
knocks again, she waits, she knocks once more, and finally . . .

"Can I help you?" a man asks through the door.

"I'm here for Friday-night services," she says.

"Are you sure?"

"Am I late?"

"A little."

"Can I come in?"

"I guess so," the man says, opening the door. "We have to be
careful. You never know who's knocking."

The synagogue is small and lost to time. There are about thirty
people between her and the rabbi.

"What is it to be a Jew?" the rabbi is demanding of the group.
"Has it changed over time? We are reminded of our forebears, who
were not free, who had to say yes when they meant no. We are all
transgressors, exiles; there is none among us who has not sinned.
It is not about the size of one's sin or one sin being greater than
another—but that we are all human and thus flawed, and only by
recognizing those flaws can we come to know ourselves."


She listens, a stranger in the rear of the room, looking at the backs
of heads, contemplating. Would Lisa go to temple with her? She's
never asked, because she and Lisa are forever in a push-pull, needing space, room, time. Lisa says they're together so much that it's

hard to know where one ends and the other begins. But she always knows where she ends—she ends before she begins. She's not what she calls a "classic lesbian," a merger, who brings the U-Haul on a second date. She is perpetually frustrated and disappointed. She wonders, is it a Jewish thing, a relationship thing, or is it just her?

The sound of a crying baby brings her back into the moment. As the woman with the crying infant leaves, she notices that he is there, up front. She recognizes him from his hair, the nape of his neck. He is four rows up and deep into it, dipping his head at key points.

Surprised but pleased, she used to think of him as serious but thought that his success had eroded that. She imagines him now as a bit more of a wartime playboy, hanging out with people like the fearless woman journalist with the eye patch who was killed in Syria. She imagines he plays high-stakes poker and has drunken late-night sex with exotic women who speak no English.


"Those saying the Mourners' Kaddish, please stand," the rabbi intones. He stands, prays. She can tell from the rise and fall of his shoulders that he begins to cry.

And then it is over. The Shabbos has begun, and the congregation is invited to stay for a piece of challah and a sip of wine—in tiny plastic cups like thimbles.

"I didn't know you were Jewish," he says, tossing back the tiny cup like it was a dose of cough medicine. "I thought you were gay."

"Like they're related, Jew and gay? Different categories. I thought you were married."

"Divorced, but I am living with someone."

"So am I," she says. "See, I knew we had something in common. What about the deadline?"

He shrugs.

"How did you get here?"

"Taxi. Thirty dollars. Do you know that the taxis are shared? You pick up people along the way—a toothless woman and groceries, a fat man who couldn't walk any farther."

"Do you go to temple a lot?" she asks.

"No," he says, wiping a tear from his eye.

She pretends not to notice.

"I'm starving," he says. "The last thing I ate was the death tuna at lunch. Do you think there's Chinese around here? In my family that's the way we do it, temple and then hot-and-sour soup."

She shakes her head. "No, but there's a famous ice cream place near here, wins all the prizes at the state fair."

The ice cream stand is set back from the road in the middle of nowhere. They find it only because a long line of cars, trucks, minivans is pulled off and parked in the dirt.

WE MAKE OUR OWN BECAUSE WE LIKE IT THAT WAY is written in bubble-lettered Magic Marker on poster board. The long summer season has taken a toll; thundershowers and ice cream drips have caused the letters to run. The posters look like they've had a good cry.

Enormously large people lower themselves out of their minivans and wobble toward the stand.

"What I like about these gigs is the local color," he says, taking it in.

A few late bees hover.

"Yes," she says. "It can be really hard to get out of one's own circle."

"I'll go for the medium Autumn Trio," the War Correspondent tells the boy behind the counter.

"Small chocolate in a cup," she says.

The War Correspondent pays.

"Chivalrous."

"Taxi fare."

The ice cream scoops are like a child's fantasy of what an ice cream cone might be, the scale both magical and upsetting.

"This is what's wrong with America," he says, digging in.

"Entirely," she says.

They sit at a picnic table in a grove of picnic tables.

"Was your family religious?" he asks between licks.

"No," she says. "Yours?"

"My grandmother and my aunts are observant, but not my father, who adamantly refuses."

"Where were they from?"

"From a town that no longer exists."

"Mine came in a pickle barrel," she says. "When I think about it, I imagine the ocean filled with grandmother floating on pickle barrels all the way from Latvia to Ellis Island."

He's like a kid eating his ice cream, happier with each lick. She reaches over and wipes drips off his chin. He smiles and keeps licking. He has three flavors, the house special: butter pecan, maple walnut, brandied coffee.

"Taste it?"

She takes a lick, eyes closed. "Maple," she says.

"Try over here," he says, turning the cone.

"Brandy," she says. She slips a spoonful of hers into his mouth, noting that there is an immediacy to ice cream, that it travels through you, cold down the middle while the flavor stays on your tongue.

"*A schtik naches,*" he says.

"*Naches.*" She laughs. "My grandmother used to say that when she brushed my hair. She pulled so hard that for years I thought *naches* meant 'knotty hair.'"

"It means 'great joy.'"

"A *yiddisher kop,*" she says. "Mr. Smarty Pants."

She has another lick of his ice cream, and then there's a pause, a moment, realization.

"You okay?" he asks.

"The ice cream is so delicious and you look so happy," she says, and then pauses. "I'm haunted by the survivors who refuse to enjoy life because it would be disrespectful to those who were lost. They feel an obligation to continue suffering, to be the rememberer."

She tells him about Gerda and her chocolate ice cream and then asks, "But why are we here? Why do you and I choose to live in the pain of others?"

"It's who we are," he says. "*In di zumerdike teg zol er zitsn shive, un in di vinterdike nekht zikh raysn af di tseyn.* On summer days he should mourn, and on winter nights he should torture himself."

"But why?"

He shrugs. "Because we're most comfortable when we're miserable?"

"I have to remember to tell that to my therapist on Wednesday."

He bites his cone. "I've never been to a therapist."

She looks at him like he's crazy. "You've been an eyewitness to a genocide but you've never been to a therapist?"

"Nope." He crunches.

She can't help but laugh. "Meshuga."

"Now, that's funny. You're calling me crazy for not going to therapy."

They walk back to the car. "The only Yiddish I know is from my grandmother. She wasn't exactly an intellectual," she says.

"*Az dos meydl ken nit tantsn zogt, zi az di klezmorim kenen nit shpiln,*" he says. "If the girl can't dance, she says the band can't play."

They get into the car and fasten their seat belts. "So, Rakel, you who are so good at arranging everything. Where are the *kinder* this evening?"

She sighs. "Ah, Erike, I wanted a weekend like when we were young and used to play hide-and-seek in the pickle barrel, before we had so much responsibility," she says. "So the children, I loaned them to your brother and my sister. She needed help with her children, he needed help with the harvest." She pulls out onto the two-lane road.

"It's true," he says. "Our boy is a little no-goodnik who has no idea of what hard work is, and our girl is soft in the head and will have to marry well."

"Remind me, how many *kinder* do we have?" she asks.

"Ten," he says.

"So many," she says, surprised. "And I gave birth to them all?"

"Yes," he says. "The last three it was less like a birth and more like they just arrived in time for dinner."

"It's true. I remember I was making soup when the eighth came along, and I was bathing the fifth when the ninth announced himself, and the tenth, she arrived at dawn while I was having the most wonderful dream."

They are quiet; a truck passes, blasting heavy-metal music.

"You know," she says, "after the tenth child, I went to the doctor and said, 'I've lost all sense of who I am, and everything down there feels inside out.' The doctor patted me on the head and said, 'When the children grow up and are married, you will know who you are again. And for the rest, I'll put in a thing.'"

"A thing?"

"A pessary," she says, and then pauses and adds in her regular voice, "I've never used that word before, but I always wanted to."

"Can you have sex with a pessary?" he asks.

"You haven't noticed?" she says, back in character.

"When the doctor put it in, what did he call it?"

"He called it a 'thing.' He said, 'I'll put in this thing, and you'll feel better. And I said, 'Will I be able to go?' And he said, 'Yes. You will go, and everything will be beautiful again.'" She continues, "The women talk about him, about whether or not he gets excited when he sees us. He stuck his finger in Sylvie's ass."

"We're digressing," he says.

"We're talking dirty," she says.

And as they drive into the town, it's as though they're coming back from where they've been, lost in time.

At the hotel, the crowd from the conference has spilled out of the bar in heated debate. Across the street the local convention center is hosting a gun show, and some of the conferees are considering a protest. There are mixed emotions. Some are desperately urging people not to take to the streets, and others feel that they must act—to do nothing is to allow the show to go on at every level.

"How do we stop the violence? I'll tell you how, we organize a group, Nothing Left to Lose. We go in shooting and keep shooting until they realize a gun is no defense," one of the men says.

"He lived this long to be a moron?" someone asks.

"He lost his wife recently," another says. "He's been very depressed."

Another man spots the War Correspondent. "Can I buy you a drink?" the man asks, already drunk.

———————

Before the War Correspondent can answer, she is leading him away, down the hall. "You want a schnapps?" she asks.

*"Makhn a shnepsl?"*

"Minibar," she says.

When they get to her door, he flicks her Do Not Disturb sign. "Are you sure it's safe? What if something gets disturbed?"

"Like what?"

There is a pause.

"If I kissed you, would you hit me?" he asks.

"Is that a question or a request? If you kiss me, would you like me to hit you?"

He doesn't say anything.

She does it, she kisses him. No one hits anyone. She puts her hands up to his face, feels the scruff of his whiskers.

She likes the way he feels. Lisa is small, her skin smooth—she's a sliver of a person, like a sliced almond.

And then the door is open. He takes a scotch from the minibar, swallows it like medicine.

"Have you ever slept with a man?"

"Is that an offer or a question?"

He doesn't answer.

"Yes," she says. "Have you ever slept with a lesbian? Maybe that's the real question?"

"Who initiates? Like, is it always the same lesbian each time, or do you take turns?"

She untucks his shirt. His skin is warm, the fur on his belly is long. His body is both soft and hard, fit but not muscle-bound.

"This is not what lesbians do," he says.

"You have no idea what lesbians do," she says.

"Tell me," he says.

"We give each other blow jobs."

"What do you blow?"

"Giant dildos and chocolate cocks," she says, pointing to the still-unopened box.

"You're exciting me," he says.

"You've always excited me," she says. "It's been a long time. . . ."

"How long?"

"Sometime in college," she says.

"Is it scary?"

She laughs. "I thought you were going to say liberating." She unzips his pants and takes him in hand.

"I really like your . . ."

"Member?" he suggests.

"Friend?" she says. "Seriously, it's beautiful."

"Thanks. But are you just going to examine it, or . . . ?"

"I can't help it. I love a penis."

He laughs. "You are so not what I expected."

She is teasing him with her mouth, her hands, her body.

"You're killing me," he says.

"We are at a genocide conference."

"It's not a joke," he says.

"Behave," she says. "Would it be easier if I tied you up?"

He snorts.

"How about you just lie down and be quiet," she says.


His body is the other, in opposition, distinction, in relation. The weight of him, the musky scent, is delicious. His mouth tastes of scotch and ice cream.

"I bet you get laid a lot," she says. "Do I need to worry?"

"No," he says.

"Is that true, or do you just not want to be distracted?"

"Do you want me to use a condom?"

"No," she says. "I want to feel it."

Their sex is meaty, almost combative, every man for him/herself. When he turns her over and takes her from the back, his desire is apparent. She is humbled and overwhelmed by the power of the male body. It wants what it wants and will take it until satisfied. A penis connected to a man is entirely different from the strap-on or the rabbit wand Lisa brought with her from a previous relationship. All of them are like artificial limbs, prosthetic antifucks, but this, she thinks, this is amazingly good.

"Is this making love?" she asks, not realizing she's speaking aloud.

"It's fucking," he says.

"Is it okay?" he asks, suddenly self-conscious.

"Yes," she says, not thinking about him but about how much she's enjoying herself.

And then, as they're getting close to the good part, she can't help herself and anxiety pulls her out of the moment.

"Is it true that once a guy starts, he won't stop till he comes?"

"I don't know," he says, annoyed.

His annoyance exacerbates her anxiety. "I think it's true," she says.

He slows down for a moment. "What about lesbians?" he says. "Do lesbians stop?"

"Sometimes," she says. "Sometimes right in the middle they just give up and stop. It fails to escalate, or someone says something and it de-escalates."

"Do you usually talk the whole time?"

"Yes," she says.

"Maybe that's part of the problem."

They finish coated in each other.

The Sabbath lay is a very good thing, a blessing.

There is quiet and then sounds from across the street. "You want to shoot someone, shoot me," Gerda Hoff says, standing in the street.

"You like guns so much," Gerda says. "You have no idea. Those don't protect anyone. You want to feel like a big boy, so shoot me."

"She's asking for it," a young guy from the gun show says. "Shoot her."

"That's not amusing, Karl," the other guy says.

"Karl. What a name, like Karl Brandt," Gerda says.

"Who's he?"

"Exactly," she says. "You have no idea who you are or where you come from. Karl Brandt was the Nazi who came up with the idea of gassing the Jews."

The guy from the gun show is impressed, like he thinks this Karl is cool.

"He was hanged for his crimes on June second, 1948. He should have been hanged six million times."

The Novelist is at the window—the War Correspondent behind her.

"Is Gerda okay?" she asks.

"Yes," he says.

"This isn't going to turn into some fucked-up thing where a little old lady dies on Main Street?"

"No," he says.

"She's going to come inside and eat chocolate ice cream?" She starts to cry. "We cheated," she says.

"Have you ever done it before?"

"No," she says. "You?"

"Yes," he says.

"You asshole," she says, punching him.

He laughs. "I'm an asshole because I've done it before?"

"Yes," she says. "If you cheat, it should be something special, not something you just do all the time."

"I didn't say I did it all the time. *Noch di chupeh iz shpet di charoteh.* After the wedding it's too late to have regrets." There's a pause. "Now you're mad at me."

She doesn't laugh. "I'm not mad, I'm disappointed. I should get some work done," she says.

She can't imagine actually sleeping with him there.

"Is that what you do?" he asks.

"I'm a night owl," she says. "And there is no 'Is this what I do?' because I don't do this!"

She looks out the window again. A small crowd has formed. The guys from the gun show have no idea what's going on, except that they're in a standoff with a bunch of senior citizens. A police car rolls up, the crowd dissipates, Gerda and her gang walk back across the street.

He gathers his things. "See you in the morning."

She turns—he's wearing the hotel robe. "You're going out like that?" She sounds exactly like her mother.

"Yes," he says.

"Someone might see you."

"I'll tell them my shower was broken and I used yours. P.S., now I've seen you naked."

He opens the door and stands for a moment half in, half out of the room. "Do you want to go apple picking tomorrow afternoon?"

"What?"

He makes the gesture of picking apples from trees. "Now's the moment, this is the season, the guy who gave me a ride from the airport said there's a nice orchard near here."

She almost starts to cry again. "Yeah, okay, after our panels we'll go apple picking and we'll play Jew again."

"Play Jew? Is it like a game show? 'I'll take Torah for two hundred'?" he asks.

"I have no idea," she says, closing the door.

*Do you want to go apple picking?* It's the nicest thing anyone's ever said to her.

She turns on the television and calls home, not because she wants to but because that's what she does.

"Why so late?" Lisa asks.

"I was kibitzing with someone."

"Your voice sounds funny. Are you getting sick?"

Her voice sounds funny because she just had a dick in her mouth. "I'm just tired," she says. "And you?"

"All fine," Lisa says. "I'm here with the cat and beating your mother at Words with Friends online. She's super proud because she just got 'jest' for thirteen, but she doesn't know I'm sitting on *x* and *y*, and I've got big plans."

"Nice," she says, thinking of apple picking.

She sleeps badly. At some point there's something cold and slithery crawling up her leg, but then she realizes it's the opposite, it's "stuff" running down her leg. She dabs at it with her fingers, tastes it.

At breakfast a handmade Post-it hangs over the steam trays of scrambled eggs and gray sausages that look like turds:

FYI—NOT KOSHER

There are single-serving boxes of cereal and a plate of what looks like homemade babka someone has cut into pieces.

She takes a piece of babka with her coffee. Her eyes sweep the room, looking for him and glad not to see him—as long as he's not somewhere else, avoiding her. On a wipe board someone has written, "Otto Hauser's Accepting Responsibility has been rescheduled for 9:30 this morning in Ballroom B."

Coffee and babka in hand, she locates Hauser, the self-described obsessive-compulsive whose guilt about civilian passivity during the war led him to relentlessly collect and catalog the personal effects of those who disappeared. He is "the" Holocaust-ephemera specialist, the man who doesn't want to be known.

"Mr. Hauser?"

He looks up. His eyes are a beautiful blue clouded by the watery milk white of old age. "I'm sorry to bother you. . . ."

He pats the chair next to him. "Sit."

"I'm sure you get asked all the time, but would you tell me a bit about how you came to be the Accidental Archivist?"

He pours hot water from a pot into a teacup. "My mother was very tidy," he says as he dips his tea bag up and down. His English is that of a German who learned to speak by listening to radio shows. "She wasn't an intellectual, but she knew right from wrong. She was very German, very organized. So when people were taken, she would slip into their houses and recover things, before looters, mostly soldiers, came. Slowly it became known in the Jewish community, and people would bring her things to hold for them, knowing soon would come the knock on the door. My mother was very clever, good at hiding things—she put them in boxes marked as Christmas ornaments, sewing supplies, or Papa's military uniform, and they never looked. She took them to her father's farm and buried them in the field as they harvested crops. She didn't keep a notebook, but she made a code. She kept track of everything and waited for the people to come back. Near the end of the war, quite suddenly she died. I was a young man. I carried on my mother's work so she would be proud. The war undid us all."

"And did the families come back?"

He shakes his head. He begins to cry, and she finds herself surprised by his tears, as though after so many years he wouldn't cry anymore. "No," he says. "And still, in the fields of my grandfather's farm, we find things—a silver teapot, a pointer for the Torah, candlesticks. For years I waited. Now I'm an old man. I never married, I have no family. I'm so old that I am actually shrinking." He gestures at his pants, which are held up by suspenders. "I kept everything, but I realized these things should be in circulation, not in a box somewhere, unable to breathe. I started to give them to schools, museums, synagogues, to people who needed something to hold—an object of remembrance."

"And why did you want them to edit you out of the film?"

"Because I am not a hero," he says. "I am just a man." Otto stands, and he is almost elfin. "What I have come to comprehend is that it is less about the object and more about the head." He taps his head, the aha moment, and takes off toddling toward Ballroom B.


"So nice," one of the women says, catching her more than an hour later, as she's leaving the room. "You don't just come to talk, you also listen."

"You're late," her mother says. "You usually call at eight-thirty. When you don't call, I don't get up. I don't brush my teeth. You're what starts my day. So what happened, your alarm didn't go off?"

"I love you," she says. "You are what starts my day, too." She is thinking about what Otto said about the head and the transformation of the heart and the way one moves through life.

"So," her mother says. "If you have me as the woman in your life, what do you need Lisa for? She can't spell. What you need with your dyslexia is someone who can spell."

She laughs.

"I'm not kidding."

She finds the War Correspondent after his panel has ended and waits while he signs copies of his book. "Yes, we did wear vests that said 'press' so people knew who we were," he tells a man, "but we stopped when we became higher-value targets." What is he like as bullets are whizzing past or when men with machetes appear in the middle of the night? What is the balance between excitement and terror?

When he's finished, they escape into the day. She hands him the keys. "You drive."

"Rakel, I live in New City," he confesses. "I am a perpetual passenger. I have no license."

Even Lisa drives.

The orchard is ripe with families and children and bumblebees buzzing. They debate between buying a half-bushel basket and a bushel and agree that a half is only a half, and so they buy a bushel basket and head into the fields.

"Erike, how was it today in town?" she asks as they walk down the rows of the orchard, past signs that say RIPE THIS WAY.

"I got new shoes for the horse, and I saw my cousin Heschl. He has troubles that one cannot speak about."

"His daughter?"

"No, his son."

She shakes her head, tsk, tsk, and thinks of her therapist, clucking.


Picking apples off the trees, they search for ones that are ripe, that come to them with only a tug. They polish the apples to a shine on their shirts and bite from the same apple at the same time—the skin crisp, the flavor sweet, the texture meaty and young. A few bites and then it is discarded as they hunt for the next one. He lifts her to get the perfect one from the top of a tree and then asks her to wait while he runs to the farm stand and buys a jar of honey.

He pours the honey on the apples they eat. Honey runs down his hands; his fingers are in her mouth—it's sticky.

They celebrate early New Year. Rosh Hashanah is next week, the beginning of the Days of Awe.

"I want to have you right here in the orchard," he says, lifting her skirt, unzipping his pants, his shirt hiding the details.

Does anyone see them pressed into a tree, his comic humping causing ripe fruit to fall on their heads?

She pushes him off, laughing. "Erike, put that away. You're acting like you've got pickles in your *keppe*. We're in public."

Reluctantly, he zips up. "I'll tell you something about genocides that people don't talk about."

She waits.

"They fucked a lot. They fucked all the time, because they needed the relief, they needed not to think for a brief moment, needed to remind themselves that they were human, and because they knew they were going to die."

"Even when the world is not at war, we all still die," she says, picking another apple, dropping it in the nearly empty basket. There is the sound of apple hitting apple—bruising.

"When we used to hang around together, none of the guys ever asked me out."

Another apple dropped into the basket.

"They just wanted to get laid. They didn't want to contend with someone."

"And that's why I'm gay," she says, dropping in a sour green apple.

"Because you couldn't get laid?"

"It's not like I couldn't get laid. I just couldn't get laid by a peer, because the girl has to be less than equal," she says, climbing a short ladder against the trunk of a tree. "The girl has to tell you that you're wonderful and powerful and all those things, but what about her? Isn't she also wonderful and powerful, or is she just the girl you fuck? And I'm not so much talking about you—you were married to your wife, whatever her name was. . . ."

"Marcy."

"You were married to Marcy, and I was busy fucking Saul Stravinsky."

"You were fucking Saul Stravinksy? Did any of us know? He was my hero."

"He was everyone's hero," she says. "And he was an ass. The thing he liked about me was that I didn't care—I treated him worse than he treated me, and he seemed to like that. And he taught me a thing or two."

"About sex?"

"About editing."

"Marcy and I went to hear him read at the 92nd Street Y with

Philip Roth. It was an incredible pissing contest. He and Roth clearly hated each other, which makes sense—they were practically the same person."

"I am aware," she says. "I was there, giving him a pre-show blow job in the bathroom of the green room."

He shakes his head.

"You know about the ball hairs?"

Again he shakes his head no.

"Saul's second wife wrote a memoir about their marriage, *The Door Was Always Open*. She went on about how much he loved his balls because they were so big—'Bigger than Brando's,' he used to say."

"Stop!" Erike cries abruptly. "I can't hear any more. Some things should remain a mystery."

"I have one of his ball hairs," she continues. "It's what the women who slept with him did. We'd take a hair, put it in a clear glass ball, like how people do with dandelion pods, and wear them on a chain around our neck. Hairs from the nut. Twice a year we have tea, usually eight or ten of us."

He stares at her in disbelief.

"Google it," she says. "One of them rather famously wrote about it."

"We're sitting in an apple orchard on a beautiful day, we escaped a genocide conference, and you're telling me about Saul Stravinsky's balls?" He is genuinely dismayed. "Seriously—it was all incredible. I was humping you, eating Granny Smiths, and celebrating the coming New Year. I was about to put an Empire in your mouth, truss you up against the vines, and you start talking about Saul Stravinsky."

"Do you think you might be overreacting?"

"No," he says. "No." He sits on the ground, like a child sulking. "Really?"

"I don't know," he says.

"Can I change the subject? This morning I heard a guy ask you about wearing a press vest, and you said that press are high-value targets now."

He nods.

"How close are you to things when they really get going?"

"I'm standing right there. I have a flak jacket, a helmet, a recorder, a pad and pen, and a camera, even though I'm a lousy photographer."

"And if you see something bad happening or about to happen, do you do something, like say, 'Hey, I think there are bad guys coming' or 'Wait, there's a kid in there'?"

"I'm a journalist, not a soldier."

"But what does that really mean?"

"As I said to the guy who called me a pussy, I'm there to observe and report, not to interfere. I am a witness."

"You stand by and watch while people are killed?"

He says nothing.

"Is there something more you could be doing?" she asks, and immediately realizes she sounds just like her mother; she's blaming him for not doing enough.

"Even if I got in the middle of it, it wouldn't change things."

"You sound defensive."

"I am," he says. "And by the way, I do get involved. I try to bring humanity to the situation. My pockets are always full of treats for the children, Starbursts and Twizzlers, because everyone likes candy and they don't melt in the heat."

"You're involved because you give away candy? Is that what you just said?"

He stands up and faces her, like a gorilla making himself big to intimidate. "Yes, that's what I do. I go through war zones with Smarties in my pocket. You have no idea what you're talking about," he says. "Your stuff isn't even real, you just make it up."

"Are you picking a fight?"

"You're the one picking it."

"Clever, trying to make the pickee the picker. Just because it's fiction, that doesn't mean it's not true. What you're saying is that your observations, standing there and doing nothing while people are being killed, are more important than my spending seven years developing a layered, multigenerational narrative that spans decades, giving voice to those who aren't here to represent themselves."

"Truth is stronger than fiction."

She almost says, "You're entitled to your opinion," but catches herself. "Truth isn't synonymous with history. The point of fiction is to create a world others can inhabit, to illuminate and tell a story that stirs empathy and compassion. And, asshole," she adds, "fiction helps us to comprehend the incomprehensible."

"I repeat, you have no idea what you're talking about." His voice is both full and tight with emotion. "I have seen a mine explode under a woman's feet as she's carrying her baby, watched as the woman is sheared off below the waist and the baby becomes a projectile flying through the air, a vision that in another context might be magical, but here it is magic turned to murder as the baby lands on a car, still, eyes fixed, heart stopped, a life smashed. The dying mother is asking about her baby while others are gathering the parts of her body that have been separated. A man comes with her leg, carrying it like an offering, like perhaps it might be reattached. Dark blood is staining the ground. That night the mother and baby were buried together. It's too much for the brain to process, to see bodies no longer whole, parts of a person. It's a shattering of the self. I helped dig the grave," he says. "I have helped dig many graves. How's that for the incomprehensible? Does that help? Is that doing something?"

"You win," she says, noticing that it's the same thing she does with Lisa. She wants the fight, and then she can't deal with it. "You saw it happen. You wrote it. You carry it with you—full score. It's both beautiful and devastating."

"It's not a competition," he says.

"It is, and that's what's pathetic. A minute ago you told me that what I did somehow wasn't weighty enough, or real enough. Is the desire to dominate, to win, fundamental to human nature? Is man's cruelty to man a fact of life? Are we such animals? There is a rank and an order that over time inevitably lead to extinction. The big question is, what are the obligations of consciousness? Can we train ourselves to do things differently? That's why we're here, asshole."

"You keep calling me 'asshole' like you've decided that's my new name."

"We're not real," she says. "The true witnesses are those who died, those who were stripped naked and gassed, those who were hacked to death by neighbors they grew up with, young men covered in sarcoma sores, wasting away, whose parents wouldn't even come and say good-bye. We are the witnesses' witness. I come to these conferences to acknowledge them; they need each other, but they also need the rest of the world to say, 'I see you.'"

Silence.

"There is something wrong with me," he says. "I keep having to go back, again and again."

"I'm the same," she says.

"I go around the world, to different places, to see things that no one else should see. I need it to have an effect on me, to get through to me and wake me up."

"And then what? What would you be if you were awake? Would you realize that you're an impostor, that you're just a man in pain, not a hero, just human? And then what would you do?"

"I have no idea," he says. "It's like I need to be punished. Again and again I go back."

"Well, let's find out. You're walking home from here," she says. She has no idea where that idea came from; it just came out of her mouth.

"Have you been taken by a dybbuk?" he asks. "It's miles."

She carries the almost-half-empty bushel of apples and the jar of honey to the car and drives off. She has no idea what she's done or why, has no idea about anything that's happened in the last twenty-four hours. A dybbuk indeed—would that hold up in court? She drives toward town and then five minutes later abruptly turns around and goes back, expecting to find him walking along the side of the road. He's nowhere. Feeling horrible for having left him, she drives up and down looking—nothing. She leaves telling herself he's a big boy, he's been in war zones, he can get himself home from an apple orchard.

Whatever it was, whatever it might have been—done. Over. Finis.

As she's driving, she's thinking about what they were doing, the way they were playing with each other, the freedom of their conversation as imaginary others. Her mind goes back to Otto that morning at breakfast.

"The games children play—war, cops and robbers—always good guys and bad. There is something there, something about human behavior?" He paused. "I had a frightening thing happen to me last time I was in America. I was speaking at a university in

Virginia, and I went to walk around the town. There was an antique store. I was wondering what is an American antique, what objects do they keep. So I went in. There were old ceramic bowls, heavy wooden benches, a thick black kettle one would put over an open fire, American flags, a sign from a feed store. And near the back of the store, I see something hanging; at first I think it is a decoration, a ghost for Halloween, white hand-sewn muslin, and then I realize it is something else. The head comes to a point, like a cone. . . . It is a white sheet with a pointed hood."

At the hotel she washes the apples in her bathroom sink. She writes a note, pausing to look up the number of the Jewish New Year: *"Fresh-Picked Happy New Year 5778."*

She brings the apples and the jar of honey down to the bar and leaves them on the table near the juices from Be My Squeeze. Philanthropy is the opposite of misanthropy.

"You see what's happened, don't you?" Otto said to her that morning over babka. "It spreads from generation to generation. It becomes the child's task to mourn because the parents can't. They survived, but they are frozen, holding their breath for forty years, not really alive. It is the job of the children, representing the dead."

Back in her room, she calls her mother again.

"She cheated," her mother says.

Her heart hears before her head—tachycardia. "Pardon?"

"Lisa cheated."

"Mom, what are you talking about?"

Her mother starts again, louder, slower. "Your girlfriend,

L-I-S-A . . . and I, we were playing Words last night on our phones, and I think she cheated. 'Xyster.'"

"I have to call you back," she says, hanging up.

A break. A moment. What happened? She can't say what she did, she doesn't know; did she lose consciousness? Did she throw something, smash her own head against the bathroom wall? Vomit? She has no idea except that time passed.

She calls Lisa.

"You mother is mad at me because I beat her at Words," Lisa says.

There is silence.

"Hello?" Lisa says.

"My mother says you cheated," she says, too calmly.

"Are you out of your mind? Your mother kept telling me that my words weren't real. She said that 'scry' was an Internet abbreviation and didn't count. . . . And that tone. You're speaking to me in that tone, imperious, as though you're sure you know something."

"Fine, then tell me I'm wrong," she says.

"I don't need to tell you you're wrong, because you know you're wrong. And you know what, little Miss Permanent Griever, that's what I call you in my knitting group, the Permanent Griever. You're the girl who goes to Holocaust conventions all over the world and grieves for others because she can't feel anything in her own life."

"Are you sure you want to go there?" she says, stunned. It's not like Lisa to be mean or go off.

"You know what? I don't have to go anywhere," Lisa says, "because you're the one who goes. You run away, you never deal with anything, you never even play Words with your own mother. Damn you," she says.

"This is the fight," she says.

"Yes. Damn it," Lisa says. "This is the fight I thought we'd have before you left, but I guess we're having it now. I guess we're having it while you're away because it would be too hard to have it when you got back, because then we'd have to deal with things."

"Exactly," she says.

"Exactly what?" Lisa says.

"Exactly what you said. You're right," she says. "You win. Touché."

"I'm not trying to win, I'm actually trying to talk to you—but apparently that's not possible."

"Right again," she says.

"Stop it," Lisa says. "Just stop it."

"I'm not doing anything except saying that you're right. All the things you just said are entirely right. Now what?" Silence. "What do you want to do?" she asks.

"I don't know," Lisa says. "Are we supposed to do something? I just wanted to talk. Why don't we just put a pin in it?"

*"Aroyslozn di kats fun zak,"* she says.

"I have no idea what that means," Lisa says.

"It's Yiddish for 'letting the cat out of the bag.'"

"I'm sorry we fought," Lisa says.

"So the note says," she points out. "I have to go."

"That's it? A thunderclap argument and you have to go?"

"I have a panel."

"You do not. I have your schedule right here. Your last panel was this morning."

"It's a pop-up panel on Gerda Hoff, the survivor who wrote the cancer memoir, *Living to Live*," she says, surprising herself with her impromptu fib. "Gerda is a remarkable woman, feisty. And she loves chocolate."

"Bring her a thing," Lisa says.

"Not funny." A pause. "And I'm sorry, too," she says. "I really am. Everything you said is true. I suck at talking about things. And yes, for some strange reason I am deeply attracted to the pain of others. I can't say more—except to agree with you."

"Fine," Lisa says. "Do me a favor?"

"What?"

"Be nicer to your mother."

She sits, she tries to meditate, her mind is spinning in all directions. She thinks of Otto; how was it that without knowing him she had been so deeply drawn to him, had been determined to find him, to hear his story? And without knowing her, he knew her so well. She thinks of Lisa and sees that she herself is the one who is a child. She expects Lisa to demand something of her that she needs to demand of herself. She can't wait to tell the therapist, who she imagines will be impressed or worse. The therapist might say something like, You seem pleased with this idea, but what can you tell me about what it means to you?

She hears Otto's voice from this morning: "I recently read a book that had been translated about a family where the uncles had been sent to the camps. The children, who never knew the uncles, grew up playing prison camp the way others played house or school. 'Dance for me,' the guard says, and the little boy dances. 'Tell me stories,' the guard says, and the little girl tells stories. 'Make me some lunch,' the guard says, and the children sneak upstairs and make sandwiches and bring them back down. The guard does not share. 'We are hungry, too,' the children say. 'No food for you.' 'But it is lunchtime for us, too.' 'Eat worms,' the guard says. 'Now I'm tired,' the guard says. 'Take care of yourselves for a little bit. And while I am sleeping, walk my dog and do my homework.'"

———————

"The Reenactments," she said to Otto. "That's a scene from my book."

"It was beautiful," Otto said. "But you see from the way the children handled the box that had been so carefully carried from place to place for many years and how frightened they looked when it broke open and spilled across the floor that it had become a myth. And then, when the box was broken, what did they do with the treasures that had belonged to the uncles? They put them in their game. They didn't make them precious, they brought them to life."

She wrote it. She lived it, too, in the basement of her cousin's house.

"What you see," Otto said, "is that history can't be contained, cannot be kept in a box. As much as we might want to keep the past where it was, it is always present. We carry it with us, not just in our grandmother's silver but in our bodies, the cells of our hearts. And that is why I am here. I am the person with the containers who wants to tell everyone—dump it out, pour it, let it spill. This is it, *bisl lam*, this is all you get. And, I might add, even for those who believe there is another world, a place we go when we are no longer here—they're not kidding when they say you can't take it with you."

She sits, she tries to meditate, but instead she weeps inconsolably for a very long time. She weeps until she runs out of tears, and then she sits silent and dry.

He knocks on her door, face flushed pink, dripping with sweat, shirt stained, smelling like a buffalo.

"What are you so happy about?" she asks, blotting her eyes. "You look ecstatic."

"At first I was furious. You left me there by the side of the road. It was like you dropped me on my head. But then the walk was amazing. I crossed a Revolutionary War battlefield with the rolling hills in the background, and for the first time I had the physical sense of what it was our ancestors fought for. When I got tired, I hitchhiked. I got a ride in the back of a pickup truck with a pair of giant, very well trained German shepherds."

She touches something brown on his shirt. "What is this on you, shit?"

"I think it's chocolate. I stopped for ice cream."

"The walk was supposed to be your punishment, and you got ice cream?"

He nods, guilty, like a small child. "I had a vanilla-and-chocolate twist with a dip into the chocolate that hardens. They called it a Brown Cow. It was fantastic. I hadn't had one since I was a kid on Cape Cod."

"You went to the same place we went last night—it was in the opposite direction of where I left you?" she asks, incredulous.

"No," he says. "A different place, the Farmer's Daughter."

She's irritated, almost jealous; he got ice cream and rode in a pickup truck. "Everything for you is a sublime experience."

"What have you been doing?"

"Me?" She's tempted to tell him there was a pop-up panel with Gerda Hoff. "I was fighting," she says. "With my mother and then with Lisa."

"Ah," he says, nodding. "Do you know what's happening downstairs right now?"

She shakes her head no.

"Stand-up comedy," he says.

"Holocaust humor?"

"Actually, a black guy from South Africa, followed by an open cabaret: 'Songs and Stories from Distant Lands.' Do you mind?" he asks as he opens the minibar. "I don't feel very good. Everything hurts."

"You walked too far. Too much sun. Tylenol or Motrin?" she asks. "Do you have any allergies?"

"And now you're a doctor?"

"At least you didn't say nurse."

He washes down Motrin with scotch and pulls her toward him.

"You stink," she says, pushing him into the bathroom, turning on the shower. He can't tell if she's really mad, and neither can she.

"Do you know that I'm named after Harry Houdini? And I think that's why I slip through so many situations," he says from inside the shower.

"What?"

"Harry Houdini's real name was Erik Weisz. He was the son of a rabbi."

She's giving herself a cold, hard look in the bathroom mirror. She is thinking about what they both do; they are professional witnesses, reminding others to pay attention, keeping the experience alive, hoping that the memory will prevent it from happening again. She is wondering what they're both so afraid of that it has stopped them from living their own lives. She is not paying attention to him. He splashes her with water. Her shirt quickly becomes see-through. "You want the world should see what is private to me?"

"Yes," he says, "I want to see you. I want to look at you the way you looked at me yesterday."

He is pulling at her clothes.

"Stop, you're ripping it."

"I don't care. Tomorrow I'll go to Orchard Street and buy you new underwear."

"I hate you," she says. "You ever suck cock?"

"No."

She brings the box from Lisa into the bathroom and rips it open. Three chocolate cocks fall out: pink, milk, and dark.

"Are you going to fuck me with those? Is that what lesbians do?"

"You're going to suck it," she says.

They both almost laugh but catch themselves.

"Do you have a safe word?" she asks.

"Like my password?"

"No, a safe word for sex play, like a way of crying uncle if you want to stop."

"Roth1933," he says. "It's my password, too. Now you can take me for all I'm worth. What's yours?"

"Ovum," she says, slipping the dark chocolate dick into his mouth.

His hands find her female form in ways that are entirely different from Lisa's. Lisa likes her arms, the cut of the biceps, her shoulders. His hands are on the curves of her hips, grabbing her ass, lifting her onto him.

They are doing things with each other and to each other that have them on the verge of hysteria—they are laughing, crying. They are outside themselves, and they are themselves, and then they are asleep.

In the morning there is a circle on his chest like a bull's-eye.

"You have Lyme disease."

"It doesn't happen that fast," he says.

"Sometimes it does."

They kiss. The kiss is deep and filled with a thousand years of longing, a thousand years of grief. They part for breath, laughing—

they both know. She bites him hard on the shoulder, her teeth catching the muscle, leaving a mark.

The conference is over. There is no good-bye, because if they said good-bye, it would mean that something had ended.

"What I've learned after being the keeper of the grief," Otto said, "is that letting go doesn't mean you forget, but you find freedom, the room to continue on. There is the fear of forgetting, but it doesn't happen. One learns to live with the past and allow oneself and others a future. One never forgets."

She drives to the airport, drops off her car, and gets on the plane. She wishes the plane were a time machine, a portal to another world. She wishes it would take her somewhere else.

She is home before Lisa gets back from work.

"How was the conference?" Lisa asks.

"Good," she says as they are making dinner. "I met Otto Hauser."

"Your hero," Lisa says.

"My hero," she says.

Are they going to talk? Are they going to break up?

Lisa says nothing more about the fight, and neither does she. She brought two chocolate cocks back with her. After dinner she offers them to Lisa. "Which do you want?"

"I just want you," Lisa says, patting the sofa next to her. She sits next to Lisa. The cat jumps up and gives her a big sniff and makes a couple of circles before jumping across her and curling up on Lisa's lap.

Time passes. She writes the War Correspondent into a short story. He's disguised as a Buddhist poet and she as a brain surgeon. They meet when he bumps his head. They have nothing in common except a koan.

She forgets about the chocolate cocks until she discovers them one day at the back of the fridge. She melts them down and bakes them, pink and milk chocolate, into a chocolate swirl bread—a babka of sorts.

She thinks of Otto. "You know who comes to my talks these days? People who are still fighting. In Israel they call ahead into Gaza and say, 'You have five minutes. We are coming to bomb your neighborhood. Get out.' They call it 'the knock on the roof.' It seems polite but strange—you tell people ahead of time that you're coming to kill them? It reveals to me we have made a habit of treating each other like this. Old habits are hard to break."

And then he took her head between his hands and kissed her on the head. *"Shepsela,"* he said. *"Du bist sheyn."*

# Hello Everybody

She hears his car grinding up the hill. At the edge of the driveway, the engine shudders, continuing on for a few seconds before falling silent. He buzzes the front gate; Esmeralda, the housekeeper, lets him in. The gate closes with a thick, metallic click.

"Where are you?" he calls out.

"I'm hiding!" Cheryl yells from the backyard.

He comes in through the pool gate.

"Shouldn't that be locked?" she asks.

"I remembered the code," he says.

"The pool boy's code, one-two-three-four?"

He nods. "Some things never change."

"Is that good or bad?" she wants to know.

"It's difficult," he says.

She is right where he left her—on a recliner by the edge of the water.

"You look pale," she says, raising her sunglasses, squinting to examine him.

He looks down at his arms. "I'm regular," he says.

"How can you see anything? Your glasses are so dark."

"They're for sailing," he says. "You know, the reflection off the water."

"They're wraparound, like an old man with cataracts wears," she says.

"Cadillacs," he says. "I always used to wonder what was so bad about being old and having Cadillacs. I'm blind," he says, taking the glasses off. "In the east the light is softer, gentler, more shadows. Here it's klieg-bright, like living on a film set. And you?" he asks. "How are you?"

"Blind, too," she says. "But only when I go indoors. When I go inside, everything is black and I crash into things."

Walter sits on the recliner next to hers and puts the glasses on again.

"I'm glad you're home," she says, only just realizing how much she's missed him. "Do you remember when we first met?"

"Yes," he says. "I smiled at you, and you threw up."

"Spit up," she says. "When you're four months old, it's called spitting up. I didn't throw up on you until much later."

"And so the story goes," he says.

"It was in a Music Together class," she says.

He nods. "My mother has a theory that in twenty years a spaceship will land, the doors will open, the song 'Hello Everybody' will play, and our entire generation will march, without a second thought, onto the mother ship."

"Wouldn't surprise me," she says. "So do you feel different? Was it the way you thought it would be?"

"The same and different," he says. He has been away at school, and—although she didn't realize until now—she felt thoroughly abandoned.

"I had my logo branded onto my butt," she says, rolling over and pulling her pants down; her "monogram" is a deep scar on the curve of her ass. "You can touch it," she says.

With his finger Walter traces her cursive initials. "Does it hurt?" he asks.

"No," she says. The skin is surprisingly absent of sensation. She thought it would be more sensitive, but instead of feeling more she feels nothing. She pulls up her bathing suit and rolls over.

He sticks out his tongue—there's a metal stud in the center; it wasn't there in the fall when he left for school.

"Does *that* feel good?" she asks.

"I don't know yet," he says, grinning. "I was hoping you would tell me."

She laughs. Her teeth are exceptionally white.

"Your smile is amazing," he says.

"Oh," she says, blushing, "I had a crushed-pearl polish last week."

"Nice," he says.

She cocks her head. "Are you wearing makeup?"

"A little," he says. "It has a sunblock effect." His acne is covered in thick pancake makeup, like the kind a television actor wears; his skin reads like a topographic map of adolescence. Twice a day he wraps his face in hot washcloths, drawing the hard, hot eruptions to a head. He thinks it's horribly ironic that this should happen to a young man—like rubbing his face, literally, in the pus of puberty. He wrote a paper on it at school, "Acne as Expressed in Contemporary American Childhood." They are forever marking and unmarking their bodies, as though it were entirely natural to write on them and equally natural to erase any desecration or signs of wear, like scribbling notes to oneself on the palm of the hand. They are making their bodies their own—renovating, redecorating, the body not just as corpus but as object of self-expression, a symbiotic relation between imagination and reality.

Neither siblings nor neighbors, they grew up together—each

other's witness and confidant. He was the first one to see her nose job, her breasts—both the original ones and the add-ons. She saw his chin even before he did, and his eyebrow piercing.

"How's your head?" he asks.

"Medium," she says. "Yours?

"Dented," he says. "Transitions are hard."

"Are you medicated?" she asks him.

"Lightly."

"And you?"

"Moderate," she says.

"It's hard to be depressed out here," he says. "It's paradise."

"The medication has to work twice as hard." She pauses. "I keep wondering what analysis is like. Does anyone actually do it anymore?"

"Do you mean does anyone practice analysis or is anyone in analysis?"

"Either," she says.

"I think you have to be older and have more of a history," he says.

"You have to go five days a week. It becomes your life," she says. "I think I'd rather just lie here talking to myself."

"It's probably just as good," he says.

"I went to see my mother's psychiatrist," she tells him.

He's genuinely surprised. For years they discussed the fact that they thought the psychiatrist was out of his mind, based on "quotes" her mother repeated. They also suspected that her mother was having an affair with him. After so many years of hearing her mother say *Dr. Felt says* and *According to Dr. Felt*, "I needed to see for myself what it was all about. I thought I'd reached a point where I could handle it." She takes a breath. "Honestly, I'm not sure what made me do it. It was more like a compulsion. I just had to see who he was."

"And?"

"Not good," she says.

"In what way?"

"It was a really weird office, very not L.A., modern but old at the same time—there was a black leather sofa, Oriental rugs, weird African statues with big genitals, and it smelled funny."

"Like what?"

"A combination of meat, sweat, and sadness."

"What was he like?"

"Overinflated," she says. "I asked should I sit or lie down. He didn't answer. So I simply took a seat. I couldn't tell if he didn't hear me or just didn't want to say anything.

"Then he spun around in his chair, stared at me, and asked, 'Do you want a boyfriend?'" She goes on to repeat the dialogue, imitating Dr. Felt.

"I said, 'Yes.'

"'You need to lose ten pounds,' Dr. Felt said.

"'Not that kind of boyfriend,' I said.

"'Maybe you're gay,' Dr. Felt said.

"'Maybe I'm normal. Maybe I want a boyfriend who likes me for who I am and not who you think I should be.'

"'Gay,' Felt said.

"'Not,' I said.

"'It must be hard for your parents. You're so defiant. Is there anything you enjoy?'

"'The sky, the earth, the wind, the sea,' I said, 'and food. I love food.'

"'Gay,' Felt said.

"'Isn't it interesting? If a woman wants to be appreciated, accepted for who she is—you think that makes her gay? Why doesn't it make her attractive to a man?'

"'Men want women to look like people in a magazine. They want women to have tits and look good on their arm. They don't want to be challenged, they don't want to take care of you—for a man it's all about them.'

"'If that's true, why does my father put up with my mother?'

"'Don't be naive,' Felt said.

"'What?'

"'The money is all hers.'

"'Okay, then why does she put up with him?'

"'Why do you think?' Felt said, very shrinklike.

"'Why do you think?' I asked the shrink. 'You've known her longer than I've been alive.'

"'Is it that long?' Felt asked me, suddenly vulnerable.

"'Yes,' I said.

"'It's very hard to leave a marriage,' Felt said, snapping back into his shrink affect. 'Especially when there are children involved.'

"'Are you saying that it's my fault that my parents are still married?

"'Am I?' Felt asked.

"'Are you talking to me or to yourself?' I asked him. He made a sour, patronizing face. I stood up. 'And *you* need to lose at least twenty pounds. I don't know what she sees in you,' I said, and left."

"Then what happened?" Walt asks.

"He billed my parents six hundred dollars for an extended consultation. I intercepted the bill, wrote 'SCREW YOU' on it, and mailed it back. Not a peep about it since," she says. "I don't mind feeling paralyzed. I think I'm used to it. In fact, I'm not even sure that what people would call paralyzed isn't just normal for me. I don't move a lot."

"Unless you're in a spin class," Walter says.

"Yes, of course, in spin or yoga or dance, but when I'm not in a class, I'm very still."

"Do you think this is where you'll always be?" he asks.

"I don't know how to be anywhere else."

He glances at her thigh, as thin as someone's arm. "Remember when they used to call you 'Chunky'?"

"Like I could forget?"

"Was it after the candy bar?"

"Yep. The only good thing about my brother dying was no one ever called me Chunky again."

"How does anyone recover from that?"

"You don't," she says. "You can go see his room if you want; it's all still there like he'll be home any moment."

"Maybe your family should move," he says.

"We all just walk faster past his door."

"Anyone ever go in?"

"My father used to take naps in there, and Esmeralda feeds his fish."

"The same fish?"

"I don't know; I just know there are fish."

"What about your grandparents?"

"We don't talk to them anymore."

"Wasn't he with them when he died?"

"Yep," she says, adjusting her bathing suit.

"Imagine how they must feel?"

"He told them that he'd been bitten by a poisonous snake, and they said, 'It's just a bug bite, put a cold washcloth on it.' And then he was dead."

"How long has it been?" Walter asks.

"Almost three years," she says.

"What about your other grandparents?"

"Moved to a gated community in Phoenix where there are signs that say 'Watch Out for Walkers,' with illustrations of bent-over old people pushing walkers with tennis-ball halves on the bottom across an intersection."

"Do you visit them?"

"Not so much. They don't recognize my mom; they tell her she reminds them of someone, they can't remember who, and ask how long she's been working there."

"Do they know you?"

"They think I'm my mother's sister who died years ago. 'We've been so worried about you,' they say. 'Are you feeling all right? How is your health?' I don't know what to do, so I just pretend I'm her and I try and tell them about my sister, meaning my mother, and they look confused and ask, 'Do we have another child? How odd that we don't remember. . . .'" She pauses. "You know, I really always liked your grandmother. In my head I used to pretend she was my grandmother. Remember, we used to make cookies with her when we were little. She makes good cookies."

"Very good cookies," he says.

"We never had cookies in our house. My mother said they were 'dangerous.'"

"Do you want to swim?" he asks.

"I don't like getting wet," she says.

"Since when?"

"Since I got this haircut. If I get it wet, I have to redry it, and it's really hard to make it look right. I have to hot-iron it. I should have gotten a Brazilian blowout." She takes a breath and then blurts the things that have been most on her mind. "Are you seeing anyone at school?"

"It's not that kind of place," he says.

"What kind of a place is it?"

"All boys. What about a bike ride?"

"A real bike? Not like a spin bike at the gym?"

"A bike," he says. "Like the ones that are in the garage just sitting there."

She wrinkles her nose.

"I'm surprised you can still do that," he says.

And she bursts into tears. "Am I even real?"

The light, the sun, the reflection off the dry sandy earth, the flagstone, the pool water—it's all blindingly bright.

"It's hard to know, isn't it?" he says, gazing upward. "Look at the sky. Isn't it amazing? So blue, so open."

"My tears taste like sun lotion," she says.

He stands up. "I have to take a leak."

Going into the house is like passing through an air lock. There are newly installed thick plastic flaps over the screen door, like on the entry to the grocer's meat locker, meant to minimize the loss of purified cool air, to keep what's outside out.

Everything in the house is white, everything is new. Cheryl's mother has an "allergy" to old things. She has a profound fear of things that are used, including antiques, vintage clothing, books. Everything has to be new and smell factory-fresh.

He uses the guest bathroom in the front hall and can't help but notice open cans of Play-Doh purposely left on the top of the toilet tank.

The dog lies on the cool tile floor in the front hall, panting heavily. Her tail thumps as he approaches.

"Hey, Rug, how are you?" he asks, bending to say hello to the shaggy white dog. The dog's name is simply Rug, because . . . well, she looks like a rug.

"A special rug," Cheryl's mother once said. "Nonshedding. Her fur is hair like a human's, and so she needs to be groomed but not vacuumed."

"Are you hot?" he asks the shaggy dog. "Do you need a hairdo? Is it time to get out from under?"

"Is that you?" Cheryl's mother, Sylvia, asks. She is in the living room, laid out on the white sofa in her bathing suit—a one-piece in marine blue with a sarong loosely wrapped around her legs. The tan skin on her arms hangs a bit loose, as if the meat is missing and the sinew that remains has pulled slightly away from the bone.

"It's me," he says.

"I was thinking you'd be back soon. I can't see with this pack on my eyes. How are you?"

"Good," he says. "And you?"

"Fine," she says. "Except I can't see."

"Seems to be going around," he says. "I got special glasses from the doctor. Would you like to try them?"

She raises her arm, and he hands her his glasses. She slips them on over her ice pack.

"Oh, thank you, Walter, that helps." She's the only one who calls him Walter; everyone else calls him Walt or W.W.

"You might need to take the ice pack off," he says.

"This is perfect for now—there was light leaking in—making matters worse. I had a little bit of an accident," she says, and says nothing more.

"Can I get you anything?" he asks.

"Like what?" she asks.

"A drink?"

"That would be lovely. What are you having?"

"I don't know, maybe a Coke?"

"Just some bubbly water for me, with a wedge," she says.

"Ice?"

"No, it bruises the bubbles. There's a covered bowl of wedges in the small fridge under the sink," she says. And then she adds as a complete non sequitur, "Soon they'll be able to fix noses in utero."

Walter brings her a glass of water, no ice, with a wedge of lime. Cheryl's whole family, except her father, wears bathing suits all day, all the time, even at Christmas.

"They're pool people," Walter once told his mother. "They just want to go in and out."

"It's because they live so high up the hill," his mother said. "You can walk around half naked in a place like that because no one can see you."

"They don't care if people see them."

"Can you imagine if I wore my bathing suit all day?"

"No," he said.

Cheryl used to say that the bathing suit was what kept her honest; in her bathing suit she could tell if she was getting fat right away, in ounces.

"And," Sylvia, on the sofa, goes on to say, "did you know that the first use of liposuction was for women whose thighs pronate?"

"Pronate?" Walter says.

"Tip inward," she says. "It's a tricky business, you know. I've known of several women who had a poor outcome. Mrs. Lipmann lost a leg to a post-lipo infection."

"Sounds bad," he says.

"What about you, Walter?" the mother asks. "How was it in the East?" She asks this as though the East were the Far East, as though it were long ago and he'd ventured to an unexplored territory in the far reaches of Hong Kong or Shanghai.

"Good," he says. "I saw the fall for the first time in my life. The leaves turned, the air got cooler, the wind blew—it was just the way they say it is in books."

"I never liked it," she says. "Everything dying and falling down, then the cold, cold days. I hate being cold."

He nods, but she can't see him. There is a silence.

"Are you still there?" she asks.

"Yes," he says. "Just heading out."

"Go forth," she says, and he does.

He pushes back through the heavy plastic flaps and out onto the patio. The air outside, at least twenty degrees warmer and chock-full of microdebris, catches in his throat. He coughs and then takes a sip of his soda—the can is sweating.

"Did you see my mother?" Cheryl asks.

"Briefly," he says. "She's on the sofa."

"And?"

"Hard to tell," he says. "I didn't get a good look."

"She tried to have the color of her eyes changed. It didn't work, burned the corneas."

"Is she really blind?"

"Temporarily blurry," she says.

While Walter was gone, she'd dug her brother's old G.I. Joes out of the pool house and has set them up in a noncombat tableau under her chair—she won't go into his room, but she still likes to see his toys.

"The dog looks different," Walter says, not noticing the G.I. Joe situation.

"She had surgery for fatty tumors. They aren't dangerous, but they're really unappealing."

"Is that why she's panting?"

"She's recovering. Mom wants to keep her hair long until it's all healed so we don't have to look at it."

"And the Play-Doh in the bathroom? Is it supposed to inspire you to 'go'?"

Cheryl laughs. "She smelled some at a friend's house whose grandchildren were visiting and fell in love with the aroma. And she thought yellow and brown were 'funny' for the bathroom. You should see what's in her bedroom. She's addicted."

"And the fridge?" he asks.

"Too much pressure. She says we're more 'prepared-food' people than cooks, so we gave Esmeralda the big one and got two small under-the-counter ones."

"Your whole family is living out of a bar fridge?"

"Two bar fridges, plus I have one in my room that no one knows about. It's in my closet."

"Wow," he teases. "I go away for a couple of months and everything changes."

"You didn't even mention the flaps," she says, pointing to the door.

"It's my favorite part," he says. "Very vulval or grocer's dairy case."

"My idea," she says. "I wanted to go green. What's it like at your house?"

"Same as it ever was. You should come over sometime," he says.

"I can't," she says.

"My mother likes you," he says.

"You showed her a nude photograph of me."

"I didn't show her, she found it."

"Whatever," she says, annoyed. "I can't go to your house."

Cheryl slides off her lounger and crawls underneath to play with her brother's old G.I. Joes.

"We used to call them G.I. Jokes," Walter says.

"I gave them names, Tommy, Paul, and Pedro—the twins." She holds up two dolls that are exactly the same.

"Remember when Abigail got her prescription for medical marijuana and we all went to the top of Doheny and sucked on those marijuana lollipops and watched the sun set?" he asks.

"That was a perfect day," Cheryl says, definitively. "And remember when I used to lie in bed reading and eating pistachio nuts and I'd get the red dye all over the books, literal fingerprints on the pages?" She hides the G.I. Joes under the bushes by the pool.

"Reconnaissance mission," she says to no one in particular.

"And on your sheets, and Esmeralda yelled at you and made you switch to the natural nuts?"

"I like the red ones better," she says. "It's not really dye. I think it's just beet juice," she says. "Or not."

"Remember when we were younger and had such good imaginations?" he says.

"We didn't worry what other people thought?" she asks.

"We made our own tattoos," he says.

"Out of Elmer's glue and Magic Markers," she says.

"We spoke in other languages," he says. And for a magical moment, they revert to speaking in accents, his a kind of Russian-Yiddish. "Von day ve vill goh to zee place where I vas born. Et es so cold you vear a coat all year roundt, no von worries vhat you eat, no von ever sees your body. You vill lov it."

She responds in faux French, "'Ow do you say en français? You and I will promenade off into the Siberian sunset."

"Remember when we were kids," he says, reverting to English, "your mother would drop us in Beverly Hills for pizza?"

"She didn't like me to have pizza at home. It was too challenging for her—the scent was overwhelming, the temptation too great."

"You would order pizza with pepperoni and sausage, and then when it came, you'd pick off the toppings."

"I just liked the juice of the pepperoni," she says, climbing back onto her lounge chair.

"The grease," he says. "You liked the shiny pink grease."

"Is it weird that I was conceived during one of the Iraq wars and my sister was conceived the night the space shuttle blew up?"

"Do you think your parents only have sex in times of national emergency?" he asks.

"I think they only have sex when they're at a loss for words. Do you want to go to my room?" she asks, code for, *Do you want to have sex?*

"No," he says, "I'm kind of post it these days."

"What does that mean?"

"I'm not over it, but I'm not into it. I'm trying to inhabit myself in a different way?"

"Gay?" she asks.

He doesn't answer.

"You can tell me," she says. "If there's anyone you can tell, it's me."

"I just got back," he says. "I need time to readjust."

"He's adopted," she long ago told Abigail, in an effort to explain Walter to her sister.

"What is that supposed to mean?" Abigail said.

"Literally adopted," she said. "Like his parents gave him up. I mean, does he look like a Walter to you? I think he's more a Marc or an Adam."

"That's why he's always at our house? Because he has the wrong name?"

"He's at our house because he feels comfortable here. I'm his oldest friend in the world, and he thinks we're fascinating, like specimens he can study. He wants to be a scientist."

"He has no parents?"

"He has parents, but they're too milk-and-cookies, always asking, 'Do you need anything? Do you want to talk?' He needs a reality check."

"That's why he comes here?"

"Pretty much."

"It's not because I give you guys all the pot you want?" Abigail wanted to know.

"It's not about bribing us," she says. "We have a pool."

"They don't have a pool?"

"No."

"Are they poor?"

"I don't think so. They're just not pool people," she says.

"I don't get it," Abigail said.

A large white cloud passes in front of the sun, and there's a sudden drop in temperature. A cool breeze sweeps through, spinning tiny mini-tornadoes of loamy soil at the edge of the flagstone. Cheryl glances at her skin. "I'm covered in goose bumps."

"Pilomotor reflex," Walter says. "Same as what happens to a porcupine when its quills go up." He says nothing about the fact that due to his heavy makeup he feels no breeze on his face. He feels nothing except the sensation of being painted over and, when the sun is high, melting.

"The weather is changing," she says.

"Nothing stays perfect forever," he says.

"You're making me nervous," she says. "Are you sure you don't want to go to my room?"

"I'm sure."

"Okay, no biggie," she says. "How about we go hang out in the dent?"

The "dent" is what she calls the den, the odd room between the living room and before the long hall that leads to the bedrooms. The dent spans the full width of the house and is divided by a central passageway—the road by which all must pass. On either side of the passage is a dent, a room without doors that has no specific purpose. And despite the fact that the room is neither here nor there, it is in fact the most casual and most used space in the house. On one side of the dent there is a giant television mounted on the wall, always turned on with the volume down, and on the other side are built-in bookcases and a desk. It's the one "human" part of the house; there are family photos on the bookcases, all of them taken before Billy died, no photos from after. Walter isn't sure whether there really have been no family photos taken or if it's just too painful to put them up—family minus one.

"Is this a picture of you or your mom?" he asks.

"My mom when she was younger. She recently had all her childhood photos retouched so that everything is perfect—no snaggletooth, no cut on her cheek, no acne," she says, and then abruptly stops. "Acne" is the word not to be spoken.

"Do you want to play a game?" she asks.

"Like what?"

"I don't know, one of the games we used to play, like Operation, Clue, Life, Monopoly, Twister?" While he's thinking, she flips through glossy magazines, inhaling deeply from the perfume-scented pages. "I just love looking at pictures of food."

Her father walks though the room in a bright pink golf shirt and bright green pants. He's holding a hand mirror in front of him, staring at himself as he walks.

"Look at me," he says, speaking to no one in particular. "I look miserable, my eyes are falling. Why didn't anybody tell me? Why didn't one of you say something? If your own family can't tell you the truth, then who can?"

Her mother follows after him. "Use clear tape," she says. "That's what people do. There's some in my medicine cabinet."

As her mother walks through the dent, the channel on the television changes, the background music shifts, the lighting dims, Carole King begins to sing. It stays that way until she's five feet out of the dent, heading down the hall toward the bedroom, and then a quiet mechanical voice, like a small frog, says, "Revert, revert," and the television is back on the Weather Channel, the lighting brightens, and the unidentifiable but calming "earth sounds" music returns.

"What was that?" Walter asks.

"She's wearing her sensor. It's like a magic amulet around her neck. We all have them—the entertainment computer is programmed to adjust music, lighting, and temperature to the preset preferences of the sensor wearer."

"What if you're all in the room at once?"

"There's a hierarchy of who tops who—oldest to youngest," she says. "I personally never wear mine. Abigail once was so pissed at them that she reprogrammed hers and hid it in the bookcase. She turned the dent into a heavy-metal sound-and-light show. The only way to get it to stop was for one of my parents to remain in the room until the computer guy came—my father slept on the sofa for three days."

"Do you think your family was always like this, or did something change?"

"I'm not sure what you mean?" she asks, confused.

He lets it drop.

Her mother is descended from a long line of goddesses—Emma Goldman, Eleanor Roosevelt, Janice Dickinson, all of them powerful, some of them elongated—supermodels. Her father is a second cousin twice removed to Twiggy. Abigail is a model as well; she has the unique ability to look totally spaced out but be focused enough to follow directions—she's a natural. Malleable, pliable, Abigail wants to be seen but not as herself. She is forever putting on costumes, makeup, different personas, trying to find the right fit.

"You should be an actress," people used to tell Abigail.

"You should be yourself," Cheryl says.

"No idea how to do that," Abigail confesses.


The mother comes back through, again the music, lighting, channel change. "Walter, will you join us for dinner—we're going out to celebrate."

"What are we celebrating?"

"Abigail completed her parole."

"Great," Walter says.

And the mother leaves the room—and the little voice announces, "Revert, revert," and everything does.

"What was she on parole for?"

"Vomiting in public," Cheryl says. "It turned out that it was food poisoning, bad sushi, but my parents were convinced it was bulimia. So they let the police press charges, and Abby had to go to a Scared Straight program for people with borderline disorders."

"Is your mother still mad about our accident?"

She shakes her head no. "It just really frightened them. The timing was bad."

"We were running an errand for her," Walter says, defending himself. "Going to Costco to buy a hundred rolls of toilet paper. Who buys a hundred rolls of toilet paper?"

"She likes to be prepared."

"We were almost home, climbing the canyon, my foot was on the gas. A dog crossed the road. I swerved," he said. "I couldn't bear to hit an animal."

"I feel the same," she says.

They rolled over and over and then BAM, loud crash, dust, black. Silence.

"Are you still there?"

"Yep," she said.

"A dog crossed the road," he said.

"I saw it."

"Can you move?"

"Yes and no. What about you?"

"I can't get out."

"Are we going to burst into flames?" she asked.

"I hope not."

"Do you have your phone?"

Sirens, the Jaws of Life, cervical collars, tape. They are surgically removed from the car.

"It's a miracle," his parents say. "They both had their seat belts on. They're good kids."

"Her face is ruined," is the first thing her mother says when she sees her in the emergency room, still taped to the board.

"Thanks, Mom."

"I didn't say you were ruined, but your face is a mess. I'm calling Dr. Pecker, my plastic surgeon. If there's anyone he'll come in off the golf course for, it's me."

"Leave it," she begged. "I'll look like I've lived."

"Plastic surgery is recommended," the ER doctor said. "Better to fix it now while it's fresh."

Despite her protestations, her face was repaired; to the untrained eye, the damage is imperceptible.

"Will you come to dinner?" Cheryl asks Walter. "Abigail only eats foods that are ten calories or less, so it should be great."

"It will be," her mother says, chiming in from the other room. "We're trying a new place. It's called Micro-Macro. They serve tiny, designer-size macrobiotic bites."

"Sure," he says. He doesn't know how to say no.

In the late afternoon, the air stagnates. It stops moving entirely and fills with dust. They go back and forth from the pool to the dent. There is no spot that's truly comfortable.

"Hot out?" the mother asks from the sofa.

"Blistering," Cheryl says.

"The view is diminished by the smog," the mother says.

"Are the air filters working?" the father calls out from the other room. "I can't breathe without the air filters."

At four o'clock the mother extracts from the mini-fridge a frozen concoction her trainer makes and gives them each a shot glass full of it, and, oddly, they all feel better. They shower and dress for dinner. Cheryl puts a dress on over a bathing suit. "It's how I live," she says. "You can borrow a shirt." She opens her closet to Walter, who is wearing jeans over his swimsuit and a T-shirt. "Shop," she directs him.

He picks light blue gingham.

"Nice," she says. "Very summery."

In Los Angeles men wear a lot of pastels. In fact, they wear almost only pastels, or white or black—pastels go well with the setting, a hint of color, neither overwhelming nor negating.

"Are my eyes open or closed?" Sylvia asks when they gather in the living room.

"I'm not sure," Cheryl says. "Can you see?"

"Sort of," the mother says.

"Can you drive like that?" Abigail asks.

"I think they're more for being driven," the mother says. "Do I look sultry?"

"You look swollen and like you're sleepwalking," Abigail says.

Sylvia turns, announcing to them all, "You know I named her Abigail after Abigail Van Buren—Dear Abby—hoping that I would have a daughter who was a friend, a person I could share my troubles with. Apparently there was some confusion with my order, and instead I have this—a daughter whose middle name is trouble."

"Should we go in one car or two?" the father asks.

"Two," Abigail says. "That way no one straddles the hump."

"Did you ever get a new car?" the mother asks Walter.

"A new old car," Walter says.

"What kind is that?"

"Used," Walter says. "Cheap."

"Good on you," the mother says. This is always what she says when she doesn't know what else to say.

The children and adults divide into teams. Abigail takes the kids in her small Mercedes, and the father follows in his larger one.

"Is that a girl's shirt?" Abigail asks Walter as they're driving to the restaurant.

"What's the problem?" Cheryl wants to know.

"The buttons go the wrong way," Abigail says.

"What do you mean, the wrong way? They open and close—what else are buttons supposed to do?" Cheryl asks.

"On women's shirts the buttons are on the left, and on men's the buttons are on the right."

"Never knew," Walter said.

Abigail shrugs. "It's cool. The shirt looks good. I just didn't know if you knew. And I like your makeup. It looks good, too."

"It's not makeup," Cheryl says. "It's sunscreen."

"Whatever, it looks nice. You've got such nice eyes, you could actually wear a little eyeliner."

Walter says nothing.


They pull up to the restaurant, and a valet takes their cars, the maître d' leads them to their table.

"Do you have a menu that lists the calories?" Abigail asks.

"We don't, but if you tell me what your calorie limits are, I can speak to the chef and see what she suggests," the waiter says.

"Ten calories," Abigail says.

The waiter doesn't blink. "Is that total or per item?"

"Per item," the mother says.

"Got it," the waiter says. "Let me see what the chef can do—any allergies?"

"None."


When the food arrives, the mother sends her plate back and asks the waiter to take half off. "It looks overwhelming. I want just enough, but not too much," she says.

Abigail's plate is beautiful—a menagerie of foams, pockets, juices, reductions, whips, mousses, and a small tower of dry ice smoking in the center.

"Bravo," she says to the waiter.

Sylvia takes a taste of her no-cream creamed spinach, dabs the corners of her mouth with her napkin, and is instantly waving her arms, summoning the waiter.

"Uh-oh," she says. "I think these napkins are part polyester. I have a profound polyester allergy. Are my lips puffy?"

"Don't ask him that. He's a waiter, not a doctor," Abigail says, not even looking up from her phone and her food.

"Have you got any paper napkins?" the mother says.

The waiter returns with a large stack of paper napkins. "Gracias," she says.

"You're welcome," the waiter says.

At dinner they are all on their devices. The only person they talk to is the waiter. Occasionally and without warning they will speak randomly and out of context.

"Dinitia got sideswiped by a trailer on the 110," the mother says.

"Roger's going under," the father says, shaking his head.

"Again?"

"That's what he says. 'Film at eleven. The feds taking me out of the office in handcuffs.'"

"Poor Alice," the mother says.

The father appears deeply shaken.

"Can you turn away from me while you're talking, I can't look right at you—your face tells me too much," the mother says to the father. And they go back to their devices.

"You're not tied to Roger, are you?" the mother asks. "I mean, financially bound."

"No," he says. "We're just friends."

"Mindy got the cover of *Vogue*, fucking amazing," Abigail says.

"Language," the mother says.

"It's big—she's American. Almost no American girls get the cover anymore."

"Where do we go from here?" Cheryl asks Walter. "I don't know if this is the whole world or just this place."

"In what way?" Walter asks.

"Like, is this a place that only exists in this place and couldn't exist anywhere else? Like a state of mind or a moment in time?"

"You may have to leave the country," Walter says.

"Am I equipped?" Cheryl asks.

When they are done eating, the plates look much like they did when they were put before them. "Was everything satisfactory?"

"Delicious," the mother says.

"Would you like us to wrap the leftovers?"

"Yes, please."

The plates are cleared, and the waiter returns with an enormous doggie bag—actually a shopping bag filled with food. "Dessert or coffee for anyone?"

"No room," the mother says.

And the father takes the check.

As they wait for the valet to bring the cars, Abigail says, "Did you know that there's a park in Los Angeles, a well-known place not far from here, where people go and leave their doggie bags? Because the fact is, most of the people who don't finish their food really don't want to take it home with them. Someone wrote an article about it—'Eating Well Without a Home.' Every night hundreds of people leave doggie bags. You can just pull up, and someone will come right to your car and take the bag from you."

"Someone like who?" the father says, counting out cash to tip the valet.

"Someone like a homeless person will come to the window of your car and take your doggie bag."

"And your Cartier watch," her mother says.

"I think you use the other hand," the sister says.

"The wedding ring?"

"You could just feed it to the dog," the father says.

"Oh, no, I would never feed this to Rug. She gets only raw food— raw chicken, pheasant, beef, and organic grains in patties that are in the freezer. I'll give it to Esmeralda. She loves hand-me-downs."

When they get home, it's still light out. The adults go inside, Cheryl and Walter return to the pool, and Rug comes with them and lies on the flagstone at the edge of the water, dipping the toes of her front paws in. Cheryl pulls her dress off. He takes off the shirt and his pants. They are both as they were, as they have always been. The sky is charcoal, powdery black, reminding her of another day, another time.

Two goldfinches fly in and land on her knees. "Horatio and Ray, meet Walter," she says, introducing them.

"How do you know they're male?" Walter asks.

"Their markings," she says. She tells the birds to play dead, and they both lie on their backs, feet up.

"Weird," Walter says.

"I've been training them," Cheryl says, giving Horatio and Ray each a sunflower seed; the birds hang around waiting for more. "They also like poppy-seed bagels and watercress sandwiches," she says.

"So are they your new best friends?" Walter wants to know.

"Are you jealous?" she asks.

Annoyed, Walter stands.

"Okay, so tell me," she says. "Where's the exit sign?"

"It's not like the freeway," he says. "There are no signs, no ramps. You just have to decide for yourself when to take the leap." And with that he plunges into the water. When he breaks the surface, she's gone. Panicked, he climbs out, making wet footprints like dance steps on the flagstone, turning every which way, looking for her, frantically calling, "Cheryl, Cheryl!"

"What?" she finally says, punching her way back through the bushes with Rug, the dog, following her.

"I jumped in, and then you were gone. I thought you'd left me."

"Someday I may go somewhere, but I'm not leaving you. Rug went after something, and I went after Rug," she says.

"You're bleeding," he says, pointing to a scratch on her arm.

"I'm still hungry," she says, licking the blood. "Want some?" She offers him her arm.

Walter takes Cheryl by the hand and jumps, pulling her into the pool. "No matter what anyone says, this is it," he says.

"This is where we are," she says.

"This is the life," he says.

# All Is Good Except for the Rain

She rushes in, shaking the deluge from her jacket and her umbrella, quick to be rid of it. The maître d' takes the umbrella, lowers it with a swift shake, and slips it into a stand, where other, more relaxed umbrellas are already waiting.

"Your coat," he says.

"Please." She turns, spinning her coat off in a practiced twist.

"How are we this afternoon?" he asks.

"We are as expected," she says. "Take a look outside."

"It's good to see you again."

"You've become a habit," she says. "Best be careful—certain habits are often to be gotten rid of. Apologies," she says as she approaches the table where Genevieve is waiting. "I'm drenched." She sits and uses her napkin to blot her face.

"It seems like it's getting worse," Genevieve says, glancing up from her mobile.

"Of course it is. Would you expect otherwise?"

"One can hope," Genevieve says, and for a moment she is all thumbs as she finishes a text, hits SEND, and then slips the device into her purse.

"In these times the only way to remain optimistic is to side with the darkness and then be pleasantly surprised," she says.

"I suppose."

"Oh, we're not having one of those 'woe is me' lunches, are we? I was looking forward to a good time. I've had a week of a juice fast, and I'm desperate for food."

"Pig's-bladder chicken?" Genevieve perks up.

"Perfect. I'd make it at home or at least try, but I have no idea where you get a pig's bladder."

"Perhaps a butcher?" Genevieve suggests.

"And then how do you get the chicken into the bladder?"

"You just put your lips together and blow."

"Touché." Sarah glances at the menu. "You know, I may just have the salad, rocket and parmesan. So tell me everything," she says. "And quick."

"The big news: After a thousand nights alone, I'm finally seeing somebody."

"I know," she says. "We all know. But no one ever sees you with him."

"We're very private."

"Are you enjoying yourself?"

"I think so."

"What happened to your idea of going gay?"

"I suspended it."

"Water?" the waiter asks.

"Yes."

"Still or with gas?" the waiter wants to know.

"Still," they say.

"You don't want to go out? Make the scene? See and be seen? He is, after all, somebody. You'd get points for that."

"Points for what?"

"Points to use the next time around."

"As what? The former shag of somebody?"

"So you're keeping your love a semi-secret."

"Oh, I wouldn't call it love."

"Wouldn't you?"

"Not really. He's much, much older."

"Yes, I know. You act as if no one knows who he is. There's an enormous exhibition of his work at the museum."

"Yes," she says. "He took me to see it."

"So if it's not love, what do you call it?"

"An experience," Genevieve says.

"Ah," Sarah says. "And what is the experience like?"

"His hands are exceptionally strong, the hands of a worker—rough, calloused—but the insides are like an avocado—ripe, soft, untouched."

"How could he be so untouched?"

Genevieve shrugs.

"Do you feel you're getting to know him? Isn't that the big complaint? They all had him, but they never knew him?"

"I'm not sure what 'knowing' means. Perhaps if you give up needing to know, it becomes less of an issue."

"Clearly he's already had an impact," she says, somewhat snidely.

"He says the other women have wanted more than there is."

"It's possible," she says. "He may be right. We all want more than there is."

"Bread?" the waiter asks.

"No," Sarah says.

"Yes," Genevieve says.

"Yes or no?"

"One yes and one no," Genevieve says.

Sarah leans forward as though forced intimacy, if only spatial, will squeeze out the truth. "Does he appreciate you?"

"I think so."

"Is his skin falling off the bones like an old turkey's?" She pulls back, laughing at her own joke, which isn't funny. "Do you think he loves you?"

"Do you want me to be honest?"

"It's friends' lunch. Yes, be honest."

"I try not to think about love."

"And for lunch," the waiter needs to know.

"We'll have the bird, the pig's-bladder chicken, a side of spinach, some mashed, and what else?" Sarah asks Genevieve.

"Glass of wine?" the waiter suggests.

"Yes, a red, something full but nice."

"The cabernet sauvignon."

"I've been wondering about you," Sarah says, "about you and him. I've been trying to imagine it."

"Do you know something?" Genevieve says. "Is there something you know? You always know something, so if there's something you know, why don't you just go ahead and tell me."

"I don't know anything," Sarah says, and this is true.

The still water is poured. There is something between them that is brittle, tense. It's been that way since they met, as children, so the tension, the crispness, is familiar, but over time one would have hoped for a certain elasticity, a kind of give that has never emerged.

"You act like you know something. You act like you know all the intimate details, the unsaids of everyone else's life."

"I don't think of myself as acting. And if we're being honest . . ."

"We are."

"I know one small thing." She pauses. "I'm a little jealous."

"A taste from the kitchen," the waiter says, setting small plates in front of them. "House-made salami, a pocket of olive juice, and that's a mustard-ginger foam on the top."

"What about you? Are things better?"

"Sadly, I've never really recovered," Sarah says.

"It's been a while," Genevieve says.

"I'm slow to adjust," Sarah says.

"Better not to adjust. To adjust means you think it will then remain as it is, it will stay the same."

Sarah nods. "You're quite right. Don't adjust, simply carry on."

"Push forward," Genevieve says.

"'Onward Christian Soldiers,' 'Forward Through the Ages,' and all that." She sips her wine.

"How long do you maintain a grudge?" Genevieve asks.

"How long do you hold a crush?" Sarah retorts. "Time is irrelevant—what happened to me should never happen to anyone. It was one of those life-changing events. The worst part, I didn't see it coming, I didn't have a chance to prepare, to brace myself, to think, 'Here it comes,' and watch my life flash before my eyes. It was late afternoon, I was home alone."

"Having a moment to yourself," Genevieve says.

"I was having a sit-down, a moment, a cup of tea. I was trying to read a book that I'd been trying to read for months. The phone rang. It was him."

"Hugo," Genevieve says.

Sarah nods. "'Where are you?' I ask, wondering, 'Why aren't you home?' 'I'm at a friend's house,' he says."

"Who?" Genevieve says.

"'You don't know her,' he says. 'Look,' he says, 'I've got some news for you.'"

"News?" Genevieve says.

"'I don't like you,' he says. He pauses. 'Actually, it's worse than that. I loathe you. Our marriage is a sham, an ugly, disgusting excuse of a relationship.' 'Are you high?' I ask."

"No," Genevieve says.

"'Drunk?'" Sarah asks.

"Maybe a little," Genevieve says.

"'But that's not the point. The point is, I don't love you. And maybe worse, I hate our whole life—your friends, so clever, so self-satisfied, so fucking spoiled.' I take a deep breath."

"Hugo, you can't mean it," Genevieve says.

"'I do mean all this, and more,' he says. 'Your tits are hard. They're like rocks.' 'But you bought me my tits,' I say. 'They were an anniversary gift. It was you who wanted me to have bigger, firmer tits after the children were born. You said you missed my breasts, that mine hung like empty sacks, low and flat on my chest.' 'Well, I was wrong. Your old tits were better. Why would a woman get new tits just because her husband said so?'"

"You don't expect me to answer that," Genevieve says.

"There are sounds in the background," Sarah says. "'Where are you?'"

"I told you, at a friend's house," Genevieve says.

"'And are you sleeping with this friend?'" Sarah says.

"Yes," Genevieve says.

"'Since when?' I ask."

"Where did you meet her?" Genevieve asks.

"'In the park.' 'Is she there now?' There is no answer. I raise my voice. "'Did she tell you to call your wife and tell her you're leaving? Did she say no tickee, no washee? Did she put you up to this?' He says nothing. 'Is she listening to our conversation?' Still nothing. I get up from my chair. I go to the window. I open it. I think of jumping. I am overwhelmed, sickened. I look out. The streets are wet, the evening rain has just stopped, the city is wet, shining, kind of romantic, and there's Hugo on the phone telling me how disgusting my tits are and that my ass has gone flat. I remind him that he never had an ass."

"Men don't need one," Genevieve says.

"That's not true, it's a misconception. Women like to hold on to something, to give a little squeeze. 'Where are you, Hugo? Are you in the city? Are you right out there somewhere? Are you on the pay phone at the corner—someone is. Is that you, Hugo?'"

"I told you," Genevieve says. "I'm at a friend's house. I'm not where you can see me."

At the table Sarah's eyes begin to water. "I am sobbing. I hear myself say, 'Well, I've got some news for you, too. I put up with you for a long time, despite your comments about my tits, despite the fact that whenever you're supposed to show, you vanish. I got you through. Remember the cokehead episode? Remember when you sold your father's watch, when you bankrupted us, including the money my grandmother left for the children to be educated? I could have dropped you a thousand times, but did I, Hugo? Did I leave you, or did I get down on my knees, down to where you are, and tell you, "Don't worry, Bumpy, it'll be better soon, it won't happen again. Things like this, they happen once in a lifetime, and it's over now—all gone." I held you, Hugo, I talked you down, and this is what you're doing, this is my thanks?'"

"I'm calling to say it's over," Genevieve says.

"'Hugo, this is low, this is mean, it's lousy. After twenty-six years of marriage and four children, you call me from some chick's house to say you're getting head and our marriage is over. What is she like, Hugo? Is she that good? Does she do it some way I should know about, something special, a little trick in the finish?'"

"'I'm going now,' he says," Genevieve says.

"Yes," she says.

There is a distraction as their main course is whisked out of the kitchen, the pig's bladder blown up like a balloon, a thin, fleshy globe. All eyes are on their table as the waiter pops the bladder with a carving knife and reveals the chicken, which appears naked, as if uncooked. "It doesn't brown in the bladder," the waiter says. "That's what keeps it so tender." He deftly takes the skin off the chicken and carves the bird as the patrons at other tables ask, "What did they order?"

"I was left without words," Sarah says.

"He called two weeks later," Genevieve says. "Not exactly contrite."

"No, more like it was all a misunderstanding. 'It was a big nothing,' he said. 'No big deal. I was taken for a ride.' 'She dumped you,' I said. 'Yes. But not before she got ten thousand bucks outta me.' 'For what? Everything? When we last spoke, it sounded like you were getting something out of it.'"

"Did you tell the kids yet?" Genevieve says.

"'No.'"

"Why not?"

"'I didn't know what to say.'"

"You have to believe me," Genevieve says.

"'I do believe you. I believed you for twenty-six years, and I believed you two weeks ago. It's right now that's up in the air. What about the sham, the ugly, disgusting, poor excuse for a relationship? What about my hard tits?'"

"I was under the influence. Maybe we could get your tits redone, softened up a bit, put back where they were originally," Genevieve says.

"'Maybe these are my tits now and that's just the way they're going to be.'"

"Maybe," Genevieve says.

"'Come home,' I say," Sarah says.

"And what did you tell the children?" Genevieve asks.

"We had to tell them something," Sarah says.

"What were they thinking? Did they wonder where he'd gone?"

"We sat them down and said that we hadn't meant to frighten them, we were sorry for the delay, we weren't intending to keep them in the dark but wanted to wait until there was news, until there was something to say."

"And what did you say?"

"We said that Daddy had been kidnapped but now was back safe and sound."

"Kidnapped by who?"

"Whom."

"'Terrorists, of course,' our older boy said. And we just nodded. 'How awful,' our daughter said. 'Yes,' we said. 'But there is good news.'"

"What?" Genevieve asks.

"'Once this has happened, it will never happen again. You don't get kidnapped by terrorists twice.'"

"And did the children believe you? Did they believe that he was kidnapped by terrorists?"

"Yes," Sarah says. "And oddly, he believes it, too." She finishes her wine. "I think it would have been better if he'd been killed. If the terrorists had finished him off, if when I looked out the window and saw someone at the phone booth, it had been him, and then a big truck, a newspaper delivery truck, would have skipped the light, skipped the curb, and flattened him—in midsentence. That would have been good. It would be easier, would make this constant sensation of having been in some kind of accident more logical, or if not logical perhaps more natural. It would have been a more natural end for him to have been killed than for us to simply go on as though nothing has changed."

"And what for dessert?" the waiter asks. "A sweet? A pudding?"

"Tea," Sarah says.

"What kind of tea? Black, herbal, green?" the waiter asks.

"What have we come to that one can't simply order a cup of tea without it turning into Twenty Questions?"

"We'll have the Chocolate Mousse at Your Discretion."

"What does that mean, 'at your discretion'?" Sarah wants to know.

The waiter brings an enormous crockery bowl of chocolate mousse and leaves it on the table.

He brings two smaller bowls and two spoons. "At your discretion," he says.

"You take as much as you want?" Genevieve asks.

"Or as little," Sarah says.

"Fantastic," Genevieve says, serving herself heavily. "This is so good it's almost chewy." They take what they like, and then they want more, but their spoons are no longer clean. "Use your butter knife," Genevieve urges her. "Your butter knife is clean." The tension is broken; they giggle over bad behavior, gluttony, and a bowl of chocolate mousse.

"After a week of vegetable juices, a life of deprivation, this pudding is a drug. I'm getting high just eating it," Sarah says. "So what about you? What are your plans for the summer?"

"Off to Corsica. He has a place there."

"Have you ever been?"

"No. It's a first for him as well. He's always gone alone. You?" Genevieve asks.

"Here," Sarah says. "I'm staying right here." She gestures to the rain that never stops. "Look at it out there. I can't go out there." She pulls the enormous bowl of pudding closer. People can't help but stare.

# The National
# Cage Bird Show

Until now the familiar world was governed by Boy Scout
promises, God's law as relayed in the Sunday sermon,
the coach's doctrine, the military code of conduct, and the
expectations that the drill sergeant made clear when he
cited John Lyly's Euphues, 1578: "The rules of fair play do
not apply in love and war." The drill sergeant continued,
"In case it's not clear to you ass-monkeys, this is not a love
affair. We are at war." There is an irreducible truth to how
cruel man can be. Some learn early on, and then there are
others, like me, for whom it comes as a brutal awakening.
But that's not what you were looking for. You asked me why
am I in a chat room for lovers of parakeets?

It's budgies. "Parakeet" just means parrot with a thin body
and a long tail. While a budgie is a parakeet, a parakeet isn't
always a budgie, which is short for "budgerigar."

I bet you do well on crossword puzzles.

☺ Thank you.

I'm here for the distraction, the pleasure of something that is as small and clear-hearted as a budgie. And perhaps this is just a fleeting attempt to keep myself sane in a situation that is so beyond foreign that I fear I have lost myself permanently. And you?

*Just curious.*

Say more.

*I'm a child of divorce, I live in a world without life, where even an ant crawling across a counter is cause for major intervention. Mine is a sealed habitat. The only noises are the drop of the morning paper, the shower, the coffee machine, and the buzzer at suppertime when DelRoy, the doorman, calls to say the boy from Sushi Express is here with dinner in hand. This is not a home. Home was a classic six, which was sold to a Russian who's going to connect it to his classic six next door. This is new construction, freshly minted, purchased with prenuptial dollars after the implosion of my parents' marriage. It is a sterile cube, an emotional clean room, where my mother hopes her life will find balance again. P.S. Before the world fell apart, I used to want a brother or a sister, failing a dog, a cat, or a budgie.*

Are you two serious? This is a budgie chat room, not the—

Oyster Bar at Grand Central.

Or Aisle 19 at Walmart. I've seen people walking up and down the aisles eating. They open packages of this and that, sandwiches for themselves, eat and leave without paying.

Can we please stay on topic? Do any of you feed grapes to your birds?

Seedless and organic only, pesticides settle on the skin—or you can peel them.

*Mrs. PH-A has parakeets. She lives upstairs in a duplex and has a gold cage that's five feet tall.*

Gold leaf.

Brass.

"Gilded" is the word you're looking for. A gilded cage.

You always have to be right. I'd hate to be your wife.

It's funny, when I read what you all write, it reminds me of the sound of birds chirping.

We're like a Greek chorus.

It's a regular sing-along. Whether or not advice is wanted, it's given.

*Mrs. PH-A had a holiday party for everyone in the building. There was spiked eggnog for the grown-ups and sanded sugar cookies for the kids. Mrs. 8C-D discreetly licked the caviar off the blinis and passed the tiny pancakes to her daughter, who loves carbohydrates. I told Mrs. PH-A how beautiful her birds were. She smiled and said, "You're the only person who's noticed the birds. Everyone else just talks about the cage." Are you really in the military?*

I am.

*And are you in a war?*

I am at war.

Have you done this before, just come into a chat room and started talking to someone—a stranger?

No, but whenever there's a computer available, I go on it. I wander . . .

It's called surfing, not wandering.

The guy is a soldier. He can call it whatever he wants.

Sometimes I stay up all night looking at other parts of the world or just reading the news from home.

*Where is home?*

America.

Duh.

Don't be an a-hole.

Language, please . . .

*How'd you end up in the army?*

The truth?

No, lie to her, that's what we're all sitting here waiting for.

I did what a lot of people do. I walked away from all that was familiar. The only thing I knew about the army was whatever I'd seen on TV, on Super Bowl commercials.

Have a Coke and a war. That's really saying something, isn't it?

I am the local EOD, explosive ordnance disposal specialist, basically the Maytag Man for bombs. I'm good with my fingers. I can thread a needle in the dark. Anything with a detonator, I'm your man.

We all have gifts, my grandmother used to say.

Truisms like the slips of white paper in fortune cookies.

I look for disturbances in the landscape, places where the dirt is loose, where you see something where there should be nothing, where something is out of order.

*Like a wet glass on the kitchen counter, like wrappers and crumbs.*

Exactly.

*My grandmother isn't talking to my father, so I guess we're not going there for Thanksgiving.*

Last year on turkey day, I ran route clearing for eight hours. I had to dismount and investigate twice, which is pretty much the last thing you want to do. But I got my reward, a double dose of dark meat and a whole pumpkin pie with my name on it.

Uh, side note for the newbies, we usually don't talk about Thanksgiving or how good "the bird" was. A lot of us are—

Vegan.

Pescatarian.

Vegetarian.

Lactose intolerant.

Can I be weird for a minute? I just want to confirm that neither of you has birds. Is that correct?

Correct. When I first got here, I saw rainbow-hued bee eaters, long-tailed shrikes, Siberian stonechats, and red-throated flycatchers.

*I have a strong bird affinity. Mrs. PH-A asked me to bird-sit one weekend when she was in CT. My mother said I could only*

*do it if the doorman went with me. So during his break, Del-*
*Roy and I went in and just sat there with the birds. We gave*
*them millet and dehydrated mango and talked about all kinds*
*of things. Turns out DelRoy is a pigeon flier—he races pigeons*
*from roof to roof in the Bronx.*

Anyone else here not have a bird?

You're being passive-aggressive.

Is it passive-aggressive if it's totally obvious?

Is there a requirement that someone be in possession of a
bird in order to enter the chat room?

Apparently not, but they're monopolizing the conversation,
changing the subject and stuff, and we don't even know
them. They both just wandered in here.

So wait, we don't talk about TG but can we talk about how
creepy it is that birds love hard-boiled eggs?

Scrambled, as long as it's not in a Teflon pan.

I gave mine the roasted one from the Passover plate . . .

Are you still there?

*Yeah.*

Where?

*I'm here in my room on East 86th Street. My mom let me pick the decor, and I chose a forest theme. I have a bed that's made out of an ancient tree trunk. My mother and I are Mrs. and Miss 7B—the doormen refer to everybody by their apartment number. When I come home, they say, "Miss 6C is having her piano lesson but then might like to go to the park." Or "The pup in 8G wants a walk." What about you, where are you?*

I'm in deep. The landscape is like another planet: dirt, rocks, and dust, nothing more. In some places the roads are so narrow they call them goat trails. People say there used to be trees and we're known for grapes and pomegranates. At this point if I see something that looks like a pomegranate, I'm more likely to assume it's a bomb than breakfast.

Do you drive around on camels?

You're thinking of Lawrence of Arabia, not Larry of Afghanistan.

Not so much. We have trucks with radar, long mechanical arms that can scratch the dirt, camera bots we can send into a location. Back at basic they said, "In case of a dust storm, if you have a camel, ask the camel to sit down and hide yourself against its leeward side—camels are used to dust storms. That was followed by, "If you don't have a camel, tie a bandanna around your nose and mouth and try not to suffocate." It's not exactly helpful. When a dust storm hits, you can't breathe. It's like your lungs are filling with sand, and it just rips away at your skin.

*Ha, that's how my mother describes Dr. Fisher, her dermatologist.*

What does it mean when my birdie is all puffed up?

Scared, cold, sick.

*Do you live in a tent?*

Mostly we live in military squalor in things like shipping containers. It's called a company-level camp. Two hots and a cot. The running joke is that wherever we are, it's always named after a guy called Stan.

*What was today in the war like?*

Today? We were in convoy for seven hours. The whole time you're in the vehicle, you're praying you find it and BIP it before you roll over it. BIP stands for "blow in place." We blow up devices too dangerous to move. I've got my bell rung pretty good a couple of times. And then when you get to the destination and have to dismount, you start praying there are no snipers. They called it a training mission because we had new soldiers on board.

*Same. Everyone here is totally into training. At school we run laps around the Central Park Reservoir. And I play tennis twice a week. I used to take spin class but had to stop because I was getting obsessed.*

Are pomegranate seeds safe for my keet?

Yes.

Mine loves popping them, like me with bubble wrap.

I always think I'm fine until we get back. And then I vomit. Every day I puke my guts out—sorry if that's TMI.

*No, it's fine. I have a friend who used to barf every day, but that's different—she made herself do it. I don't know what upset my mother more, the fact that my father was sleeping with someone else or that she found out about it at lunch. She was eating a Cobb salad, filled with things she doesn't even like— blue cheese, bacon, hard-boiled egg—waiting for him to tell her the "really important thing." Halfway through he said, "I'm leaving you," and she got up, walked out, and threw up all over the corner of 61st and Madison. She apologized to people who were walking by, mumbling "chemotherapy" because it was easier to say than "adultery."*

As far as I'm concerned, you're both exotics.

Is newspaper okay as a cage liner?

Yes, if you don't care about inky feet.

I'd call the printer and make sure they use nontoxic ink.

The computers here are the kind from a hundred years ago, and there are only a couple of them. I waited in line to get on, like how you used to wait for a pay phone. Right now ten guys are staring me down—we're only allowed

15 minutes—but they're being nice . . . I better go. Some of these guys have families.

*Hey, wait, before you go—what's your name?*

Matthew Rose, i.e., ArMyRose.

*Is that your real name?*

Should I be using a fake name?

*I used NYCGirl2001—it seemed better than Grace.*

Grace is really nice.

*Thanks. Hey, one last question. What is it you like about birds?*

Their beauty and intelligence.

*Stay safe, ArMyRose.*

You, too, GirlyBird.

He's signed off. Seems like a nice guy. I feel for him.

For all you know, he's sitting somewhere in Florida.

I don't think so—it's a rough job being a soldier.

Maybe it's more of a calling.

Or a last resort.

*Hello, I'm still here.*

Isn't it past your bedtime?

*I just think we shouldn't talk about him behind his back.*

It's a chat room—we chat.

What about you, chickadee? Tell us something . . .

*I'm not sure what to say. My life sucks. I mean, would I be in a budgie chat room if everything were okay, really?*

Foul. Ten minutes in penalty box for insulting your hosts.

*Mea culpa. #ashamed. Tell me about your birds . . .*

Mine likes to ride around on my head. She just sits up there, and I walk around the house like that. Sometimes I forget she's there and my wife reminds me: birdie on board.

◆　◆　◆　◆　◆

Knock, knock, anyone home?

*I'm here, just studying for a test.*

You don't have to knock—the door's always open.

While I was waiting in line to talk to you, I was thinking about how much easier it is for me to type what I'm thinking rather than saying it out loud. Voices are hard for me. The last time I got my bell rung—it never really stopped ringing. It's like I'm deaf and at the same time have a superpower. I can hear the smallest sound, like a match being lit a hundred yards away. The din on normal voices just kills me—it's like a marching band between my ears. The other day you asked me why I joined the army?

*Yes.*

My father was not a nice guy.

*Mine's not winning any medals at the moment either. He thinks inviting me to breakfast with his new girlfriend is nice. Thanks but no thanks.*

My father burned down our house. That's when I left.

*OMG. Seriously?*

Yep.

*Where is he now?*

Jail. I literally just walked away from it all, while the house was still on fire. I went into the recruiting office and said, "Where do I sign up?" The guy gave me the once-over and asked, "Anyone looking for you?" "Like who?" "The cops?" "No." "Am I going to regret this?" the officer asked me. "I could ask you the same thing," I said to him.

*Wow. Was your mother okay?*

She escaped without injury. Whatever we had as a family went up in flames. She's now living with my aunt. There's no going back.

*No one thinks about how it affects the kid. All my parents think about is themselves and their reputations.*

When I got into the army, I asked them to give me the hardest job. I wanted to do the thing that other people weren't willing to do.

*I shouldn't even be telling you about my life. Compared to what you're going through, my story is boring.*

Everyone's got something.

*My mother works all the time. She says she's learned her lesson when it comes to men. Is it weird to say I just wish things could be the way they were? I wish I didn't know that a dad could fall out of love with his family. Part of me refuses to believe it— does that make me a romantic?*

GirlyBird, every bird lover is a romantic at heart. When the other guys used to come back at night and write down what kind of action we saw, I made notes about warblers in the elms.

Excuse me for interrupting while you all are waxing poetic—
but my keet hates pellets,

Some birds never eat pellets.

*My mother doesn't keep food in the house—she wants to avoid*
*temptation. There are cans of tuna but no mayo. There are*
*black coffee ice cubes and celery sticks—she eats them when she's*
*trying to solve a really tough problem. "It's not easy," she says,*
*"being a corporate woman at this stage." She does exercises at 6*
*a.m. And if I want to talk to her but the timing is bad, she*
*holds up her hand like a stop sign and says, "I'm crazed." Other*
*times she makes a sad-pouty face and asks in baby talk, "Are you*
*okay?"*

My birdie hides a little extra food in a corner of the cage
where she thinks no one can see it.

My big guy has to always eat first, before the other one. I
tried using both doors, putting in two dishes simultaneously,
but it made him crazy. He couldn't decide which to go for,
hopping around, squawking.

Mine have gone mental in general. They're biting me all the
time. How do you stop a keet from biting?

The question I'd be asking is why are they mad at you?

*Sometimes I go to 8C-D after school, because the housekeeper is*
*Irish and makes tea sandwiches with cucumber and cream*
*cheese, watercress and butter, tuna salad, egg salad, on white*

*and brown bread. She leaves them on the counter covered with plastic wrap. The kids who live there couldn't care less. The housekeeper told me that the secret to egg salad is Dijon mustard.*

I've never had watercress.

*Maybe it's just an Upper East Side thing.*

What always gets to me is when we roll into a town. Picture two streets that look like a Buffalo Bill stage set that burned down twenty years ago. People are living in the rubble, and sometimes they're running toward you screaming at you in a language you don't understand. You have no idea what they're saying, and you can't read the clues because everything from the intonation to the gestures is entirely different here.

*That sounds scary. I mostly have to deal with Alexander, who lives in 8C-D and who has started making me do "exercises" to earn the sandwiches. At first I thought it was funny that in some way I should pay for my snacks. Now I just think he's weird.*

We're beyond outsiders. We're alien insects who roll through in crazy machines. It's like the military ran out of places to blow up and rebuild, so they sent us to an ancient civilization. I wasn't even born when this war started.

*Alexander made me Purell my hands, then follow him into his father's walk-in closet and do a dance weaving between his suits. And then he told me to run my hands down each of the ties, stroking them.*

It's like there's a communication error.

Latency issues have to do with communication hops between transmitters and satellites. Uh, my day job is in software systems.

Latent: present but not visible. It's a popular crossword clue.

At first it freaks you out: these voices, talking fast, hysterically, in a language where you maybe know three words. What are they saying? Is someone hurt? Are they happy to see you? Or are they crying because their life is so awful, because someone killed their child, or because their car won't go? Are they asking where did you come from and why are you here? Do they want to kill you? The little kids knock me flat. Sometimes we come in right after something has happened—you see things that don't look real, body parts detached, kids covered in blood and dirt. We get out and give the kids things like soccer balls and dolls. We pump up a ball and throw it to them. Condolences on your mom and dad, but hey, here's a toy.

*My mother made me give away all my old toys when we moved. She gave me one box and said, "This is for the keepers." I bet some of my stuff is over there. Do the girls like Barbie dolls?*

Are birds color-blind?

How do we ever know what someone else sees?

*And then Alexander tells me to face the fridge and put my
hands up. I do, and he comes behind me and lays over me—his
hands on my hands, facing the fridge. I just try to hold my
breath.*

That's what I do all day, hold my breath. When I'm in the
operational arena, I'm more awake, more alive than I've
ever been, but I don't breathe. I have to remind myself,
breathe. My job is to make the unsafe safe, to prevent
things from exploding. The minute you stop caring if you
get out alive, you're dead, but things can get messed
up. Your superiors lose sight of the goal. And you start
wondering who is the real enemy. You find out things like
there's a "contractor" in the area paying people on both
sides for information. The contractor has more money in
his pocket than you'll see in a year, and he's handing it
out right and left, hoping some trinket of intel will fall off
a tree.

*Alexander leans against me for a long time, our breath fogging
the Sub-Zero stainless. I look down—he's wearing white sweat
socks, bleachy clean. I see the hem of his blue school shirt, the
cuffs of his khaki school pants.*

It is a war without end. We go out and we come back. We
do the mission. But it's taken a turn. There are times we
don't know what we're fighting for. One of the commanders
said, "It's not a war, it's a chronic disease."

My bird just flew into a wall—how did she not see the wall?

No horizon line—put up Post-its, that's what I do. Orange or pink Post-its like caution signs.

*I go to an all-girls school. I know nothing about boys. I have no idea what's normal.*

Every day, every night I remind myself that I am a real person, not just a piece of military machinery. As much as it feels weird pouring my heart out in front of an audience, you're the ballast.

In case you're curious, you can tell how many of us are in the room by looking at the upper left corner of your screen where it says "Number of Birds in the Room." Right now it's seven.

I find it wonderful. I'm seventy-six years old, and I look forward to it every day. I never talk about myself, but I'm in one of those motorized chairs, oxygen-dependent, and this is the most interesting thing that's happened in years.

I've been in this chat room since it started . . . Really lovely to hear what everyone has to say. BTW, I had no idea that's what the number in the upper left meant until you just told us.

Why are you oxygen-dependent? Are you really fat?

I'm going to ignore that.

As would any polite person.

And the answer is no. Stupidly, I was a smoker. I smoked round the clock for 60 years.

I'm sitting at this blinking cube, this Etch-A-Sketch of the mind, 6,000 and some miles away, trying to pour my heart into it, but maybe letters were better, scratching it out by hand.

I remember trying to draw circles on the Etch-A-Sketch, right knob slowly up and down, left knob side to side.

To erase it you had to shake it really hard. It sounded like sand scattering in the wind.

I gotta go, the guy behind me is getting agitated. Good luck on your test, Grace.

*Stay safe, ArMyRose.*

❖ ❖ ❖ ❖ ❖

I think Charlie Bird is sick. I asked my daughter to look at him, and she thought he was fine. Then a friend came by and said, "The bird is fine, but I'm insane . . ."

*Sorry to just bust in.*

You're home early.

*I need to talk to ArMyRose—does anyone have his real e-mail or a phone number?*

Everything okay?

Is it normal for a keet to vomit?

Parakeets often regurgitate as a sign of affection. They throw up for their owners or a favorite toy, a mirror or a bell.

*Everything is not okay. Mrs. PH-A jumped out the window.*

I can't help thinking something is wrong with Charlie Bird.

Is she all right?

PH stands for "penthouse," so, not likely.

What are his symptoms?

His face is squinchy, and he's a little puffy. I've been watching him all morning, and all I can say is he looks the way I feel when I have the flu.

I thought you said she was an old woman?

Maybe it was an accident and she fell?

*The doormen said she'd been very depressed and had been making philosophical statements. And Mr. 8E is in the lobby telling people that hers was hardly the fairy-tale life others imagined. Her family was wealthy, but she never got the one thing she needed.*

What was that?

*Love, according to Mr. 8E. Her last husband was a brilliant man; he helped calculate the age of the universe, but then left her with no warning. That's why she moved here, to the building so new it has no history. She's out there. I can't see everything, but I can see her shoe, a simple black pump with a three-inch heel.*

I think you should come away from the window.

*She had a certain charm, a spark, almost like effervescence. She left envelopes for each of the doormen with "Christmas Comes Early This Year" in script on the outside and a page of instructions. DelRoy showed me the part that applies to me: "The birds are for the new girl. She knows who she is. She will ask you about them first thing. My family will ask about the cage. The cage is in fact gold and was a birthday present from my father—my 21st birthday. My first husband used to say, How ironic at the age of your emancipation he handed you a portable prison. Tell the girl she should get a different kind of cage and that the birds need space to fly free. Tell her they like to sit on the tops of bookcases and pick at books—they're fond of first editions."*

Now Charlie's just sitting on his perch closing his eyes like he's exhausted, and the other one is looking at me like he's asking, "You gonna do something about it?"

That's awful, my thoughts are with you.

Really bad—but now you've got keets. You're a mum.

*Well, they're not here yet. It all just happened. The police are in the apartment now. There are news trucks outside. It's really strange. I wonder what she'd think if she saw the response. Mrs. PH-A was always very apologetic. Mrs. 9I said it was because her mother was English.*

Now the other one is pecking at him, like he's saying, "Charlie, stay with me, don't go to sleep, Charlie." I'm calling the vet.

*Where is ArMyRose?*

I'm sure he's out on a job.

I don't think it works that way. He's not like a repairman—he's a detonator.

Fine, a "mission." Apologies for not using military-speak. Anyway, kiddo, is there someone you can call? A friend?

Are you still looking out the window?

*How'd you know? Maybe I could go over to the pet store on Lexington Avenue and get some supplies—suggestions?*

Seed, millet, treats.

Always with the food. How about cage, water bowl, food bowl, bath, some toys?

From what you've said about your mother, I'm thinking maybe you need one of those cage skirts that catches seeds and maybe a little mini-vacuum.

✦　✦　✦　✦　✦

Hey GirlyBird, I know it's late there, really sad to hear about Mrs. PH-A. We had a 24-hour communication blackout.

*It's okay, you're in a war and I'm like in 8th grade.*

Did you get the keets?

*Not yet—the police sealed off the apartment. Maybe tomorrow they'll let them out.*

Last night a crazy thing happened. I'm not sure if I was asleep or awake, but I heard a sound from when I was a kid. It was the sound of my bike wheels with a playing card in the spokes. We used to stick a playing card between the spokes and pretend we were riding motorcycles. It was an excellent sound, the stop-and-start clack, clack, clack. Then I woke up and realized it was mortar fire. I'm hating myself for enjoying the memory, lost in time, the deep blue sky at twilight, the summer crickets, so loud, my bike, riding, flying toward home. They're goddamned firing on us, and I'm dreaming of crickets, lightning bugs, and the smell of sparklers. I remember the science teacher telling me iron makes orange, magnesium makes white, ferrotitanium makes yellow-gold.

*It sounds like it was really good until you woke up.*

Have you ever noticed that when things get strange, you go back in time, to a particular moment? Like the thirty seconds when the guy at the carnival is turning a paper cone in wide circles inside the machine—just before he hands you a puffy cloud of cotton candy.

*I think about smells. Hot dogs. Fried clams.*

For a treat I let my birdies pick on a Nilla wafer.

I give mine pasta, 'cause I'm Italian.

What do you like better, blue or pink cotton candy?

*Pink. Blue seems unnatural.*

Fried Oreos.

Mushy ice cream sandwiches—the outside skin of the chocolate cookie stuck to your fingers.

Funnel cake with powdered sugar.

It's amazing what a bird can tell you if you're willing to listen. Charlie was sick. I took him in, and the doc gave him subcutaneous fluids and antibiotics, and he's a new man. Four hundred bucks, but he's alive.

✦ ✦ ✦ ✦ ✦

It's been crazy here. We were doing unmounted searches in a village. I was moving around with my battle buddy, and then there was a sound, not even a sound, more like a punch through the air—you feel it coming, but there's nothing you can do before the sensation of something exploding into a punching bag knocks you back. I look at my buddy, and I don't even understand what I'm seeing. He's spitting out his face, his teeth, his chin, his jaw. There's a gaping hole tearing through his nose, one eye is gone, the other panicked, thinking is this how it ends? I can taste his blood in my own mouth, a sour metal tinge. He can't talk—he has nothing left to talk with. I take a step toward him and see a thin wire through the dirt, a daisy chain of IEDs. Despite all that's happening, he sees it, too. And before I can figure out how to get to him, he reaches for his gun and fires directly into what is left of his head. Brain matter splatters across me, thoughts not spoken, every idea he ever had, his life not yet lived, spraying me with the last of his consciousness. The gun falls like a tin toy. The body, heart still plump and pounding, veins coursing with the chemistry of survival, takes a moment to buckle, crumpling toward me and onto the ground. My friend, an open wound, an uncapped well, spilling sticky human reds and browns into the dirt. In the distance I hear the thick thud of a chopper. The other IED guys eliminate the threat, and the medics rush in and take him. I am left in the dirt, clutching the knit hat he used to wear and wondering what are they going to try to save, what can be revived.

*I just vomited into my mouth. ArMyRose, I'm so sorry.*

At a loss for words.

Don't know what to say—condolences.

I'm not sure why, but on the ride back I kept thinking about my 7th-grade field trip to the Smithsonian in Washington, D.C. We saw the flag that flew at Fort McHenry in 1812. The actual "broad stripes and bright stars," except I remembered that parts of it were missing, blown to shit. I'm not supposed to be telling you any of this. I could get in so much trouble, but I just can't sit on it. Not to be creepy, but I kept a couple of his teeth—I thought his family might need them for DNA evidence.

*Does every school go to Washington, D.C.? I saw that same flag.*

One can only imagine what you've been through, soldier.

You've been traumatized.

Right now, I need my head washed out. I wouldn't mind being spun around in the Vortex, paralyzed by centrifugal force as the bottom drops out. If they could spin it fast enough, maybe it would wipe my memory clean.

When I was a kid, they called it the Gravitron.

It's actually called the Rotor.

I was all about the Himalaya—fast and tight.

Tilt-A-Whirl for me.

Am I the only one who likes the Madhatter's Tipsy Teacups?

*Is it weird that I don't like rides? I don't even like elevators.*

There's no way you go through something like that and come out unaffected.

I had an uncle, a World War Two veteran, who suffered from Guadalcanal syndrome. He was like a feral cat, jumpy, couldn't take loud noises, and would weep at news of any kind, good or bad.

Shell-shocked, they used to call it.

Fucked is what I'd say, pardon my French.

*Love does not begin and end the way we seem to think it does. Love is a battle, love is a war, love is a growing up.*

GirlyBird, that's great. Maybe one day you'll be a writer.

*I wish. That was written by James Baldwin in "The Price of the Ticket." We're reading that in my school. Have you ever been to a bird show?*

No.

*Maybe we could go sometime?*

That would be nice.

*What do you think it's like?*

Loud. Squawky.

I got two of my best boys at a show.

You meet the most wonderful people.

*The National Cage Bird Show is in New York in January. Come with me? I'll take you to the Empire State Building. I've lived here my whole life, but I've never gone to the top. And we could go for a carriage ride in Central Park—it's corny but fun. There's a place called Serendipity that makes Frozen Hot Chocolate, which is so good.*

Sounds good, GirlyBird, something to look forward to. I wish I had more to say, but nothing makes any sense anymore. It's getting hard to imagine a way out of here.

Do budgies glow in the dark?

Have you been doing edibles again?

Breeding feathers absorb ultraviolet light from the sun, so if your birdie has been in the sun for a few hours, he might come in with a little glow, like ring around the collar.

How long have you been over there?

This is my third ride ticket.

*ArMyRose, I'm changing my name from NYCGirl2001 to GirlyBird01 in your honor.*

Thanks, Gracie.

I think my bird is bleeding. There's a drop of blood on the paper towel.

Just one drop?

Yes.

Maybe he has a broken blood feather?

He looks unhappy.

Any signs of injury?

I'm scared. It's like making me feel panicky.

I've got eyes on my back and a long line needing to call home. Signing off for now.

*Sleep well, ArMyRose.*

You, too, GirlyBird.

I think it's his wing.

Wing or a feather?

It looks like he bent his feather.

You're gonna have to pull it out.

I don't think I can.

Birdie can bleed out if you let it go uncorked.

Here's what you do: Get a washcloth and have someone hold the bird.

I live alone.

Okay, so you're going to hold the bird in one hand and extract it with a hemostat.

A what?

You can use tweezers or even needle-nose pliers.

Get as close to the skin as you can and then pull the feather out, firm and swift in one go. But before you do anything, get some cornstarch ready.

I'm so freaking out. I need cornstarch?

To stop the bleeding.

Is that the yellow box with the corn on it?

Yes.

So weird—I never made the connection. I'm dumb.

What's the bird doing now?

Just looking at me. And— Oh, no . . .

What?

I just spilled tea on my keyboard.

Put it in dry rice. Right away.

What's happening with the blood feather? The suspense is killing me.

I'm scared.

If the bird is bleeding and you can't get to a vet, you have no choice.

Okay, okay.

Does anyone want to play the theme to Jeopardy?

I did it! OMG.

Is the bird okay?

Yeah. Startled—but fine.

What a night. I don't even have to watch television anymore.

✦  ✦  ✦  ✦  ✦

*Good news! I met Mrs. PH-A's daughter. She buzzed this afternoon and invited me to come up and get the birdies. When I got there, she said she wanted to make sure I understood that the cage was not included, "It's a family heirloom." She gave me the birds and their supplies and some books that she said they liked to peck at. "It's ironic," she said. "My mother used to give them pages of the social register to shred. She always wanted to use it as lining for the cage—the idea of her birds shitting on everyone gave her great pleasure—but the book would be used up too fast, and it was better they spend the whole year pecking away at it. I'll see to it the subscription is renewed," the daughter said, and then she ushered me out the door. As I was leaving, I asked her, "What are their names?" She looked baffled. "It never occurred to me that they'd have names," she said. "We always just called them Yellow and Blue."*

Am I the only one worried sick?

He's on a mission, special ops or something.

If he were killed, we would hear about it.

What if that wasn't really his name?

Where was he from?

Did he say Florida?

No, you said Florida.

They report the military deaths every day. You can look online.

They don't report until 24 hours after the next of kin have been notified.

He wasn't in good shape when we left him.

Grace, is that you?

*It is. I'm just home from school.*

How did the English test go?

*Meh, I got like an 88.*

That's pretty good.

*Not at my school. That's what they call borderline . . . Has anyone heard anything?*

No, we were just talking . . .

Question: I just got a new keet. Do I need to keep it in a separate cage from my other one?

Think of it like this: How would you feel if someone moved into your house uninvited, with no warning?

Okay, I'll keep him in his own place for now.

*I hope you guys won't be mad.*

About what?

*I have a confession to make. I went to their apartment again. I just couldn't stand being home alone, and I was craving egg salad.*

Do you have a picture of your fat budgie to share? Or are you lacking a wide-angle lens?

My budgie is pudgy, too, a real a chunky monkey.

*It was totally weird. I asked Alexander where his sister was, and he said in her room. I went to check on her, and the door was locked. I called to her through the door. "I'm fine," she said, "just go away." I should have taken that as a sign.*

The world is filled with signs that go unread.

*I went into the kitchen with Alexander. "Assume the position," he said. And so I leaned against the fridge. And then he said, "Spread 'em," like he was going to frisk me. He leaned against me, really hard, flattening me against the fridge. It all felt a little weirder than usual, rougher, and I was thinking maybe Alexander was on drugs or something. I kind of knew what was happening, but at the same time I didn't really get it. I could feel him pressing against me and then something happening with the back of my skirt. Then, abruptly, he stopped and told me to go home. As I was riding up in the elevator, I looked over my shoulder. The rear of the elevator is mirrored, and I see this spot, like phlegm, on my skirt.*

Seventy-seven years old and never have I heard something so disgusting.

You really need to tell someone.

It's lewd.

It's not lewd, it's assault. You were assaulted. Let's call it what it is.

Make us a promise—you won't go back there again?

Tell your mother!

*Are you mad at me?*

Of course we're not mad at you.

*I wish ArMyRose were here.*

We all do.

Do keets go underwater?

Mine dives into his bathtub.

Charlie Bird likes being sprayed by the plant mister.

I have one that sits in the soap dish while I take a bath.

◆ ◆ ◆ ◆ ◆

*Okay, so I took your advice—I told my mother. First thing she said was, "Where's the skirt?" Stuffed into the bottom of my hamper. She said we could use the DNA evidence to extract a price from his parents. At first I thought she said "a prize," and I asked, "Like what?" "Therapy," she said. She thinks I'm troubled because of the way I described the sandwiches in great detail. She's worried that I've lost my faculties. Can you imagine the humiliation, my mother confronting his parents with my skirt in hand? "There goes your naivete," she said. I thought she was going to say my virginity. Talk about blaming the victim. And if I question her authority, she reminds me not that she's my mother but that she was top of her class at law school and editor of the Law Review.*

It's a strange reaction for an educated woman.

You'd think she'd feel guilty for not having protected you.

The anger is her way of dealing with the guilt, which is too painful.

*She told me I'm no longer allowed to stay home alone and that she's going to go into my college fund and hire a babysitter. When she finished, I told her that I'm going to take Yellow and Blue and go live with my father.*

I bet that didn't go over well.

*Let's just say the perfect white cube of an apartment isn't perfect anymore, so I guess that's progress. She threw a mug at the wall. It made a deep impression.*

I didn't want to say anything to jinx it—but for the last few days I've had the sense something special is about to happen, and voila this morning I've got a little keet, fully hatched, looks like a nude alien. It's the first for my girl, who is on it and ready to be a mom.

Cause for celebration.

Smiley faces all around.

*I'm about to be cut off. She's unplugging me until I come to my senses. Will log on from school. Good night.*

◆   ◆   ◆   ◆   ◆

Hey, sorry to be MIA. I hit a rough patch, and I'm in Germany of all places.

Loud chorus of hallelujahs.

Answered prayers.

*ArMyRose, you're alive! I was so scared. I have a lot to tell you.*

I'm dictating this to someone, so forgiven any errors. I'm near Naturpark Pfälzerwald, the forest and the ruins of medieval castles. Citizens hike the trails, stopping for a glass of the local Gewürztraminer. The earliest traces of human settlement in Landstuhl are from 500 B.C.

You don't quite sound like yourself.

Something may be lost in the transition.

Does he mean translation?

Yes.

What town are you in?

Landstuhl. 250 miles from here to Dachau.

That doesn't sound good.

I don't think it's him. I think he's been hacked.

You're always so negative.

*ArMyRose, something happened. I was savaged by Alexander, and then I told my mother about it, and now I'm back to*

*having a babysitter, which isn't so bad. She's like two years*
*older than me and better at French, and she brings snacks for*
*both of us.*

The young lady was molested.

I don't think it's right to tell other people's stories.

Sometimes when she speaks, it's as if we need an interpreter.
New York is not like the rest of the world.

If I'd been there, GirlyBird, I would have punched his
lights out.

*I know you would.*

Are you all right, soldier?

*My mother . . .*

Honey, let ArMyRose have some space to tell us what's
going on. We know you've been missing him—but give him
a moment.

*Fine.*

My battle buddy's name was Melvin. He lived long
enough to be an organ donor: Someone here in Germany
is carrying his heart. I am wearing Melvin's hat, a knitted
cap his mother made that he wore under his helmet. It's
stiff with sweat and blood and smells terrible. I can't take

it off or I will come apart. I need the compression on my head. It's the only way I can feel.

*ArMyRose, things here have been very strange. Word gets around. I think the doormen know—they're looking at me funny. It makes me self-conscious. And I'm at a standoff with my mother. We're not speaking, so I can't even ask her.*

GirlyBird, growing up is the work of a lifetime. When your parents named you Grace, they had something in mind— let that be your guide.

*They named me after a dog.*

Is there anything we can do for you?

The thing about budgie owners is we are all mothers at heart, caretakers of the most innocent.

There's an old man who comes through every day asking if I want anything—newspapers, books, phone cards. Every day I tell him I want nothing. Regardless, he hands me a chocolate bar. I have 16 chocolate bars in a drawer by the bed. His eyes are a beautiful blue gone cloudy. I think the chocolate is his personal version of community service.

Soldier, are you injured?

We were on a routine clearing mission. I got out to investigate something, and the earth erupted beneath me, like a volcano. I don't think I ever hit the ground. I was flying through the air, and then the air became a plane and then a blur, almost like being underwater for too long, a kind of fog.

*Same. It's like pea soup here, murky.*

I wake up, and a man is standing over me. The man is holding a small wooden house in his hands. "Öffnen die Tür," he says. Just outside the house, arms outstretched toward a spot where her husband once stood, there is a female figure in a red skirt and a white top. "Öffnen die Tür," the man says, and then he opens the top of the house and music starts to play. The female figure spins in a circle, dancing by herself. When the song is over, the man closes the top, opens his other hand, and shows me the husband— the missing figure who used to be attached. The figure is wearing lederhosen and brown pants. "Father?" I ask. The man shrugs. I fall asleep again. Is it my father? Is that my house in his hands? I am home running in the woods behind the house, I am jumping over a fence, I am climbing a tree, so high that I can see everything, only it's not my yard—it's entirely bombed out, a ghost town. I wake up, and the man with the music box is gone. Was he ever there, or did I dream the whole thing?

*My mother told Alexander's parents about my skirt. Twenty-four hours later, he got shipped off to wilderness therapy in Oregon. That was the prize. It's pretty funny, because he's seriously afraid of the dark.*

I look down and think am I shorter than before? I don't even think I was done growing. I fall asleep wondering, do they plant the legs they cut off? Are there limb forests somewhere in Germany?

We're glitching again.

Awhile back, when I had the dream about riding my bike at twilight, I left out something. I was riding from my best friend's house toward home so fast, diving into the night. I could hear my mother calling me, her voice cutting through the ringing crickets. When I got to the house, she was crying. She told me my grandfather had been called home.

So weird, every time it's about to rain, my girls pack a bag. They put all their favorite things in the far corner of the cage and wait.

Hurricane season is upon us: a reminder birds need a go-bag same as people—current photos in case you get separated, wire, pliers, duct tape, travel cage, blanket, food and water, bird leash.

I'd like to see a keet on a leash.

Animals are the first to know when things are getting weird. When I first got here, I used to see all kinds of birds, magpies, laughing doves. I always knew it was a bad sign if we rolled into a place and there were no birds.

I'm sure you know they're doing excellent work with prosthetics.

Maybe instead of a keet you'll get one of those wounded-warrior dogs?

There is great solace in the animal kingdom.

While I was sleeping, someone left me a questionnaire. "When you have been in difficult situations in the past, how have you handled them? Describe the activities you were doing before this happened. Which of these activities do you expect to resume?" What I really want to know is how you jump up and run outside when you hear the bells of the ice cream truck.

*ArMyRose, does that mean you're not coming for the bird show?*

GirlyBird, my arrival is delayed.

# Your Mother Was a Fish

*À l'oeuvre on reconnaît l'artisan.* You can tell an artist by his handi-work.

She is sewing a story, stitching a tale, line by line. This one is about her great-grandmother who sewed herself a mermaid costume and swam to America. The journey was long, arduous, and by the time she arrived at the state of Maine, her costume had fused to her flesh. She had a dressmaker split the center seam, separating her legs so she could walk, and she went through life with her legs covered in thick green scales, a brocade, fossilized by the sea into leathery chaps like the kind a cowboy would wear. Men found her scales incredibly attractive; it was considered good luck to rub her thighs. They all wanted only one thing: to get into the space be-tween the scales, the alligator purse that had been perfectly pro-tected. But the sweat of their palms stung her skin; she found them repulsive.

She moved to Massachusetts and took a part-time job doing wom-en's work sewing tassels on loafers in a shoe factory.

———————

*Suck cock, suck cock,* the sound of the sewing machine.

At a country circus, she met Ray, a boy with powdery hands, like buttery talc, who worked the spinning cups in a traveling show. His mother was a bearded lady, his father the world's tallest man. His beloved Uncle Meurice, a merman, who'd died long ago, was laid out, taxidermied in a vitrine that traveled wherever the family went—a quarter a peek.

Ray asked her about her homeland, and she told him about the veiled life, she told him there were places she couldn't go, she told him she was invisible there—people saw only what they wanted to see, they didn't look very far. She told Ray that when she left, she knew she would never go back. Her family wept as she sewed herself into her disguise, their tears filling the river that floated her down to the sea—her home was lost to history. As she told Ray the story of her past, her eyes welled up and heavy tears dripped plink, plunk onto Uncle Meurice's vitrine. Ray wiped the vitrine dry and never asked her about it again.

When their daughter was born with an extraordinarily long needle-sharp index finger that featured a bony eye for thread to pass through, they thought it a plus. They named her Penelope. She could thread herself through fabric, through wood, and drill through metal. Penelope was incredibly good at math, winning a scholarship to a prestigious engineering school. She graduated with honors and took jobs building ships, airplanes, skyscrapers.

Their son, Morris, named after Ray's famed mer-uncle, was born with wings, transparent fire-resistant flesh webbing from his arms to his ribs. His shirts had to be custom-made. A more successful Icarus, Morris completed the first successful shipless solo flight into space and returned with an incredible tan. At a very young age, he married an ornithologist, and they nested on the top floor of a high-rise.

"Yours is a family of unusual traces," a soothsaying neighbor said.

"We are bred to survive," Ray answered, accidentally clipping the woman with his weed whacker, lacerating her ankles. "It is evolution—we keep what we need, we lose the rest."

Morris had an irrational fear of infants of all kinds, and so he and his wife lived with their two ancient Labradors, their deaf screaming cockatoo, and various geriatric gray parrots and macaws, each adopted at an advanced age. They opened their doors to any kind of elderly animal. "Don't put your pet out to pasture. Give it a new life at Ye Olde Animal Haus" was the slogan on their matchbooks.

Penelope, so smart and successful, was lonely. Strolling the seaport, she met a sailor from far away; they married that night and immediately returned to the water. Helping her pack to go, her mother gave her the family heirloom: the scrap saved from her center seam. Penelope, recognizing its significance, affixed it to her skin—a scaly merkin mounted with crazy glue.

———————

Given the family's history, it came as no surprise when Penelope's parents received word via carrier pigeon that identical twins had been born on an island off Key West, with gills and organs of both sexes—identical hermaphrodites Tasina and Tasi.

"Grandchildren!" the newly minted grandmother announced to the ladies of her sewing circle, leaving out the spawny details. The sewing circle clucked approvingly. Long ago when she'd joined the sewing circle, she told anyone crass and curious enough to ask about her scales that she was a burn victim. It was easier for people to understand and she wasn't looking for trouble.

*A stitch in time saves nine, a fish in time saves mine.*

Thimbles and Threads, the ladies called themselves—a ministry that stitched for salvation: "Charity Never Faileth—Sew What's New?" They knitted hats for cancer patients, socks for orphans, afghans for Afghans, lap blankets for cold old women and men, the grandmother donning a thimble to finish watch caps for the Holiday at Sea, "Leave No Keppe Cold," a Jewish military relief organization.

But soon Penelope's sailor mate met a bad end. Not used to living on land, he had gone ashore and failed to look both ways when crossing train tracks, and even though the conductor slammed on the brakes, nothing was spared, and his bodily mash was returned to the sea in a potato sack covered with Penelope's salty tears.

A youthful widow, a single mother, a woman with needs of her own, Penelope began an affair with a dolphin. In a dispatch to her mother, she described him as a great conversationalist, incredibly loving, and gifted in special ways. "He can curl his member like a finger beckoning. . . . I won't say more lest you think me crude. Swimming with him reminds me of when I used to dance standing on Daddy's feet, waltzing in time. For the moment I am content to live as a fish."

Her sailor's children, Tasina and Tasi, matured quickly and were ready to replicate—both able to complete the process entirely on their own. To her dismay, Tasi, her he/she daughter, declined—she felt the need to hang on to herself to be, in essence, copyrighted, but Tasina, her she/he son, turned out little ones by the dozen. Some stayed on land, some on the sea, some sold seashells, another had fleas, four go to Harvard, two go to Yale, a dozen go to Trinity, and one goes to jail. Another spends his days surfing big waves in Hawaii, and the oldest is a federal judge, swearing in people who promise not to tell tall tales. Tasina, having spent so many years raising children, found it difficult to get a job and worked as a temporary secretary—she/he's pretty, but can she/he type? Penelope, now twice widowed, having had enough of it all, returns to the city. A septuagenarian who looks forty, well preserved from a life in salt water, she comes back to New York. Having learned a thing or two from her kids, she tells everyone that she wants to be called Tom. She packs a plastic penis bought on the Lower East Side at Babes in Toyland and tends bar down by the water at a place called Henrietta Hudson, spinning her yarns to any available ear. One of the girls at the bar tells her the story of a straight businesswoman who packs just because she feels it gives her a competitive edge. "No one knows what you've got tucked in your pants until you get hit by a train," she says, and Penelope Tom nods knowingly.

One night spindly Sarah Spider, a sex therapist, sits down next to Penelope Tom near closing time and starts spinning a handsome web. Penelope Tom admires the handiwork, and the mating dance begins. "It's been so long I wouldn't know where to begin," Penelope Tom confesses as Sarah's expert hand travels up her thigh. She remembers the sensation her mermaid mother spoke about, and having inherited her hypersensitivity and not forgetting that she's still got the old scaly merkin crazy-glued over the spot, she feels her/his packy getting moist and squishy. Sarah spins a wicked web, leading Penelope Tom back to her apartment after closing up shop. Sarah ties her/him up and down and is just about to cuff her/him to the bed when Penelope Tom realizes that there's more to it than that. Lost between her legs, a latex hothead, Sarah is a cannibal and a carnivore, and she's the midnight snack. As Sarah is using her pincers to pry the merkin loose, Penelope Tom comes to her senses and with her elongated index finger—the needle nail grown tough over time is now like an ivory tooth—pierces Sarah's shell. The stabbed spider spurts bug juice everywhere.

Penelope Tom takes a taxi to her granddaughter Tess's house in Harlem, leaving her cock and balls behind, hoping she can hide out for a while. Tess, a fashion designer, has a boyfriend who, nostalgic

for the ontogenetic past of life in the womb, internalizes the water—
he drinks his morning urine. It harks back to the water of his early
life, the amniotic, the oceanic. His habit has prompted many
women to leave him. Tess just nods. She brings him a tall glass to
pee in. "Bottoms up," she says, liking the way his penis fills the glass,
like a soda siphon. "Aqua vitae!"

While recovering at Tess's, Penelope Tom catches up on her reading and finds that during its journey the space rover *Opportunity*
discovered evidence of water on the surface of Mars and is in-
trigued at the idea that at some unknown time in the distant
past there was life on the Red Planet. She gets it in her head to
do one thing before she dies—with her engineering skills she will
build the bimodal nuclear thermal rocket.

Because of her age, because she is a woman (before she is a man),
because of all of history and everything that has come before, she
is once again invisible. No one notices the little old lady man in
Harlem sewing herself a spaceship. *Nautilus Neptune.* She confides
the details of her project to Tess, who supplies heat-resistant fabric
and helps her grandmother saw off her index-finger needle, which
they affix to the spaceship as an evolved antenna of Darwinian
evolution. As Penelope is preparing to go, she affixes what has become the family seal, the historic remnant of scaly merkin, to the
nose of the *Nautilus Neptune.* On the appointed day, Tess stands on
the roof of the building and lights the long fuse. Wearing welder's
goggles, she watches as her grandmother takes off, a bright blast, an
eruption, carrying the past into the future with a sonic boom that
echoes around the world.

# The Last Good Time

"Are you going?" she asks as she spoons cereal into the baby's mouth.

"In a moment," he says, looking out the kitchen window—the sky is what he calls a winter mouse gray.

"How long will you be?"

He shrugs and adds a small folding umbrella to his bag.

"She's not dying today, is she?"

"I don't think so," he says as he goes into another room, returning with an old photo album.

"Again?" she asks.

"She likes it," he says.

"You like it," she says.

He nods. "I like it."

She looks at him as if she's waiting for something. He ignores her, focusing instead on the way the room has become punctuated by brightly colored pieces of plastic—the high chair, a cup, a ball, assorted pink toys.

"Why can't you just say it?" she asks.

"I'm not sure," he says as he's putting on his coat.

"You're so careful that you're going to end up with nothing."

"I live in my mind," he says.

"But you have a heart, I know you have a heart," she says. "You made the mistake of letting me know."

"A fatal error," he says.

"It's like you're already gone," she says.

"I should go, I'm late," he says, taking a piece of dry toast off her plate. "Bye-bye, baby," he says, bending to kiss the baby on her head. He inhales as he kisses her, and her downy-soft hair brushes his lips. The child's scent is clean and sweet.

"Say 'Bye-bye, Papa,'" the mother tells her, picking up the baby's hand and waving good-bye with it. The mother accidentally bumps the enormous cup of black coffee in front of her—it rocks, coffee splashing back and forth suddenly like a stormy sea. "After a while, crocodile," the mother says.

"In a minute, schmidgit," he says, trying to be playful as he's leaving.


He takes the long way around to the nursing home to visit his grandmother. Driving, he becomes obsessed by curbs. As the population ages, should the height of curbs be lowered? Would four inches be better than six inches? Would more cars jump the road and hit pedestrians? Would it be worse rather than better? Trained as an architect, he now works as an urban planner; his job is to make sense of things, to order the growing sprawl of what once was a small town. It's up to him to figure out where things intersect, where the overpasses should go, and if a new road is to be built, in what direction it should go. He is supposed to be able to think about the future without forgetting the past—something he finds difficult.


He was born nearby, in a place that was often cold and wet. His earliest memories are his feet and fingers perpetually chilled. He grew up obsessed with socks, wet wool socks, the smell of wet wool, of damp animals and fur. Since he was a little boy, he has dreamed of cowboys and California. He imagines it as a place where you wake up and the sun is always shining. He imagines that it is the most American place in America—dreams are made there. In his imagination it is a place where the Old West meets Marilyn Monroe, where every street is decorated differently—he is conflating Disneyland with Hollywood and doesn't even know it.

He drives to the nursing home, checking on various works in progress along the way. As he's driving, he's thinking of the photos in the album, remembering ones of himself as a boy, building the world of the future with plain wooden blocks and the expression of rage and disbelief on his face when his buildings fell down. He remembers that he liked wearing his fringed cowboy vest and gun belt day and night—over clothing or over pajamas, everywhere he went—the suede made him feel safe. He remembers a photograph of himself on his first day of school, posing outside the building as a cowboy in full costume. And he remembers that on the first day his teacher told him she was pleased to have a cowboy in the class but that he had to leave his hat and his guns in his cubby, and then later that day she came up and whispered that for reasons beyond her control he could not bring his guns to school anymore. "Times have changed," she explained. "Just being a cowboy isn't so simple these days. Someone might take it the wrong way, so perhaps it's best to go undercover." He remembers not really being sure what that meant but in general thinking the teacher was nice. He remembers the photograph and wonders if that is all he really remembers. Perhaps he made the rest up, or is that really what the teacher said?

"Good morning," he says as he enters his grandmother's room. She smiles, and only half of her face moves—the left side remains expressionless. He kisses the good side. Her breath is not sour, not like she's rotting from the inside out, but sweet like lavender, like wild grasses, which remind him of a trip they once went on long ago. Her fingers trace the purple scar across her skull—she has brain cancer. On the wall around her bed are posters made by the staff to remind her of her name, what year it is, and who the prime minister is. FOR FUN YOU LIKE TO SING, the poster says.

His grandmother is not so old—but her hair has always been white. He's thought of her as old since he was a child, even though she's now only in her mid-seventies. As a child he would spend long weekends with his grandparents. He would sleep between them in their bed, their heavy scents and sounds deeply comforting. His grandparents took him on trips; they liked going camping in the forest. When he was young, they bought him a Polaroid camera—he took it on every holiday—the pictures now fading, like they're evaporating. When he was fourteen, his grandfather died, and there was a large space—like an unbridgeable gap—in the bed, and he stopped spending weekends. It felt too awkward. Still, it was his grandparents who were the stability in his life, and he hates that he is losing her—she is the only thing that has stayed the same.


"You look tired," his grandmother says.

He shrugs. "I've had a lot on my mind."

She nods. "What season is it now?"

"Almost Christmas," he says.

"How is the baby?"

"She is plump and happy."

"And the baby's mother?"

"Not happy. She accuses me of living in my head. And she's right," he says.

"What is it like in your head?" the grandmother asks.

"Better," he says. "It's like in the movies. The sun is always out. When it rains, it pours. Life is large, dramatic. The men are heroic, and the women are beautiful. Things are clearer, life is not so confusing."

"We all have our dreams," she says.

"I find it very difficult to stay in the present," he says. "It wears me out. I get too angry. When she says she loves me, I become afraid. I go cold, and I don't talk."

"You must bring something to it," the grandmother says.

"I have nothing," he says. And they are quiet. "How about you—how are you doing?"

"I don't sleep so well," she says. "Day is night and night is day."

"This place is not a home," he says.

"Some people live here for a long time," the grandmother says.

"Would you like me to take you out? I could get a wheelchair and walk you around the garden."

"What is it like outside?" she asks.

"Cold and wet," he says.

"Let's not and say we did," the grandmother says. "How is the baby?" she asks again.

"She is plump and happy," he repeats.

"And your mother?"

"She is with her husband and family," he says.

"I was always very fond of your mother," she says. "I liked her more than my son. How big is her new child?"

"There's a boy and a girl. They are ten and thirteen," he says, speaking of his half siblings.

"Has it been that long?"

"Apparently," he says. "Do you want to look at pictures?" he asks, holding up the album. When his parents divorced, neither wanted the photo albums. They wanted no record of their time together, of life as a family. He became an outsider in his own life, an unwelcome reminder. His father was an only child; he is his grandmother's only grandchild.

She likes looking through the pictures.

"Whatever there was, he took it all," his grandmother says as she's flipping through the pages. "It's odd," she says. "Your father won't come to visit me if he knows you are coming."

"He doesn't like to bump into things," he says. "He doesn't like the unexpected."


A nurse comes to get his grandmother, to take her for a bath. He tells her that he'll wait and goes down the hall to have a coffee. "This is my daughter and her mother," he says, showing a picture that is not in the album to a young nurse—he keeps it in his pocket.

"Your wife?" she asks.

"No. The baby's mother," he says. And then he laughs. "She recently asked me to leave, said I was just occupying space."

The nurse smiles at him. "I'm sure she didn't mean it."

"I think she did," he says.

The nurse pours herself a coffee and goes back to work. He sits waiting.

He flips through the photos of his childhood again—the last good time.

"I am going on a journey," he tells his grandmother when she is out of the bath. "I don't know for how long."

"So is this good-bye?" she asks.

"Would you like me to stay, to wait?"

"No," she says.

"Where are you going?"

"In search of something," he says.

"Where will you look?"

"In America," he says. "I want to go to the desert to put my feet in the sand."

There is a pause.

"What?" he asks. "You look sad."

"I just wish you could have found it here," she says.

He nods. "I have always been somewhere else."

"I have something for you," the grandmother says, sending him to her closet, to her bag, and there is a sealed envelope with his name on it. "It's been here all along," she says. "It's for you from your grandfather and me."

"What is it?" he asks.

"It's your ticket out," she says.

He opens the envelope, and it is a ticket he made years ago—a pretend ticket to take a spaceship around the world. And money, a lot of real money. He can't help but smile.

"I thought you might need it," she says, laughing.

"This is too much," he says of the money.

"Take it," she says. "I have no use for money."

"I'll take the ticket and save the rest for the baby."

"You do what you choose."

"I love you," he says, bending to kiss her, and then he has to turn away—it's too much.

"You always have," she says. "Let me know what happens."

On the plane to Los Angeles, the movie starts to play, then stops, then repeats itself from the beginning. Each time it starts again, it gets a little further, and after the fourth time the passengers beg the crew not to try again. "It's enough," they say. "We can't keep watching the same thing over and over"—but of course he can. For him each time it is different. Each time he looks at it, he sees something entirely other. He looks at the ticket he made years ago—the flight is like a giant ride, the turbulence like the up and down of a roller coaster, the whole thing is an adventure.

Upon arrival he puts on his sunglasses—Ray-Bans; he never wears them at home, but here the glare is too much, the shadows bold, directed like slashes of light and dark, dividing the world into patterns, grids playing off the concrete, the parking lots, the chrome of the cars. He gets into his rental car and heads downtown. He is fascinated by what he sees, the cracks in the roadway, curbs that dip down at the corner for handicapped people, confusing intersections with flashing Walk and Don't Walk signs. He drives for hours and hours, up, down, around, stopping only to look, to think. He drives just to drive, for the pleasure of driving. He drives despite its being decadent and wasteful. He drives because it is something you don't normally do—just drive with nowhere to go, driving for the satisfaction of watching the road unfold. The wide boulevards— Santa Monica, Wilshire—are appealing for the straightforward rise and fall of it all. He drives to the tar pits, to the place they call the Grove, and then toward Hollywood—sex shops, tourist depots, and from there up the hills toward Mulholland Drive and what he

thinks of as the top of Los Angeles, looking out over it all, the industry of Los Angeles. On the way back down, he stops for a hot
dog, and the guy behind the counter laughs when he calls it a sausage. Still hungry, he gets a burger from a place that you have to
have a kind of code word for—a friend told him it's not enough to
just get a cheeseburger, that he should order it "animal style,"
meaning with sauce and pickles and onions. It's like he waited to
arrive in order to eat. He drives, he eats, he consumes everything
and feels optimistic for the first time in a long time. He checks in
to his hotel, takes the car out again, and drives to a bar downtown.
Sunglasses on—the sky is still blue, the day bright, the street entirely empty. He is a foreigner who feels less foreign when he's away
from home.


"Just coming in from the cold?" an old guy in the bar asks him,
noticing his winter clothes. He wears ginger-colored corduroy
pants, his shirt is dark green—basically he looks like a tree lost in
a forest. The old man is lingering over a scotch. His face is heavily
weather-beaten, he's thin, his hands are gnarled. "I know what
you're thinkin'," the old guy says, aware that he's being looked at.

He shrugs.

"You're wondering if I've got a cigarette."

He shakes his head no. "I don't smoke."

"I used to carry them on me all the time—I used to get 'em for
free, cartons and cartons of 'em—'Just give 'em away,' they'd tell
me. 'Give 'em to anyone you run into and tell them your story.'"

He listens a bit more carefully.

"I still have the story," the old guy says. There's a pause. "You
wanna buy me a drink?"

"Sure," he says.

———————

"I grew up in Texas," he says. "My daddy worked horses; I did, too. Only went through sixth grade, and then I just couldn't be bothered." The old guy is playing with the short straw in his drink, knotting it with his gnarled fingers. "I learned a trick or two, rode in the rodeo for a bit—roping horses, was a rodeo clown. You know what that is?"

"The fool in the pickle barrel who lets the bull come toward him," he says.

"That was me," he says. "Till I got kicked too hard, and then I thought there had to be a better way. I came out west and got into the industry, mostly building sets, doing a little of this or that. Tough when you don't have much of an education. Anyway, it ended up that sometimes they needed a cowboy, someone good with animals, someone who could stand in and do a trick or two." The old guy looks at him as if to ask, Are you following what I'm telling you?

He nods.

"I'm it," he says, tossing back his drink. "I'm the last cowboy."

"Is that it? Is that the whole story?"

"No," the old man says. "But you gotta put another quarter in the jukebox."

He signals the bartender to pour another round of drinks.

"Back in 1955 this fellow Leo Burnett—that name ring a bell?"

"No," he says.

"Leo Burnett came up with this great idea for an advertising campaign—to sell cigarettes. He thought of a cowboy, rugged, masculine, and so it was born—the Marlboro Man."

"Are you saying that you were the Marlboro Man?"

"Not exactly," he says. "I was the stand-in for the Marlboro Man. I was the one that came early and left late and stood around for hours under the hot lights—I was the one who ran. I got paid a few bucks and a fuck of a lot of free cigarettes, that's what I'm trying to tell you." He shifts his weight on his chair. "I'm in pain," he says. "My hips are crap. I fell off horses so many times it's amazing I can walk a single step. But despite it all, I'm the last man standing. Hey, so what about you, Mr. Man, what planet are you from?"

"I just got into town," he says. "Just passing through."

"Do you need a place to stay? I've got a sweet corner spot in a shelter downtown. It's pretty crowded, but I could put in a good word for you."

"No," he says, "I'm okay. I'm heading south tomorrow."

"It's comin' on Christmas, you know."

He nods.

"You got plans?"

"Not really, just kind of playing it as I go."

"Well, I'm not one to preach, but if you want to go to church, we've got some good Christmas Eve services, and there's a bunch of places to get a hot meal. Some of us, we don't have much, but what we've got we share."

"I'll keep that in mind, thank you," he says, getting up to go. He digs in his pocket and finds a twenty and tries to give it to the guy.

"I can't accept," the man says. "It was good enough of you to buy me a drink—I need nothing more." And then he stops to think. "I'm lying," he says, taking the money. "I've got nothing—twenty bucks and I can live another day."

"Merry Christmas," he says, still feeling the old man's fingers on his hand as he exits the bar. The old man follows him out. They step onto the sidewalk—it's still bright and warm and so different from anyplace else.

A car cruises by and stops at the light, blaring loud music. The old guy leans toward the driver's window and shouts, "Make it louder!"

He laughs at himself for still being in love with the idea of cowboys—wondering what it is he thinks is so magical about men learning to be tough, to hold on to their feelings—to say less rather than more. He thinks of cowboys as loners, rebels, lovers with wounded hearts, rule breakers, fierce, brave, like John Wayne, Roy Rogers, and Clint Eastwood.

"God love ya," the old man says, slapping him on the back before he ducks into the bar.

He goes to his hotel, orders a pizza, and looks through his photo album, turning to the pages he thinks of as the Last Good Time: the family trip to Disneyland the Christmas before it all went wrong. His plan is to drive to Disney in the morning—in search of what he has left behind.


Exhausted, he tries to sleep but has lost track of time and finds himself dressed, ready to go at 4:00 a.m. He forces himself to lie back down, remembering that his mother used to say, "Rest—even if you can't sleep—just rest."


Checking out of the hotel at 5:30 a.m., he arrives at Disney before the gates open. He drives in meditative circles around Anaheim for ninety minutes before parking in the enormous structure and finding his way to the train that will deliver him to the Magic Kingdom. At the train depot, he feels himself begin to recede. What had seemed so clear, so obvious, a return to the place where things were good, becomes opaque. He feels small, in need of direction, lost in a sea of families. He lets the first train leave the station and then the second, and finally after a while the train conductor, noticing that he's been standing on the platform, asks, "Are you waiting for someone? Do you need assistance?"

"I don't know where to begin," he says.

The conductor ushers him into the first car on the train. "It may sound corny, but . . ." The conductor begins to sing, "'Let's start at the very beginning, a very good place to start.'"

"Thank you," he says, thinking the tune sounds familiar.

He passes through the ticket booth and enters the Magic Kingdom. Surrounded by people in a frenzy, rushing to get to this world or that, he stands still for a moment, feeling both excitement and trepidation, knowing that there's a good chance his first reaction is not going to be one of relief—nothing is the way it used to be.

Last night he made a map for himself—a kind of agenda based on the photos in the album. His plan is to visit each of the attractions he went to with his parents. He hopes to conjure his memories of that day and of his childhood in general.

He breathes deeply; it means too much to him. He looks at the faces of the children and their parents around him taking in the whole thing for the first time, the look of surprise and enchantment, joyous and over the top. His parents came to America because he wanted to, he begged for it. Walking through the park, he tries to think of himself as shorter, smaller, his experience less broad, his understanding only half formed. He tries reimagining himself as naive. It occurs to him that the different lands within the park are like sets for a film, that each tableau is an unfolding scene and the guests are in fact the actors. It is all a fairy tale, all make-believe, and he wants to go in deep, to be the boy he once was, the boy who thought it was real. And at the same time, the brute force of reality, the intrusion of truth, is inescapable, and with it comes sadness. People with FastPasses hurry by, conspiring to find their way around the long lines for each ride. He doesn't remember there being long lines, doesn't remember there being such a competitive edge to everything.

At the Mad Tea Party, he gets into his own spinning teacup. He tries to spin fast. He went on this one with both parents; he remembers that he sat in the middle, his face stretched in a smile of exaltation. As he turns the center wheel, round and round, faster and faster, the cup begins to spin and his memories unspool; in his mind's eye, he sees his mother and father, youthful, athletic, playful, taking turns with the camera, taking turns posing with him, and then sometimes asking a stranger to take a photo of the three of them together. Looking back, he's always wondered if he missed the clues, if he should have seen it coming or if the whole thing happened offscreen.

His father never told him he'd left. One day while he was at school, his father came and packed up his belongings. He also took the train he'd given his son for his birthday—the boy was not sure why.

He didn't realize what his father had taken until after he told his mother that his train was missing. "Why?" he wanted to know.

"Ask your father," she said.

"Where is he?" the boy asked.

"I have no idea," she said.

"When is he coming home?"

"He's not," she said.

"But he was here," the boy said.

"While we were out," she said bitterly.

"When is Daddy coming home?" he asked again, and again sure he was just misunderstanding something.

His mother got angry.

"Did he take anything of yours?" he asked.

"He took everything," she said. The boy followed his mother into his parents' bedroom, and she opened the father's side of the closet—empty except for the Christmas sweater his mother had recently bought him.

"Even his toothbrush?"

"No," she said. "I suspect he has another."

"Why?" the boy asked.

"Because there was nothing left," she said, and shrugged, resigned.

"Me?"

"That's not a reason to stay together." She took a moment to collect the shoes he'd left behind and put them in a bag. She set the bag out by the trash along with the Christmas sweater. The man who lived downstairs, who was in charge of taking the trash to the curb, took the bag. More than once the boy saw the man wearing his father's Christmas sweater and felt his heart accidentally jump, thinking his father had returned.

Dumbo, the flying elephant, is crowded. He waits patiently, and when the family in line ahead of him asks if he minds sharing an elephant with the grandmother, he says he'd be happy to and smiles. Her thick-soled shoes and coiffed white hair remind him of his grandmother. They board their elephant, buckle in, and take off. At first he drives, dipping the elephant up and down with the joystick, pretending they're catching up on the grandkids in the elephant just ahead. And then he asks if she'd like to drive, and she's thrilled. When it's over, she beams. "Thank you," she says, "you're a very nice boy." He wishes it were true. In the canal boats of Storybook Land, he remembers that his father would take him out on Sundays. He wouldn't come into the house—they'd have to meet somewhere. Often they'd just go to a park, and before bringing him home his father would buy him an ice cream. On rainy days they'd sit in a museum or sometimes, still in the park, under the shelter of a tree.

"Where do you live?" he asked his father.

"I'm staying with a friend," his father said.

There was great formality, a distance between them. Who are his friends? he wondered but couldn't bring himself to ask.

He found out his father was staying with a woman who was a math teacher at his school—one of his friends told him. At first he thought it was a joke and pretended it wasn't true, but when he saw the math teacher in the halls, he noticed she went out of her way to avoid him. She would see him and pretend she didn't.

"Does she have any children?" he asked his father after some time had passed.

"No," he said. "She never wanted children."

"Why does she work with children if she doesn't like them?" he asked his father awhile later.

"No doubt she would have done better in a university, but there are very few jobs and she's a bit older."

He remembered being with his parents at Disneyland, laughing, his father being silly, the world seeming magical, unreal. "It's unbelievable, there's no dirt here," his father said.

And then he remembered his parents at home after the trip to California, his father becoming more serious, losing his sense of humor, and as he did, his mother became more playful, almost as if mocking him, and it made his father angry. "Grow up!" he remembers his father shouting. He glances at the photographs. What he remembers is true, there was no dirt, everything was spotless, perfect, everything was in its right place. There was a parade down Main Street. There were wonderful old cars, tooting horns, and a float carried Snow White and the Seven Dwarfs, assorted fairies and others. His father lifted him high, sat him down on his shoulders—a change of perspective. And then there's a photo of his mother and father, each holding him by an arm and swinging him through the air—he recalls the sensation of flying like an airplane. He sees it now and realizes how sentimentalized it is—the railroad station, city hall, the opera house. It's small-town America comes to the big city, a utopian vision of a world that might have been but never really was, the budding landscape of power. He is in it, and the conflict remains; is that consciousness or bitterness? he wonders. Is it his adult self mourning a lost childhood? Is it his own anger at himself for being stuck in this place—needing to make sense of it, needing to make it right?

He doesn't know what happened, who left whom—no one would say.

Within a year his mother married a man who was younger and who didn't like him at all. The feeling was mutual. Suddenly he'd become an intruder in his own life, and he didn't like competing with a stranger for his mother's affection, so he spent less and less time at home. His stepfather didn't go to any of his school events, didn't do anything for or with him; at best they tolerated each other. Time passed, and his mother had a new baby.

"He's a good father," his mother would say.

"To his own children." He remembers watching his mother breast-feeding the baby.

"Not in front of him," his stepfather declared, pointing a finger at him.

He went outside and spent the night among the trees. Later he got a job working in the movie theater, sweeping stale popcorn. The owner trusted him so much he went away for the summer and left the place to him. For all intents and purposes, he lived at the theater, watching the films over and over again.

He goes on each of the rides multiple times. He tries to stay focused. The disorientation of going up and down, high and low, and round and round allows him to reprocess his experiences. He is whirling, dizzy, nauseated, thinking about everything. There are moments he believes he may be hallucinating, or maybe it's just dehydration.

"Are you running from something or toward?" a young woman asks.

"Pardon?"

"I'm Candace. I'm one of the cast members here at Disneyland. I just wanted to make sure everything is going all right."

"I think so," he says. "I mean, as expected."

"Are you with a group?"

"No," he says. "I'm on my own."

"Most men don't come to the park alone," she says.

"I came with my parents." He pauses. "Long ago, when I was a boy. This time I came in search of something."

"What?"

"I'm not sure, I felt I'd left something behind." He glances up at the tree over his head. "But perhaps I'm just in search of a palm tree."

"Did you know the palm trees aren't really from California? They came from Latin America a hundred years ago," she says.

"I didn't know," he says.

"And worse yet, they're dying of a fungus."

"After I came to Disneyland, I went home and told my friends I met Mickey Mouse and Abraham Lincoln. They laughed. Now I've returned to revisit the dream, Tomorrowland and the future— to find out if it's still alive."

"And is it?" she asks.

"It's hard to tell," he says. "Nothing is from here anymore. It's all from China—it's like China owns the United States. If I pick up a Disneyland snow globe and turn it over, on the bottom of the world it would say 'Made in China.'"

"You're funny," she says, laughing.

"A regular clown," he says.

"I've finished work for the day," she says. "You were my last assignment."

"I was an assignment?"

She doesn't answer. "Do you want to grab a bite?"

"I haven't eaten all day," he says. "Is there someplace you like here at Disney?"

"No," she says. "We're not allowed to eat with guests, but we can go off campus. I live nearby."

"Sure," he says.

As they're walking toward the exit, she tells him that the 1955 dedication plaque reads "'Here you leave today and enter the world of yesterday, tomorrow and fantasy.' I love that," she says. "Every day as I come and go, I repeat that phrase, as a mantra."

And then she explains that "cast members," the Disney words for employees, check out at a different place and have their own parking area. She tells him that she'll meet him at the parking structure. She circles and finds him walking up and down the rows in the parking structure, unable to locate his car.

"I have no idea where I left it."

"What color was it?"

He can't quite remember. "Gray? A silvery, grayish green?"

"It happens all the time," she says. "I'll let the security people know. Worst case they don't find it until late tonight, after the park closes."

"I've never lost something so large," he says, getting into her car, which is small, white, and rusting from the bottom up.

"It's worse when people misplace their kids—that happens multiple times a day. We have a whole system set up to reunite lost children with their families," she says as they exit the parking lot.

Along the way they talk about the weather.

"Is this normal for here?" he asks.

"Normal how?"

"Is it always this hot?" he says.

"The heat comes and goes—there is no normal anymore," she says. "Is it warm where you live?"

"Not really," he says. "It rains a lot."

"Here," she says, "it's usually a little bit better than this—a little more perfect. That's what everyone likes about it. Have you been to America many times?" she asks.

"A few," he says. "Have you ever been to Europe?"

She shakes her head. "I wanna go to London sooo bad, but I haven't even been on a plane yet."


She drives to a small, low apartment complex about ten minutes from Disney. The complex, called The Heights, has a big sign by the entrance that says ELECTRIC AND A/C INCLUDED. The buildings look like what they used to call factory housing—meaning that it was made to house factory workers, but the truth is it's so undistinguished that it looks like it was made in a factory and simply deposited here one night. The buildings are numbered—that's the only way to tell them apart. Her apartment is on the middle level of a three-story building.

Before opening the door, she warns him, "We have cats. We're not supposed to, but we do. And roommates. I have three roommates, but they're at work right now. We're all cast members, which is nice because it gives us something to talk about."

He nods.


She leads him into the dark apartment. She opens the metal vertical blinds, and a small cloud of dust snaps off, rising into the air, catching the light, glittering like fairy dust.

"Would you like a drink?" she asks.

"Sure," he says.

"We have beer and Tang."

"Beer would be nice."

She takes out two and marks a paper inventory sheet held onto the front of the fridge with heavy magnets. "Are you married?" she asks, handing him the beer and a package of saltines.

"Not really," he says, following her lead and eating the crackers first before taking a sip.

"What does that mean?"

He swallows, washing down the stale crackers with the beer. "A crisis of confidence?" he suggests. "I live with someone, we have a baby. But I'm not as into it as she would like me to be."

"Does she know you're here?" she asks.

"She knows I'm gone, but I didn't give much in the way of details."

"What do you tell her?"

"Not a lot. I mostly talk only in my head." He laughs at himself.

"Where did you meet?" she asks.

"At a party. She's a photographer, a lot of weddings, family photos—no one calls you to photograph a funeral. After the baby came, she wanted more, I wanted less. It got harder."

"Are you hungry?" she asks.

"I am," he says.

"I don't know if I should charge you for it or give it to you for free."

Startled, he chokes and beer comes out of his nose.

"We call that snorfing," she says. "When you laugh while you're drinking."

"Is it funny?" he asks.

"Yes, because you weren't sure what I meant, were you?"

He blushes.

She opens the freezer and shows him it's full of frozen meals. "One of my friends works in a hotel, and he sells whatever he finds in the rooms on the black market. I pay like fifty cents a meal for food that's good as new—still frozen. I've got lots of macaroni and cheese and frozen pizza. Things like this one." She pulls out something called a Hungry Man dinner. "This one is a delicacy—very few and far between. I think I paid a dollar for it. The gluten-free stuff belongs to my roommate—it's very expensive."

He moves to take out his wallet.

"No," she says. "Be my guest." She pops the meal into the microwave and sets the timer.

She's looking at him, wanting something. She moves a little closer, raises her beer, and they tap their bottles together. He knew that something might happen when he accepted the offer to go to her house. She kisses him. "I don't do this," she says. "I don't pick up men at work and bring them home." The microwave beeps. She opens the door, peels back the wrapper, and sets it for another minute, then kisses him again.

"Then why are you doing it?" he asks, knowing he should be asking himself the same thing.

"I've never slept with someone from another country. I'm wondering if it's different," she says.

"And I've never done it with an American," he says.

He puts his beer down. Again they kiss. "What do you think?" he asks.

"You taste foreign," she says, leading him down the hall toward her room, stopping first in her roommate's bedroom to look for condoms.

Her bed is low to the floor and surrounded by stuffed animals.

"It's like the enchanted forest," he says nervously, and then asks, "How old are you?"

"Don't worry, I'm old enough," she says. "I just really still like toys. A lot of these I won. I've got good aim when it comes to games of chance."

He follows her lead. There's something rather mechanical about her approach to lovemaking. "I haven't done it so much," she says, shy but clearly proud of what she might think of as her technique. He finds the youthful roundness of her figure sexy. Her skin is fresh and at the same time filled to the edges, like a balloon blown all the way up—she is taut, almost bouncy.

"My roommates are wilder than me," she says. "Like, have you ever done it from the back?"

"I have," he says.

"Should we try it?" she asks, as if it would be some kind of experiment. And as he's behind her, just breaking a sweat, there is a turn in her mood.

"Something really bad could happen here," she says.

"Like what?"

"Like if others came in and things slipped out of control?"

"Who would come in?"

"People," she says.

"And what would happen?"

"They might make us do stuff we don't want to?"

He pauses. "Do you want me to stop?" She says nothing. "Am I doing something you don't want me to?"

She seems frightened, undone by what she is doing.

"No," she says. "I'm just saying." And she starts to sniffle as though she's going to cry. "I just really have a hard time letting go. Let's start again."

"It's okay," he says. "Nothing bad is happening here. I thought you were having a good time."

"I was."

They begin again. This time he lies back and she straddles him—she calls this "grown-up sex," and says she saw it once in a porno movie. "It's kind of like being on a ride," she says. "Up and down. I've only had like two boyfriends, and both of them were a lot like me."

And when they are done, she puts her top back on and, half naked, she carries the used condom into the kitchen, wraps it in a wad of paper towels, and buries it in the garbage.

"Getting rid of the evidence," she calls down the hallway.

She comes back into the bedroom and gets down on her hands and knees and starts rooting through her closet. It's a rather odd view of her from the back, naked from the waist down. "What size shoe are you?" she asks.

"I take a forty-three," he says.

"No, like in regular numbers. You know, eight, nine, ten . . ."

"Oh," he says. "I think it's a nine and a half."

"Perfect," she says, still digging. Finally she pulls out a pair of shoes. "These were my grandfather's," she says, handing him an elegant pair of dark loafers with tassels. "Genuine alligator. Put them on."

He slips his feet in, trying to hide the holes in his brown socks. "What do you think?"

"I like the contrast, your socks, the shoes. You should have them," she says. "He wanted his shoes to go to a good soul—I've just been waiting to find the right person. Most American men have bigger feet."

"Did you grow up here?" he asks, walking around the apartment in the shoes, test-driving them, not wanting to take them unless they are a good fit.

"No," she says, "my family is from Utah. I'm kind of different from them, so I left." She pauses. "It's more like I ran away, but I really had to—it was the only way out. My friend's brother did the same thing—we went together to Los Angeles, and then we got into this Scientology church thing there that wasn't so great, and I had to run away again. And I came down here. This is the first place where I felt really good. I'm someone who needs to be part of something—Disney is kind of like a religious experience for me, only better. I really like the values and the characters, and it's a happy place." She pauses again. "Are you hungry?"

"Starving," he says.

She reheats the Hungry Man Salisbury Steak and makes herself a Lean Cuisine. They sit on her bed and eat, surrounded by the multicolored plush-animal kingdom.

"Do you find it disturbing that some of the animals aren't their natural color?"

"Like what?" she asks.

"Like the purple bear," he says. "Or the fluorescent-orange dog?"

"No," she says, shaking her head. "I like it. I'm not afraid of color. How's your meal?"

"It's nice," he says.

"Isn't it so fun to have sex and then eat?"

He nods.

"I think this is what people are talking about when they say they have the munchies. It's like I could eat a horse," she says, sneaking a forkful of his potatoes. "So what are you doing this afternoon? Back to the Magic Kingdom for another round?"

"Actually, I was going to drive out to the desert—to Joshua Tree—but with my car missing, I'm not sure."

"I could drive you—if you wouldn't mind paying for gas."

"That would be nice," he says. "Thank you."

He finds the concrete highway soothing—flat, affectless, rolling out for miles ahead.

"What's nice about concrete," he tells her, "is that it doesn't get potholes, so it's a smoother surface, and you don't get ruts that collect water, so it's better in the rain."

"That's really interesting," she says.

He can't tell if she's kidding or not and stops.

"Seriously," she says, "how do you know so much about roads?"

"It's my job," he continues. "The average life of a concrete road before repair is about twenty-seven years, where asphalt lasts about fifteen." He goes on, telling her pretty much everything he knows about roads. The sharing of information is relaxing; it helps him to feel closer to her.

"How do you see when there is so much light?" he asks.

"We all wear sunglasses," she says. "Polarized ones work best."

She hands him a spare pair of glasses that are tucked into her visor.

"Ah," he says, "these are wonderful. The whole world looks perfect."

"They're from the Disney store," she says. "At Disney they specialize in making things look good."

"Yes, but then how do you know what's real?" he asks.

"You bite into it," she says, laughing.

"It's true," he says. "You have hot dog stands that are shaped like hot dogs, and yesterday I ate a doughnut at a place that looked like a doughnut. You have ninety-nine-cent pizzas, Happy Meals, supersized drinks, and roads that go on forever. But why, then, is no one outside?"

"It's complicated," she says. "I don't think anyone is sure why no one goes outside. But my sense is we're all nervous to be seen just wandering around, like we're out of our element. We feel more comfortable in our cars—they're like our shells."

"Okay," he says. "So what do you love about America?" he asks her.

"Well, I love being in the entertainment industry," she says. "And who knows, maybe one day I'll go back to school or I'll keep doing what I'm doing and become a customer-service manager or something. I feel that there's lots of opportunity for someone like me—as you can see, I'm really a great people person."

He nods. "You are good with people."

"What about you?" she asks.

"I might start painting again," he says, remembering that as a boy he used to enjoy making paintings of the landscape, paintings of the places he went with his family. "Maybe I'll paint my view of the world, the details of what is in my heart, the fractures."

"What really brought you here?" she asks. "So far from home?"

"I've had a hard time," he says. "It's as though I can't find my feelings, or like I left them behind. That's why I'm on this journey. I'm looking for what I lost."

"And have you found it?" she asks optimistically.

He shrugs.

"They say Christmas is a difficult time of year for people."

He nods. "It may depend on what your expectations are. Do you have big plans?"

"I go out with my friends. We take a taxi so we can get really drunk. We karaoke, and then we do like a Secret Santa thing where everyone gets a present. It's a lot more fun than when I was a kid. What about you?"

"Often I have dinner with my grandmother."

His mind wanders, and he replays memories: blowing out birthday candles, learning to ski between his father's legs, making a snowman. He sees images in his mind's eye and can't tell what is a photograph and what is an actual memory, all of it is frozen, frame by frame, into single images—moments. He remembers that when he was about fifteen, his mother's husband went away for two weeks, and for those two weeks everything was good. He took care of his mother, of the two younger children. They laughed, she was the mother he remembered, and then the husband returned and the closeness vanished.

They stop for doughnuts and coffee. "I just love that sugared-up feeling when I'm driving," she says. "I get the best rush, driving really fast, drinking hot coffee. I don't know how it is where you're from, but here lots of people practically live in their cars."

The landscape starts to change. There are fewer car dealerships, more blank spaces, and lighter traffic. The traffic thins and thins until they reach Joshua Tree, which is an odd combination of both more and less developed than he'd thought it would be. Exiting onto a smaller road, they pass a bunch of lousy-looking motels, all of which have the word "Desert" in the name. And there are run-down bars with battered old trucks parked outside. In general there's the sense of this place as other—a kind of last stop, a place people come when all else has failed, or when they just need an out. It's scruffy, sparse, and it looks rough. He pays the fee to enter the park, and they drive onward—he's simultaneously elated and depressed and asks if they might turn off the radio and roll down the windows.

The air is cold, bracing. There's something about it all that makes him feel he's able to empty himself into the desert. He wants to get out, to run, but he has no idea what direction he might go in.

"Maybe we could park and take a walk?" he suggests.

"I'm not much of a hiker," she says. "In fact—" She holds up her foot, and she's wearing sandals with heels.

"I need to get out," he says, opening the door. "If you don't want to wait, I understand. I can find a ride home."

"Oh, I don't mind waiting," she says. "I can even just drive out of view and wait."

He shakes his head. "Honestly, I think you should leave me here. I need a moment alone."

"You're not going to do something weird, are you?"

"Like what?"

She doesn't answer. "It doesn't feel right," she says. "I'm not leaving you here. I just can't do it."

They're in a standoff.

"Fine," he says. "Just give me a couple of minutes."

He gets out of the car, walks up a ways, stands with his arms open to the world—spins them in circles, like he's trying to pick up some speed, and then begins to turn to whirl to twirl around and around again on the same spot, churning up dust and dirt, making a small cloud around himself. And as he's spinning, a single dark cloud moves over the desert, and it begins to snow. Fat white snowflakes like doilies spin down from the sky.

He stops, opens his arms wide, tilts his head back, sticks his tongue out, and tries catching them.

Seeing him like that reminds her of something. She gets out and calls, "You know, the real name for a Joshua tree is a yucca. The name Joshua tree came from some Mormon settlers crossing the desert—the shape of the trees reminded them of the bit in the Bible where Joshua reaches his hands to the sky and prays." She stands the same way he's standing, letting the snow land on her open arms, on her upturned face. "I only know that because my family is Mormon, and that's why I had to run away."

They return to Los Angeles in silence. She invites him to her apartment for "another round," but he declines. "I should be getting on with it," he says. "I met a guy in Los Angeles, the Last Cowboy, and he wanted to take me to Christmas Mass. I think he's expecting me to be there tonight." She drops him off at the Disneyland garage—the security guys have located his car. He gets out carrying his plastic bag of Disneyland loot along with a few little extra things she gives him as remembrances.

He sits in the car. From the top of the parking structure, he's got a good view of the evening fireworks—Believe in Magic—Sleeping Beauty's castle becomes a winter wonderland, the air is charged with awe and wonder, and in the end, as Christmas music plays, fake snow floats down. As he's listening, he's remembering a trip to the Alps when he was a boy, his father buying him lederhosen and telling him they were just like ones he had as a boy, and he realizing that it was the first and only time his father had ever said anything about having been a child. He thinks of the dedication plaque the girl told him about this afternoon, her mantra: "Here you leave today and enter the world of yesterday, tomorrow and fantasy."

He digs out his phone and calls home; she answers even though it is late.

"How are you?" he asks.

"We're fine," she says. "I took the baby to see your grandmother today—she smiled."

"That's nice," he says. There is silence. "I am standing here, there are fireworks going off, and a magical kingdom is in front of me."

"That's nice," she says.

Again there is silence. "It's almost Christmas," he says.

"Yes," she says.

"I'll be home soon," he says. "I think I've got what I need." He pats his jacket pocket, where the crayon-colored homemade ticket his grandmother gave him rests. "And I've got my ticket right here," he tells her. "It says it's good for one free trip around the world."

# Be Mine

"There's something you don't want to tell me," she says.

He says nothing.

"I'm not an idiot," she says. "It's not like I don't know what's going on."

He sits up in the bed.

"You're leaving it up to me," she says. "You want me to be the one to say it."

He looks at his bare chest and does tricks with his belly. The muscles ripple up and down like waves washing ashore.

"You never loved me," she says. "That's the thing you don't want to tell me."

He shakes his head.

"There's more," she says. "It's not like it's breaking news. I knew it from the start. It could never be that easy. Easy would make you like every other guy who can get it up but just can't get the words out."

Tears run down his face and onto his chest.

"Really?" she says, genuinely surprised.

"Really?" He gets up and puts his pants on.

"So that's it," she says.

He pulls on his T-shirt.

"It's okay," she says. "I don't expect you to get down on your knees and say you love me."

He puts on his shoes and looks at her. "I don't know what love is," he says. "Does that make it any easier, that I don't fucking know what love is?"

"Fine," she says, "but it's not like you get all this for nothing. I expect something."

"What?" he asks.

"Breakfast," she says.


"What about the baby?" she asks over coffee and toast.

"What baby?"

"The baby we didn't have."

"It doesn't exist," he says.

"Yes, it does," she says.

"Not really," he says.

"The baby exists—it just hasn't arrived yet."

"Are you pregnant?"

"That's not what I mean. . . ."

"Then it doesn't exist," he says.

"It does," she says. "It just hasn't been mixed. The pieces haven't been put together, but we have all the parts."

"It was an experiment," he says. "An experiment that failed."

"It didn't fail," she says.

"We didn't really try," he says. "How can we have a baby if we can't have a conversation?"

"It's not the same thing," she says.

"It's harder," he says.

"Not really. People do it all the time. If we have a baby, then we'll have something to talk about. 'Did the baby poop? Did the baby smile? Did the baby have a good day at school?'" she says.

"It doesn't last forever," he says.

"Nothing does," she says.

"The baby will grow up," he says. "It will leave home."

"We'll be back where we are now, but we'll have more in common, a lifetime of memories. 'Remember when the baby threw up? Remember when the dog ate the shoe? Remember when the cat shat in your closet?'"

"I'm not sure that's enough," he says.

"Grandchildren?" she suggests.

He bends to kiss her. "I'm late," he says.

"What do you want for dinner?" she asks as he's out the door.

"The usual."

"I'm getting old," she says at night as they lie side by side. She is reading a book, he is pretending to sleep.

"One day at a time," he says.

"Faster," she says. "Like it's speeded up, like every hour is doubling up, speeding forward."

"You're starting to remind me of your mother."

"What about my mother?"

"She always thought she was dying," he says.

"Well, look what happened to her," she says.

"She was eighty-three years old," he says.

"Death is death at any age. She was very much alive until she died. Feel my fingers, they're like ice," she says.

"Your fingers are always cold. You've got a long way to go."

"How do you know?" she asks.

"I'm being practical—people your age and in your condition don't just die," he says.

"What condition am I in?" she asks.

"Good condition," he says.

"I could be hit by a truck."

"Why don't you go stand in the middle of the street and see what happens? Maybe you'll get lucky."

"You're just trying to get rid of me," she says.

"I'm trying to sleep," he says.

"Fine. I'll go stand in the street, but I doubt anyone will hit me. More likely they'll swerve and squash some poodle out for a walk, and I'll feel guilty—like I'm the ass for standing in the middle of the street. There has to be another way." She pauses.

"Just live," he says.

Silence.

"You have the worst ideas, and you're so fucking optimistic," she says. "You think everyone can be just like you—perfect."

"I'm glad you think I'm perfect," he says.

"I don't think you're perfect—you think you're perfect."

He rolls onto his side.

"Don't do that," she says. "Don't be so fucking condescending." She sighs loudly. "Why are you so annoying?"

"Am I?" he asks.

"Yes. You answer every question with a question."

"Do I?"

"You just did it again," she says.

"Did I? I wasn't aware. . . ."

"How can someone training to be a shrink be so unaware?"

"I compartmentalize," he says. "I separate work and home."

"You work from home," she says. "Let me ask you something, why did you marry an artist?"

"I didn't know it would be such a responsibility," he says.

"What do you mean, a responsibility?" she says.

"To be not just the spouse but also the material," he says.

"Any regrets?" she asks.

"Plenty," he says. "I should have given you more to work with. I should have behaved more outrageously."

"When?"

"At dinners, in public, in bed. I should have given you something to really write about," he says.

"Is it too late?" she asks.


The night passes.


"Oh," she says at dawn when she rolls over and sees him.

"Oh what?"

"I didn't realize you were there."

"You were expecting someone else?"

She says nothing.

"I live here," he says. "This is my side of the bed."

"It wasn't always," she says.

"What does that mean?"

"We used to switch."

"That was years ago in the old apartment. Someone had to take the hot side and someone had to take the cold. One was by the window, the other by the heat pipe—it was a coin toss."

"Is that how we ended up here?"

"Where?"

"With you sleeping with your back toward me? We used to sleep face-to-face. You'd fall asleep looking at me. Or you'd be behind me, your arm around me, spooning me. . . ."

"We were on a moving train. I was keeping you from falling out," he says.

"Call it what you will," she says, turning on the television to hear the morning news.

"Do you ever stop complaining?" he asks.

"No," she says, horrified. "It would be like I'd given up hope."

"Or accepted things the way they are."

"We should get a pet," she says.

"A pet?

"Yes, like a dog or a cat."

"I don't know if the lease allows animals."

She shrugs. "I need something living to tend to."

"What about a plant?"

"Something that can look me in the eye."

"How about fish?"

"Something warm that I can cuddle, something that will love me."

"You need more than I can provide," he says, sitting up. "And by the way, I have needs, too—needs that aren't being met."

"Oh," she says. "Like what?"

"To not have someone wanting something from me all the time, to not be inundated with senseless chatter."

"Should I change the channel?" she asks—pointing to the TV.

"No," he says. "Just turn the sound off."


"Honestly, it was inevitable," she says, staring at the muted television.

"Was it really?" he asks.

"I knew from the beginning," she says.

"That's what they always say," he says.

"You couldn't exactly miss the cues."

"Some could," he says.

"Not really," she says, moving toward him in the bed.

"There's no escaping?" he asks.

"None," she says, closing in.

"Unfortunately, we're out of time for today," he says.

"I have news for you," she says. "I won't be coming back."

"We'll talk about it next week," he says.

"I've found someone else," she says.

"He who laughs last," he says.

"Fuck you," she says.

"It's about time," he says.

And before either can say more, his mouth is on hers and hers is on his, and together they are eating their words.

# A Prize for Every Player

"Tom, I don't mean to sound critical, but why do you always park way back here and then we have to walk through the parking lot with the children?"

"Jane, the car is the size of a boat, and I like to leave myself some breathing room."

"Dad, why is that giant American flag up there—what does it mean when they fly the flag?"

"That's a good question," Tom, the dad, says as the doors of the extra-large minivan slide open and they all hop out.

"I like to think it means they're happy," Jane, the mom, says. "Everyone hold hands—it's a parking lot."

"How do they get the flag up there?" Tilda, the little girl, asks.

"I actually know the answer to that," the dad says. "There's a hole in the ceiling of the store, and every morning someone climbs up and sends the flag up the flagpole."

"I don't remember the flag from last time we were here," says young Jimmy, who is nine.

"It was raining last week—they don't fly the flag in the rain," the dad says.

"Tom, is that really true, about the hole?" Jane asks. "It's not like an automatically retracting flag that rolls itself up at night and unfurls again in the morning on a timer?"

"One hundred percent true. Remember awhile back when a guy took the whole store hostage and started giving away the merchandise?"

"The disgruntled former employee?"

"Yes, and he got everyone in the store to go along with him, and they just started giving things away. People were coming out of the store carrying things, and the cops didn't know who to stop. 'Whatever it is, take it. You earned it, you already paid for it,' was his motto."

"He was one of those Robin Hood of America guys," Jane adds.

"That's right, and the cops didn't want to shoot him, and they were going to gas the whole place, and people rioted outside—they said the place was filled with innocent victims and that you couldn't gas someone who didn't even appear dangerous, or armed.

"And in the end he surrendered. He went up to the roof—took down the flag and rose up an XXXL white T-shirt, and the police helicopter came in and took him away."

"Policemen don't shoot people in real life, do they? I thought you said that was just on TV," Tilda says.

"They're supposed to try very hard not to shoot people," Jane says.

"Did you see it happen?" Jimmy asks.

"We watched on TV from home," Jane says.

Tom and Jane each take a large cart—whose front section has been molded into a toy car complete with horn and working headlights—and push through the automatic doors.

"Do you kids want to drive?" Jane asks.

"I'm too big," Jimmy says. "My head hits the roof."

Tilda happily climbs into her mother's cart.

Tom checks his watch. "It's 0900 hours," he says. His stomach gurgles—it's the coffee, waffles, bacon, and the bowl of Tilda's cereal combining into a slurry of caffeine and carbohydrates, which will cause his thinking to become slightly fogged. "As soon as we go over our mission statement, I will start the clock. We will have thirty minutes to complete our task."

The store lighting is intense—fluorescent bulbs hum high above. All the products appear to vibrate as though about to leap off the shelves.

"In today's game sequence, the first person who gets everything on this list will receive a prize, and the first team (boys versus girls) who complete their list will also get a prize. As you know, we evaluate not just for absolute number and identification of items but also for quality of purchase: Is it on sale, in the flyer, covered by a coupon, part of a value pack?" Tom reads the rules off a piece of paper he's plucked from his pocket. He stays up too late at night—working out various game scenarios and scoring systems.

"What's the prize?" Tilda wants to know. "Is it pink?"

"If you win it, it's pink," Tom says.

"Does it have a remote control and batteries?" Jimmy asks.

"Yes, son, if you win, it has a remote control and batteries."

"Will it love me?" Tilda asks.

No one answers.

"Okay, kids. Jimmy, you've got your pager—if anyone gets lost or needs directions, just contact your mother or me. On your mark, get set, go. May the best shoppers win."

"Tildy, let's look at our list," Jane says. "We've got groceries, detergent, and hydrogen peroxide, and Daddy gave us prescriptions to refill. Let's do that first so they'll be ready." As they roll the cart toward the drug counter, Jane spots Tide on sale. "Grab it," she tells Tildy.

"It's heavy."

"Lift, girl. Good job. Okay, now go down the aisle and see the Palmolive—get the one with the yellow ticket under it. Get two at eighty-eight cents and we'll get bonus points. Hang on, I have to put the toilet paper back. This one, twenty-four giant rolls, is a better value than twenty-four double—giant is double plus half a roll, and it's only two dollars more. That's twelve single rolls for two dollars—you can't beat it. Quick now, grab those plain white mailing envelopes, a box of fifty for a dollar. Don't take the box of one hundred for two-fifty—it's fifty cents more for nothing." They pull the cart into the line at the pharmacy counter. "I'll wait in line. Can you find the milk? We need one gallon of two percent and a half-pint of fat-free half-and-half."

"Mom, I'm seven years old."

"Meaning I'm asking too much of you?"

"Meaning give me the list—what does it say? Milk, half-and-half, cereal."

"The bran flakes that your father likes."

"I'll recognize the box," Tilda says.

"This line is really slow. We may have to ask for bonus minutes—to be held against the store," Jane says, referring to Tom's very elaborately calibrated scoring system.

"Daddy loves this store—he's not going to give us bonus minutes. Go to the front of the line and see if you can pay someone to let you skip ahead."

"What?"

"I want to win. Offer the person up front five dollars to trade places." She pulls a five out of her pocket.

"I can't do that."

"You can, Mom. I want to win. It's my five dollars to spend however I choose. And the prize will be worth more than five dollars—it's at least ten."

"Then you do it."

Tildy goes to the front of the line. "Excuse me. I'm in a contest. My mom and I have to do all the family shopping in thirty minutes. Could we pay you five dollars to trade places with us? Oh, thank you, thank you so much."

Jane pulls the cart up—they're next in line.

"See, I told you," Tildy whispers. "All you have to do is ask."


"Dad, why do you like the Mammoth Mart better than the other stores?" Jimmy asks.

Tom shrugs. "It's soup to nuts, one-stop shopping. And what really sold me on the store was when I bought the casket for your Uncle Luther. That impressed me—who knew they sold caskets?"

"What aisle?"

"I did it online. Death is not something to take lightly or be cheap about, but at the same time I didn't want to get ripped off. And while your mother is right—maybe I shouldn't have had it delivered to his house while he was still alive—I didn't realize it could go straight to the funeral home until after I'd clicked 'complete order.' The good news was he wasn't too aware."

"Didn't he live for like another month—with the casket in his garage?"

"He had no idea it was there. He did, however, keep looking out the window at his own car, which had to be parked in the driveway to make room, and asking, 'Whose car is that? Who is visiting me?' I think he found it comforting."

"Dad, they don't have the tires," Jimmy says, looking at the area where the tires should be.

"Are they out of stock or not yet in stock?"

"Can't tell."

"We'll check with customer service at the end—it's on the other side of the store. Anyway, I hope you never have to shop for death, but as an interesting point of fact, buying the casket ahead of time costs nine hundred sixty-nine dollars. If you needed it overnight, though—which I can appreciate some people do—the cost jumped to four thousand five hundred fifty dollars for the exact same thing. There's too much profit in grief."

Jane and Tilda turn a corner. "Daddy didn't put it on the list, but we also have to buy things to take to Aunt Francie's house for Thanksgiving."

"Why are we going there?"

"Because she can't get out."

"Why not?"

"Oh, baby, it's a horrible story. Her husband beat her, and she got so depressed that she ate herself so fat she can't fit out the door of the mobile home, so we're bringing Thanksgiving to her. Which reminds me, everything needs to be reduced-fat."

"Is that what Daddy calls 'reduced-flavor'?"

"We'll bring hot sauce for him. We have to help her get thinner so she can get out and meet someone new, someone not so violent. Daddy thinks we should convince her to move her mobile home closer to where we live—that she'd do better with family around."

"Okay, Mama, what's next on the list?"

"Ziploc bags—snack, sandwich, quart, and gallon."

"Mama, look at that person!"

"Tildy, don't point."

"Is it a grown-up or a child?"

"Someone stuck in between."

"It looks like someone from Snow White and the Seven Dwarfs. Can I touch him?"

"Better not to touch strangers." Jane's cell phone rings, and she glances at it. "It's Daddy with a halftime progress report."

"Are you going to answer it?"

"No, he's just calling for a gloat. Let's wait and hear the voice mail. We can always call him back."

She waits a minute and then checks her voice mail: "Hi, hon, it's us. I'll take it as a positive that you didn't answer—maybe you cracked the code and are near the mop heads, where the signal is poor, which means you're right on track. Jimmy Cricket and I are ahead of schedule—snow tires are not yet in stock, the sale on D batteries ended yesterday, and we have a rain check on two items, car oil and your pantyhose. We'll see you soon."

Jane dials him back. "There is no mop head on my list."

"Yes there is, sweetie. It's in the double-point, secret-code box at the bottom."

"I hate this game, Tom, I just hate it."

"Go get the mop head and we'll meet you in electronics."

"Fine. Tildy? Where did Tildy go?" Trying not to panic, Jane hangs up on Tom.

"Tildy? Where are you? Can you hear me?" She pushes the panic button on her key chain, which makes the teddy bear on Tilda's shoes growl. In the distance she can hear it, a dim growling beacon, sometimes louder, sometimes softer. Quickly, Jane goes up and down the aisles. "Tildy! Tildy!" she calls. "Come out, come out. Ollie, ollie, oxen free."

"Mama, where are you? Did you move, Mama? Mama?"

"Tildy, you're throwing us off schedule." They talk in loud voices, just an aisle away from each other.

"But, Mama, I found the thing I always wanted." Tilda appears at the end of a row, holding a baby doll swaddled in white blankets.

"Oh, Tildy, you have so many dolls."

"It's not a doll, Mommy, it's a real baby."

Tilda is right. Jane quickly takes the baby from the child. Tilda begins to cry. "Mama, why'd you snatch it?"

"It's a real baby. I don't want you to drop it."

"I carried it all the way across the store perfectly fine. Can we get it, Mama? Can we take it home?"

"Where did you find it?"

"On top of the towels. I was on my way to the mop heads, and I saw it. Can I get it, please, please, please? It can be my birthday present and my Christmas present."

"Tilda, we're out of time. We have to hurry. Let's go find Daddy and Jimmy. Did you get the mop head?"

She shakes her head no.

"We'll grab it as we go. Let's step on it." Tilda pushes the cart, fast, while Jane holds the baby, and together they run through the store.

"You're late," Tom says as they approach.

"We had a delay."

"Potty stop?"

"We borned a baby," Tilda says.

"Where?"

"On top of the towels. Can I get it? Can I, can I? It can be for my birthday and Christmas and everything else, too."

Tom takes the baby from Jane and gently turns it around, looking it over. "Doesn't have a bar code. I don't think it's for sale. Babies usually belong to someone."

"Like their parents," Jimmy says.

"Yes, but this one doesn't have parents. It was orphanated. It was there just waiting for me."

"Can you show us where?" Tom asks. "Was it in a stroller or a carriage?"

"It was on a shelf," Tilda says, leading the family back to the spot.

On the towels there's a dent where the baby had been.

"Someone must have put it down for a moment," Tom says.

"It could have slipped off and fallen. It could have gone unnoticed and starved. It could have—" Jane says.

"But it didn't," Tom says.

"That's little comfort."

"The baby's mommy is going to be looking for it," Jimmy says.

"Or not," Tom says. He unwraps the baby. "Look at the umbilicus. It's a very rough cut, like someone did it themselves."

"An outie for sure," Jane says.

"Maybe someone brought the baby here on purpose," Tom suggests.

"Maybe it belongs to someone who works here?" Jane says.

"Let's ask," Tilda says. "And if no one wants it, we can keep it."

"What are we going to do, ask people if they're missing something? If they've lost that loving feeling?"

"They could announce it over the loudspeaker: 'Would whoever left the baby on top of the towels please come to Aisle Nine,'" Jimmy says.

"What are we going to do—have them make an announcement? What if there's a pervert in the store? What if some pervert claims the baby? Then how would you feel?" Tom says.

"You get into a lot of trouble for stealing a baby."

"We're not stealing it—someone left it here knowing that nice people come to this store, people who are loving and can provide a good home and all that goes with it," Tom says.

"Babies need clothes and diapers and wipes and bottles and formula and a crib and a car seat and a stroller and a bottle warmer and a diaper pail," says Jane.

"And toys," says Jimmy.

"Goodie," says Tildy.

"Are you ready for a new baby?" Tom asks Jane quietly.

"When is anyone ready?" she says. What the children don't know is that Tom and Jane have been trying. They have been trying for years—they'd almost gotten there this time last year, but then they didn't. Jane thinks the problem is hers—she's getting old. Tom thinks it's just the way life is.

Jane says there is no such thing anymore as the way life is—science has changed all that.

"Are we really going to buy all the baby stuff?" Jimmy wants to know. "It's not on my list—how does it affect the game? And is it a girl or a boy?"

Jane unwraps the baby and peers down into the diaper. "Boy," she says.

"Well, that's good," Jimmy says. "At least it's another one for our team."

"Before we do anything, we need to think," Tom says, stalling for time. He turns to the kids. "Go get an instant camera, shoot some pictures of the baby—the baby in the towels, the baby with the aisle number in the background—and we'll put them around the store with our phone number on the back. That way if the mother comes back, she'll know how to find us."

Tilda and Jimmy head off for the camera. Tom and Jane stay with the baby.

"What do you really think?" Tom asks.

"It seems too easy. I worry we're setting ourselves up for trouble. What about the legality? What about a birth certificate? What about health issues?"

Tom studies the baby, puts his head to the baby's chest and listens.

"He looks perfectly healthy. Maybe the woman didn't realize she was pregnant—you know how girls are."

"No, I don't know how girls are," Jane says defensively.

"I say we change it," Tom says. "Practically speaking, everything we might buy for the baby has a ninety-day return, so beyond the cost of diapers, bottles, and formula it's not going to cost us."

"What about the price for heartache?"

"The kids are into it," Tom says.

"Of course they are. They're just like you—consumers to the core. They love the idea of getting a baby from the store—more things to shop for. What could be better? And what are they going to say when people ask where the baby came from? We can't ask the children to lie."

"You're right, and you can't trust Tilda not to tell the truth—Little Ms. Honesty. When someone asks where the baby came from, we'll simply say Aisle Nine."

Tilda and Jimmy return with a disposable camera. "Is it okay to use it before we pay for it?" Jimmy asks.

"Yes," Tom says. "We'll keep the wrapper and pay later."

"Just photograph the baby," Jane says. "No people in the photos, nothing someone could recognize." They lay the baby back down on the towels, and Jimmy takes the photos—the flash makes the baby cry. Tom and Jane look around, worried someone will suspect something.

"Okay, so Jimmy and I will take the baby and put the photos up, and you and Tilda pick out the baby stuff—remember, we don't have to get it all today, just the essentials—and we'll meet you in electronics."

"How long do we have?"

"Soccer is at noon."

"But Tom, I also have to shop for Francie's Thanksgiving. None of the Thanksgiving items were on the list. I'm going to have to go to a real grocery store—one with produce."

"Later," Tom says. "Let's finish our business here."

And then Tom pretends to remember one more item and sends the kids off for it, and Jane knows he's up to something.

"What are you doing?" she asks.

"I just wanted a moment alone with you—I want you to know that if we end up keeping this baby, things aren't going to change. I'm still going to want you, want you badly. And, well, you know . . ."

"No, I don't know."

"I'll still want to play the games we play."

"Are you referring to something in particular?"

He nods to an old woman going past in a motorized cart.

Jane laughs.

She's never told anyone, but sometimes on Friday nights she and Tom go to a store, if not this exact one, then another one like it. Jane limps in using a cane she bought at a garage sale, and Tom comes separately, walking with one hip higher than the other, a dangling arm, and his baseball hat pulled low. They each ask for a motorized handicapped cart and then race up and down the aisles, remembering when they were young and went go-carting and rode bumper cars. And then they up the ante: They set a budget and pick a theme—like ten bucks' worth of something you'd want to see the other wear or do. Once they even did it in a PetSmart—a little kinky but worth it.

"Am I blushing?" Jane asks. "I feel like I'm blushing."

"I just want you to know how much I love you." Tom pulls a pair of leopard-print panties from the bottom of his cart. "Ninety-nine cents," he says, waving them.

"Not in front of the children."

Tilda and Jimmy return with half-price Halloween candy. "Is this what you wanted?" they ask.

"Yes, thanks. I have a Thanksgiving recipe that calls for old candy." He takes the candy, winks at Jane. "And it's on sale for forty-six cents. Good job."

"Can we get this?" Tilda holds up a toy cell phone that's filled with lip gloss. "It's marked 'Clearance.'"

"It's not on the list," Jimmy says with certainty.

"Sure you can," Tom tells Tilda.

Shocked, Jimmy grabs something for himself. "If she gets something, then I get something, too."

"Could you pick something other than a gun?" Jane says.

Jimmy looks down at the gun. "It shoots marshmallows, which are eco-friendly and a fat-free food."

"A gun is a gun. Mind your mother and pick out something else. Today everyone gets something. A prize for every player," Tom says.

And so Tom and Jimmy and Baby go around the store taping baby photos in random places—including on the television screens in the electronics area. They become distracted, mesmerized by the glow of the TVs, some of which are larger than the living room of the house Tom had grown up in. The screens are bursting with color, high definition, digital broadcasting, et cetera, and all show the same three programs in no particular order—an action-adventure space film, college football, and a cooking show.

Tilda and Jane make a beeline for the baby department and load up on wipes, diapers, bottles, formula, a car seat, a Pack 'n Play, and a few outfits and toys.

In front of the televisions, Tom is hypnotized, drawn in. He reflexively jiggles the baby in his arms, but his eyes remain fixed on the screens. "I remember black-and-white," he tells Jimmy. "I remember remote controls with big white buttons like teeth and an audible click. I remember rabbit ears and static. I remember Walter Cronkite—he might have been the last man I trusted. I remember listening to baseball on the radio while reading a comic book and eating pistachio nuts dyed red. I remember riding in my parents' car when there were only lap belts and no one wore them. I remember being sent out to play in the morning and being told to come home in time for dinner. I remember trying to get lost. I remember Yogi Bear and Ranger Smith. I remember when a president spoke as though he were addressing the people. And I remember Richard Nixon saying, 'I played by the rules of politics as I found them.' And I remember Martin Luther King: 'Our lives begin to end the day we become silent about things that matter.' And Robert Kennedy, although I'm not sure that I remember him while he was still alive. 'A revolution is coming—a revolution which is coming whether we will it or not. We can affect its character; we cannot alter its inevitability.' The point is, I remember America. I remember when politicians had a vision, a dream for the people of this country, and didn't run their campaign based on a tax rebate if elected—essentially attempting to buy the vote. Are we that gullible that we thought George Bush's three-hundred-dollar rebate would cover it? Think of what that vote cost, think of your retirement account, your health insurance, your mortgage, and your cost of living versus your salary. How much did you lose, and how much did you make?"

"Who is that man talking to?" someone asks.

"He's speaking to me," another man says.

"This is my America," Tom says.

"Hey, buddy, I'm in there with you," another person adds.

"Run for office—you've got my vote," a woman passing by chimes in.

"Mine, too."

People begin to come up and shake Tom's free hand. A man grabs a microphone from a karaoke machine and blows into it to be sure it's on. "Testing, testing, one, two, three. Can you hear me?" The crowd nods. And with "White Christmas" playing in the background, he announces, "Ladies and gentlemen, shoppers of all kinds, it is my pleasure to introduce you to the next president of the United States. What's your name?" the guy whispers to Tom.

"Tom. Tom Sanford."

"Shoppers, come on down to the electronics area and meet Tom Sanford, the people's candidate for president."

"I can't run for president," Tom says.

"Sure you can, anyone can. It's still a free country, and you've got to keep it that way. Plus, my friend, you have a way with people. I'll be your campaign manager. S-A-N-F-O-R-D—is that the right spelling?"

Tom nods.

"Yours will be the campaign that's about returning the government to the people. I'll be right back," the man says, and dashes off.

"Adorable baby," someone calls out. "He's got your chin."

Tom looks down at the baby in his arms—does he have Tom's chin?

The self-appointed campaign manager has left the karaoke microphone in Tom's hand. People are staring, expecting something. Not knowing what to do, Tom continues to speak into the microphone. The background song has changed. "We shop these stores, stores bigger than football fields, each one like an indoor small town, we spend our lives and our dollars in these places that we find comforting, satisfying. I have a story I'd like to share with you today. I know of a family who lived in one such store for a year while they were homeless. These were good people, working people who'd lost their home when the payments on their adjustable-rate mortgage shot up. They wanted to keep their kids in school, they wanted to keep their family together, and so they made friends with the late-night crew at a store. For food they ate what had already been opened or otherwise damaged, used the shampoo that was half spilled. To the outside world, they looked like other families—the kids went to school, played in soccer games, and did their homework in the public library, staying every night until the library closed. The only thing different was that at nine o'clock every night the family of four came into the store, brushed their teeth and washed their faces in the restrooms, and said their prayers on their knees by the mattress displays. Not only were the mattresses good, but the family also felt safe, watched over by the night crew. They felt safe and cared for and as if their community supported them—and the good news was that after a while they were able to get their lives back together, to save money and move into a place they could afford. I'm not going to tell you this family's name—or what store it was—but I assure you they are real, and they are not the only ones."

The crowd has grown. There are people, three and four deep in a semicircle before Tom. When he stops talking, they wait. They want more. "Here's what I want to know," Tom says. "I want to know what you're thinking, what your concerns are—about your family, your job, your health, and your home. What do you need from your government? I want to turn it back to us—we come first. We don't want to send our children to fight wars in places we've never been, we don't want to go into countries where we are not wanted or invited. That doesn't mean we won't help—we are always available for humanitarian aid and happy to supply our products to other countries. But let's see what we can do here at home, how we can support ourselves and our neighbors. I want to have kitchen-table conversations, I want to know what the problems are, and I want you to help me to think of solutions. Our ancestors were pioneers and inventors—we need to be that, too, in our world, in our time. It's as exciting a world as it was a hundred years ago—our borders are expanding in terms of science and technology—we are part of a global, interlinked society. This country was made from scratch, from hard labor. Let's not ruin it or poison it. Let's take what we have learned and make it work for us. And if you've just come to this country—you chose it for a reason, for the idea that it promised something more, a better life. Let's make sure we can continue to offer that to each one of you."

"Do you believe in God?" someone calls out.

"Yes, I believe in God, and I believe in shopping to Friday sales flyers," Tom says, and everyone laughs.

Jane and Tilda return, their cart piled high with baby gear, and the family of five stands together as people are holding up their phones, taking pictures, shooting video, broadcasting live.

Someone shows Tom a page from his laptop—it's Tom with the televisions in the background. "I made you a website. I uploaded your speech to YouTube. It works great."

"Thanks," Tom says, shaking the young man's hand.

Jane checks her watch. "Soccer in thirty," she says. "Jimmy, you'll have to change in the car."

"I will make myself available to you—live on the Net 24/7," Tom says. "I want to be visible, and I want to be known."

As the family makes its way to the checkout, the crowd surges toward them.

Tom holds his hand up and waves. Store security guards surround the family, forming a human chain, escorting them toward the registers. The baby is crying.

"Looks like you did some serious damage," the cashier says.

"How do you mean?" Tom asks.

"You've got two full carts—if you want to open an instant credit account, you can get fifteen percent off today."

"We've already done that twice," Jane says.

"How old do you have to be?" Jimmy asks.

"Do you have a bank account?" the cashier says.

Jimmy nods.

"Well, let's give it a try." She hands him a form to fill out.

"Wow, my own credit card!"

"For today only," Jane says.

"Buy stock," the cashier tells Tom. "That's the thing to do. If you like shopping, buy stock in the store."

"I'll buy a share for the baby, for his educational account," Tom says.

"Buy a hundred," the cashier says.

While they're checking out, a woman comes up to Jane and asks, "Are you nursing?"

"Pardon?"

"I don't mean to be intrusive, but I'm a La Leche facilitator. We meet on Wednesday mornings in the community room of the library. It's a beautiful baby—give her your mother love."

Jane doesn't respond.

"We bought Another Love," Tilda says, holding up a bottle of soy-based formula.

As they leave the store, pushing the two carts ahead of them, the family is surrounded by well-wishers. There are freshly printed banners, courtesy of the home-office demo center in the store: TOM SANFORD: THE RIGHT MAN AT THE RIGHT TIME. A news helicopter hovers overhead.

Every car in the lot has a brand-new red, white, and blue bumper sticker—proclaiming Tom Sanford as the candidate chosen by the people for the people. The local high school cheerleaders are performing in the Keep Clear Fire Lane. "Sanford, Sanford, he's our man! If he can't do it, no one can! Sanford, Sanford, he's the one! Not our pal, not our chum, and he doesn't even own a gun."

The campaign manager leads the way.

"How'd I do? Not bad for thirty minutes on the job, right? I was recently 'workforce-reduced' from a company for habitually overproducing—it was threatening to my peers and a poor fit with the 'corporate community.'"

Satellite news trucks pull up as Tom and Jane load the car. Tom reads the instructions for the new car seat and struggles to install it correctly. Reporters approach. "Right here, right now, the people's candidate, nominated in the store only moments ago by his fellow shoppers. Let's take a look at him while he does some real-world living."

"How does it feel?" the reporter asks Tom.

Tom wiggles the new car seat. "Secure," he says, buckling the baby in. "I'm pleased to meet you and would love to talk, but we're T minus ten for soccer." He slides the door closed.

The campaign manager stands nearby as Tom backs out, and the mall security car escorts them to the exit, lights flashing.

"We did well today," Jane says, looking over their receipts. "We went in with two children and came out with three. We spent four hundred fifty-three dollars, but we saved fifteen percent off the top and can expect sixty-seven dollars' worth of mail-in rebates within four to six weeks."

"And I got a credit card," Jimmy says.

"And I got a baby," Tilda says.

"And I was just another working stiff," Tom says, "and now I'm a candidate for president." He pauses. "So did you get everything on your list?"

"I've got everything I could possibly want," Jane says. "Except the turkey."

# Omega Point*

It is the kind of day that farmers, when there were still farmers, would have dreamed of. The sky is brilliant blue, the plants are newly green, the air as fresh and clean as though it had been washed, tumbled dry, and neatly folded the night before. It is the kind of day you never forget.

"Hasn't been a day this pretty since the day you were born," Mary Grace Mahon says to her granddaughter.

"You didn't know me the day I was born," Ruby says.

"Oh, but I did," Mary Grace says, tucking a bobby pin further into her hair, which is white and silky and braided like a pretzel.

---

* Author's note: Lue Gim Gong, the Citrus Wizard, was one of seventy-five Chinese young men who came from San Francisco to North Adams, Massachusetts, to break a strike in the shoe factory in 1870 and one of the few who remained there. Lue Gim Gong learned English and traveled with a well-known local family to Florida. "Everything that rises must converge" is a phrase from the writings of French philosopher, anthropologist, and Jesuit priest Pierre Teilhard de Chardin—who also coined the phrase "Point Omega" to describe a maximum level of complexity and consciousness toward which the universe appears to be evolving. Pierre Teilhard de Chardin and Walter Grange from Middletown Springs, Vermont, were among the many discoverers of the bones of Peking Man, who was discovered in a series of expeditions from 1921 to 1939 in the area called Dragon Bone Hill near Beijing. Between 1924 and 1936, de Chardin and Granger exchanged at least seventeen letters that discuss among other things the difficulty of sending specimens from China to the United States. The bones of Peking Man were en route from China to the United States when Pearl Harbor was bombed. They vanished and have never been found.

"Not possible," the girl says, twirling her own black, silky hair into a grandmother pretzel.

"In my heart of hearts, I knew you'd be here soon," Mary Grace says.

"I was born in China, Grandma. The people in China didn't even know when I was born, and when I was born, Mama didn't even know she was going to adopt a baby."

"I knew," Mary Grace says. "I knew it all along. Even before your mother was born, I knew that you'd be coming our way."

"Why do you wash the wax fruit?" Ruby changes the subject.

"It gets dusty and then sticky, and then it starts to look furry."

"Why do you even have wax fruit?" Ruby asks.

"Appearances are important," Mary Grace says. "I like the bowl to look full."

"I was old when my mother left me at the orphanage," Ruby says.

"How old?" Mary Grace asks.

"Between nine and ten," the girl says.

"But you're just seven now," Mary Grace says.

Ruby shrugs, as though that's irrelevant. "I came from China in a box. I cried the whole way home. It wasn't very nice," she says.

"You came from China in your mother's lap," Mary Grace says. "I was right there. I went along for the ride. It was you, me, and your mama, three generations of Mahon women flying to America, like life coming full circle." What she doesn't say is that in China the people she met looked her in the eye in a way no one had before. "Interesting," they said. "Very," she said, and they left it at that.

"Here is your daughter," they said, handing the child to her daughter, Eliza.

"Why did my mama leave me in a box?" Ruby asks.

"The box was all she had. It was meant to keep you safe." Mary Grace goes into the kitchen and brings out a small wooden crate that some oranges had come in. "If you put newspaper or blankets in here, this would be a safe place for a baby."

Ruby takes the box from Mary Grace, lines it with napkins from the dining room table, and arranges the wax fruit in the box.

She puts the box down in the center of the dining room table.

"Does that look comfortable?" she asks.

"Are you talking to the fruit?" Mary Grace asks.

Ruby doesn't answer.

"I have a question for you. What does it mean that today is a professional day at your school?"

"It's teacher training," Ruby says.

"Aren't they already trained?"

Ruby rolls her eyes. "They do special things like make the cafeteria menu for the rest of the year, and they do bonding exercises."

"Like gluing themselves together?" Mary Grace asks.

Ruby is looking at the pictures on the mantel in the dining room. "Why are there no pictures of your father?"

"He died before I was born," Mary Grace says.

"That's not true," Ruby says.

"How do you mean?"

"You once showed me a letter he wrote," Ruby says.

"From before I was born," Mary Grace says.

"It said 'Thank you for the photograph of our daughter, Mary Grace,'" Ruby says.

"You have a very good memory," Mary Grace says, leading Ruby to the rear window. "Look at the birds," she says, pointing to the feeder. "The birds are getting bigger and bigger, have you noticed?"

The child looks intently. "I can see them growing," she says.

"Watch," Mary Grace says. As the birds peck at their food, they realize they are being studied, and they stop, pivot, tilt their heads, and spread their wings—showing off. Then they turn toward the glass, beady black eyes meeting Mary Grace's and Ruby's, one-on-one.

"I wonder what they see when they look at us?" Mary Grace asks.

"Monsters," Ruby says.

A man, no longer young but not exactly old, wearing a black hat with gemstones around the brim, putting him somewhere between preacher and cowboy, walks into Paul's Gasoline Station and Mini-Mart, his shoes smelling of gasoline. "I can never decide if I love or hate the smell of gas," the fellow says.

"You get used to it over time," Paul says.

"It's warming up," the fellow says.

"Always does."

"It'll go cold again," the fellow says.

"That's the way it is," Paul says.

"Before it gets hot."

"Every year," Paul says.

"It's misleading."

The fellow takes a look about him. "Things seem different around here. On the one hand, we count on everything to stay the same, and on the other it's inevitable that it changes."

"I moved things," Paul says.

"Why'd you stop selling chips?"

"Had nothing to do with selling them. It was me, I kept eating them, couldn't control myself; Pringles, Cheetos, Doritos, first one bag, then two. By the time I got rid of them, I was up to four or five bags a day and I was always thirsty. Now I sell the dried fruit."

"Anyone buy it?"

"No, but at least I don't eat it. You look familiar," Paul says, ringing up the gas.

The man cocks his head jauntily to the side. "People say I bear a striking resemblance, both physical and philosophical, to Voltaire, which comes as no surprise—he's a distant cousin."

Paul shakes his head. "Not ringing a bell."

The man puts out his hand. "Peter," he says.

"Paul," Paul says, shaking the man's hand, which is large and delicate all at once.

Peter spots something on the counter. "That the Unit?"

"Not exactly."

"Give me a clue?"

"If I knew for sure, I'd tell you," Paul says. "I found it in my mother's basement. All kinds of things down there. It's like an artifact from an archaeological dig. I'm thinking it's my dad's ham radio."

"You found it in her basement?"

"Yep, you have no idea what's in that basement," Paul says.

"I bet I do," Peter says, smiling, like he knows a lot about basements.

"I'm thinking about getting it up and running. There are people out there, just floating, who want to talk. I thought I might set up a little radio station where the chips used to be." Paul takes a closer look at the fellow. "Did your father used to work at the factory?"

"Nope," the man says.

"Since you mentioned the Unit, I thought maybe he did."

"Nope," Peter repeats. "Never seen the Unit. It's just one of those things you grow up hearing about but never know if it's real or not."

"For twenty-five years, my father worked at the factory, and then he opened this gas station. He worked on the gadget. That's what they called it then when no one wanted to call it what it was—a bomb. He was proud of it, used to talk like they were making something special, something that was going to change the world, like a giant Christmas present. I always pictured something big and round wrapped in colored foil like those holiday chocolates," Paul says.

"Like the Easter Bunny," the fellow says. "My dad died on Easter Sunday 1955. I never knew him on account of how priests weren't supposed to have children."

"They made the trigger," Paul says. "It was all go, go, go until they dropped it, and then you didn't hear so much. Silence," Paul says.

"Not a word," Peter says. They each take a long breath.

"'Infinite Capacity,'" Paul says. "That was the factory motto. They thought they knew what it meant. My father wasn't the same after that—at least that's what my mother says. I was too young to remember. I don't think they knew what they were making. They weren't scientists, they were tinkerers."

The two men stand in silence. Peter looks at the television set on the counter—the ball game is on. "Who's winning?"

"The other guys," Paul says. "Was it just the gas, or something else you wanted?"

"I'll take a couple of the fruit leathers and a bag of popcorn—how come you still carry the popcorn?"

"I hate the sound it makes when you chew it, like Styrofoam." Paul hands the fellow a bag. "Take it, it's on me."

As he's leaving, the fellow reaches into his pocket and flips Paul a coin. "For good luck."

"Walking Liberty," Paul says, turning it over in his hand.

"Haven't seen one of these in a long time. We used to get 'em from the Tooth Fairy."

The stranger smiles, flashing gold rims around his teeth. "Tooth Fairy," he says. "Now, that's a calling."

"I owe you some change," Paul calls after the fellow. "Or at least more popcorn." He yanks several more bags off the rack.

"You owe me nothing," Peter says. As he walks out, the gems on the brim catch the light and a rainbow explodes out of his hat.

Deep into the seventh inning, Paul spots someone at the pumps in a black midlength coat trying to fill up a two-liter soda bottle. He rushes out. "You can't just gas up a Coke bottle. You could blow us all to kingdom come. Look at you—you're an accident waiting to happen."

"I walk very long time to your station to say hello, and this is your welcome?" The man is Chinese and speaks with a thick accent. "I run out of gas on hairpiece curl. My car just stop in the middle of the road. . . . I walk from there."

"Hairpiece curl?" Paul asks.

"No mock me," the Chinese man says. "I have accent. You have accent, too—I no mock you. I have lousy life—bad harelip, bad surgery. Everywhere I go, I deal with people like you. Your father would be ashamed. Your father was good man open to all, and you are like today's man—mean all around."

"You knew my father?"

"Of course I did. That's why I come to you now. Your father fix my father's car forty years ago, and now like bad date my car break down right in the same spot as my father's—what are the chances of that?"

"Slim."

"I say so, too," the man says.

On the ground next to the man is a wide black briefcase, like a sample case or a lawyer's attaché.

"Your briefcase is sitting in a puddle of gas," Paul says to the man.

"That okay," the man says. "Briefcase look like vinyl, but it is very strong bull."

"What's your name?" Paul asks.

"Walter," the man says. "Everybody call me Walter."

"Walter, I will help you with your car. I have a niece from China," Paul says, thinking he's doing a good job.

"You and everybody else," Walter says, carrying his briefcase into the gas station office.

The pay phone on the wall of the mini-mart rings. Paul picks up.

"It's your sister," his sister, Eliza, says. Eliza owns a flower shop downtown with a sign in the window that says By Appointment Only. She doesn't like surprises.

"Can I call you back?" Paul asks.

"Why?"

"I've got someone here."

"Who?"

"A guy."

"What kind of a guy?"

"The kind of guy who has car trouble."

"Why didn't you just say so?"

"I did, actually."

He covers the phone and whispers loudly, "My sister. She's a talker."

"I'm in no hurry," the man says. "I got where I am going."

"We need to talk about your mother," his sister says.

"Why is she 'my mother' when she's your mother, too?"

"When there's something wrong, she's your mother, and you know that."

"What's wrong?"

"She's losing her mind."

"She's ninety-three years old. It's bound to happen."

"It's not that she's senile, it's that she knows too much."

He turns off the television on the counter. "What do you mean?"

"This morning when I dropped Ruby off, she was saying things that on the one hand made no sense and on the other seemed perfectly logical, or more than logical—like she knew something. She was talking about the weather and how the weather used to let you know what time of year it was and how now, on any given day, it could be any day of the year. . . . And then she went on about the bats and white-nose syndrome and the collapse of the honeybee colonies and how everything is more interrelated than we realize and we really couldn't get much dumber, could we—and then she just glared at me like it was all my fault."

Paul is playing with the half-dollar Peter flipped him earlier. "I'm not sure what to say," he says. "Sounds par for the course. And this fella needs me to help him. Can we talk later?"

"Meet me at home."

"I can't leave the station."

"Fine, I'll come to you."

Walter is buying gum balls from an old penny machine in the corner.

"I'm not so sure I'd eat those," Paul says. "Hard as rocks."

"I like it," Walter says. "It give gum ball with fortune written on it, like 'Have a nice day.' I remember this machine, long time ago the same machine used to sell a small hand of salty peanuts."

"That's right. Back in my dad's day, the machine sold salted peanuts. He loved his peanuts. Let me just find my keys and we'll get ourselves a can of gas and drive up to your car—where'd you say it broke down?"

"Hairpin curl," Walter says slowly. And this time Paul listens more carefully.

"Hairpin turn?"

Paul drives the Chinese man to his car, all the while telling the story of how the Mahon family has been repairing cars ever since Ransom Olds and Henry Ford started making them. "In fact, my grandfather and his brothers used to sell buckets of water right up there on the hairpin turn to cars whose engines overheated. They'd carry buckets up the Mohawk Trail—a nickel a bucket. And they'd pick blueberries on the way down, fresh-picked blueberries, warm from the sun, bursting with flavor. What business did you say you're in?"

"I am low-profile deliveryman, advance man. I come and I go."

At the Holiday Inn downtown, two Chinese men wearing the same black midlength coats as Walter check in. They are given a room with two double beds. As soon as the door closes, they take off their coats and do gymnastics tricks, jumping from bed to bed, turning flips in the air. They are former gymnasts and strongmen— they lift their beds over their heads for exercise.

Back at the house, Mary Grace is making lunch for Ruby. "Would you like me to tell you a story?"

"What kind of a story?" Ruby asks.

"A true story," Mary Grace says.

"Nonfiction?"

"Yes."

"That means it's real?"

"It's a story that I've never told anyone before."

"What's it about?"

"It's about us."

"You never told anyone—not even my mother?"

"Not even your mother."

"Is it a secret?"

"It was—until now."

"My mother doesn't believe in secrets."

"Neither do I. Perhaps there's a difference between a secret and something that just hasn't been said."

"I'm listening," Ruby says.

Mary Grace takes a deep breath. "My father was Chinese." Ruby looks at her suspiciously, like it's a joke.

"He was born in China in 1860."

"Were his parents Chinese?"

"Yes."

"Does Mama know?" Ruby asks, suddenly a little anxious.

"No, she doesn't."

"How come?"

"I never told her."

"Tell me more," Ruby says.

"My father's family were poor farmers in China. He came to California by boat when he was ten to live with his uncle. And when the shoe factory here went on strike, seventy-five Chinese men from San Francisco came to town and worked in the factory."

"Your father came here?"

"Yes. And he became friendly with a local family, and soon he worked for them, and when they went south to Florida—he went with them. And your great-grandmother, who was friendly with one of the girls in that family, went to Florida, too. And she and my father become very close."

"Were they married?"

"No, they were never married."

"What did she like about him?"

"He was very clever, always inventing things, and he was very kind to animals. He had a horse that he spoke to as if she were a person, and my mother liked that."

"Pop-Pop also invented things," Ruby says, speaking of her grandfather.

"Yes, that's right."

"I never met Pop-Pop," Ruby says sadly.

"You would have liked him a lot," Mary Grace says. "So after a while my mama realized that she was going to have a baby. She bought herself a train ticket and a gold wedding band and came back home big with child."

"Why did she buy a wedding band?"

"In those days it wasn't proper for a woman to have a baby on her own. When people asked, 'Where is your husband?' she'd look sad and say, 'He was killed in the war.'"

"What war?"

"The first big war, World War One."

"Why didn't she marry your daddy and live happily ever after?"

"Because people weren't so forgiving," Mary Grace says, realizing that some things are very hard to explain. "And so she was very pregnant and tired of waiting for the baby to come, and so she went out for a walk, and she just kept walking and walking. She walked right up the mountain and around the mountain and back down the mountain, and on her way down the baby came."

"You?" Ruby asks.

"Yes."

"And when people saw me, they said my face looked a little odd. 'It's the face of grief,' my mother would tell them. 'Her father died before she was born.'"

Ruby looks at her grandmother. "I think your face looks pretty. Old but pretty."

"Thank you," Mary Grace says.

"Did you ever meet your daddy?"

"No. He died a long time ago, but he left something behind."

"What?"

Mary Grace opens her hand.

"An orange?"

"My father was known as the 'Citrus Wizard.' He invented the orange we eat today."

"How did he do that?"

"Cross-pollination. He combined the strengths of different plants, something he learned from his parents and from watching honeybees, and he created an orange that didn't freeze on cold nights."

She drops the orange into Ruby's hand. "It's a good story, isn't it?"

Ruby nods.

"Should we eat our lunch at the dining room table or outside under the apple tree?"

"I'm afraid of the bees," Ruby says.

Mary Grace opens the back door. "And the bees are afraid of you," she says, handing Ruby a plate and a glass of milk.

They go out back. Mary Grace is distracted by the weather, by the fact that everything is out of order. "Hydrangea and peony are up too early this year," she says. "Something is coming into the yard, taking over the apple tree. Look," she says, "you can see it, something dark coming up from the bottom, spreading.

"Everything is vulnerable," she says, shaking her head. "When we were kids, this fence wasn't here and we used to tiptoe next door and steal Mr. McGregor's apples. The trick was to take as many as you could before he noticed."

"Did you live in this house when you were my age?"

"I did, and then I moved out when I got married and moved back in when Mother began to fail."

"How many apples did you take?"

"As many as we could carry."

"Did you get in trouble?"

"No. I don't think he minded as long as we ate them—but Mr. McGregor used to like to try to scare us."

"How does an apple tree make apples?"

"You need two different kinds of apple trees near each other in order to make fruit. Bees to carry the pollen from one tree to the other; a tree on its own is barren."

"So," Ruby says, "if your father was Chinese, that means my mother and Uncle Paul are Chinese, too?"

Mary Grace nods.

"Do they know?"

"No."

"We should tell them."

"We should," Mary Grace says.

"Tonight," Ruby says. "How old are you?" she wants to know.

"What makes you ask?"

"I was just wondering how many peanut butter sandwiches you've eaten in your whole life."

"It's funny," Mary Grace says. "I only eat peanut butter with you."

"What time is it in China?"

"Right now?"

Ruby nods.

"In China today is tomorrow."

In the afternoon the wind shifts, becoming hot, urgent, swirling, picking up whatever it can lift, twirling what it carries, around the houses, the trees, the town, up to the mountain, in a kind of rhythmic, purposeful, twisting, turning dance, as if trying to shake something off, trying to get relief.

Eliza blows into the office of the mini-mart, carrying a vase of flowers.

"For me?" Paul asks.

"For Parker, but I didn't want to leave them in the hot car."

"Parker, the guy at the cemetery? The guy with the tattoo of Jesus on his back?"

"That's him. Just before Mr. Houghton died, he gave Parker enough money to buy flowers for Mrs. Houghton's grave every week in perpetuity."

"So what is it about your mother that's plaguing you?" Paul asks.

"I don't know exactly. She's got something up her sleeve, that smug, 'knowing' look she gets—pursed lips like she's lived so long that God himself has hired her as his personal adviser."

Paul says nothing.

"And she's been very organized like she's . . ."

"Planning a trip?" Paul asks.

"Something like that," Eliza says.

"What's she going to do, run away? It's your anxiety talking. Anytime Mom or Dad tried to leave town, even just to go to Pittsfield, you practically had a breakdown. For forty-five years, no one in this family has been able to go more than a couple of miles from home base."

"We all have our limits," she says.

"I don't know how you made it all the way to China and back," he says.

"Valium," she says. "I took Valium and I took Mom. What is that thing?" She points to the old metal box on the counter.

"That's the question of the day. Whatever it is, still works." Paul turns it on; the red light warms, then glows like a maraschino cherry deep in a glass of ginger ale. "It's something Dad made. I found this one in the basement."

"It's not the Unit, is it?"

He shakes his head. "I don't think so," he says. "You never really knew what the Unit was—did you?"

"Not really," she says. "Whenever he said anything about it, Mom would shush him. I always thought it was something related to private parts."

"He called it the Unit or sometimes the peacekeeper," Paul says.

"Whatever it was, it's probably still in the basement," Eliza says, sweeping her hair, which is black going gray, back into a ponytail.

"This thing is a receiver of some sort, like a ham radio. I'd like to get it up and running, see who I can find 'online' the old-fashioned way." He turns it off and then on again—the red light glows a little brighter.

"Is it wise to turn on things when you don't really know what they do?"

"Like what? You think by turning this on I'm dimming the lights in China?"

"You never know."

"Maybe someone will call me, a voice from the past," Paul says.

"Perhaps you're sending a signal," Eliza says.

"And perhaps someone will signal me back." Paul turns the

machine off and on again and again. "Remember how Dad and I were always making stuff with our soldering guns?"

"Who could forget the smell of burning plastic and molten whatever, toxic fumes coming upstairs? I think that's what started my headaches. What happened to the chips?" she says, looking around.

"I ate them," Paul says.

"All of them?"

"Pretty much."

"I was hoping you'd have chips," she says. "I was looking forward to it."

"Fruit leather?" he says, offering her some.

"No thanks."

Paul flips his half-dollar into the air. Eliza catches it, takes a look. "Tooth Fairy paid you a visit?"

"Perhaps," Paul says.

She puts her hands over her eyes. "Everything is too bright, too clear, like the day itself has gone past full daylight and into something like Kodacolor explosion."

"You see rainbows?" Paul asks, thinking of the man with the hat from earlier.

"I'm getting one of my headaches. Can I use your phone?" Eliza goes to the old pay phone and dials Mary Grace.

"Where are you?" Mary Grace shouts. "I can hardly hear you!"

"On the pay phone at the gas station. It's the same damn phone that's been here for thirty years. I'm surprised it still works. I wanted to see if you're okay to keep Ruby for the afternoon. I'm getting one of my headaches."

"We're fine!" Mary Grace shouts. "Go home and lie down. Drive careful, I think there's a storm coming."

Mary Grace hangs up and turns to Ruby. "Your mom has been getting headaches ever since she was a child. I think it's things she knows but doesn't want to know trying to get out. Your mother is very smart."

"Like me," Ruby says.

"Just like you."

On her way home, Eliza stops at the cemetery. In the distance two men are digging a grave. Nearby, Parker, shirtless, is down on his hands and knees with a small clipper, trimming the grass around a headstone, like he's giving it a haircut or a shave. The glossy sweat on his back coats a large Byzantine tattoo of Jesus, catching the afternoon light in such a way that Eliza feels the face of Christ looking at her, demanding something.

"Who died?" she asks, nodding toward the gravediggers.

"Don't know yet," Parker says.

"I got your flowers." She holds out the vase.

"Appreciate it," Parker says, turning around, reaching into his pocket for the money. His chest and his arms are covered in tattoos, stories waiting to be told.

"Strange weather," she says, making conversation.

"Yep," he says, "there's something in the air, almost like little invisible flakes, shards of light—just landing on things."

As the wind picks up, a hum comes over the hills, low-grade and musical, more like a chant. It starts off faint, rises up, and then stops as though to catch a breath and begins again—a hum like the wind, like a Buddhist song.


The widow from across the street comes knocking on Mary Grace's door. "We're in for it now," the widow says.

"Late for snow and too early for blight," Mary Grace says, putting on the kettle to boil. Ruby, playing on the kitchen floor, listens to every word.

"When plagues are upon us," the widow says, "deliverance soon follows."

Mary Grace says nothing. What is there to say? The widow continues, "What time of year is it—harvest?"

"Spring," Mary Grace says.

"Is that right?" The widow looks at the calendar on Mary Grace's wall. "Did I miss Christmas?" She shakes her head. "When you live long enough, you see it all—the great blizzard, the unending rain, the big fire, the quake before dawn, the rising lake, the disappearing trees, the white noise. There were always those who knew and those who didn't want to know." She clucks.

The two women have each lived a long time and speak in a kind of code. Mary Grace takes out a tin of tea.

"And those who liked it the way it was before," the widow says.

"And always some who didn't want to know, who ignored the warning," Mary Grace says.

"Was that the end of it?" the widow asks. "Wasn't there more? Didn't they know that one day it would come back?"

"You and I have lived a long time. We've been through it all," Mary Grace says. "It comes and it goes."

"What are you talking about?" Ruby demands.

"We are talking about life on this good earth," the widow says.

"Will you stay for tea?" Mary Grace asks.

"I'm going under," the widow says, turning to leave.

"Be sure to take a flashlight," Mary Grace reminds her.

"You're welcome to join me," she says, filled with hope—no one wants to be alone in the dark.

"We'll stay," Mary Grace says.

"If anything interesting happens, come get me," the widow says, leaving.

"Where is she going?" Ruby asks.

"Years ago some folks built shelters underground in case of bad weather or war and stocked them with food and water. Your grandfather and I never went for that kind of thing. We're more optimistic than some of the others. Do you know what I used to like to do when a storm was coming?"

"What?"

"I liked to ride my bike up Mount Greylock."

"That sounds dangerous," Ruby says. She is by nature cautious.

"Yes, I suppose, but it was very exciting. I saw all kinds of things. If you get up high enough, sometimes it felt like you were Zeus on top of Olympus above the storm, or you could watch it move from one side of the mountain to the other—you could almost get right up inside it. Would you like to do that with me sometime?"

Ruby shakes her head no. "I'm more of an indoor person," she says, and goes back to her game.

"Look at the birds," Mary Grace says, noticing the birds just outside, making sudden, quick preparations, as though they have some kind of backup plan, some emergency-effectiveness training that they are putting to the test. The winds are picking up, though the sky remains clear but for some high, white clouds.

"Tell me more," Ruby says, to distract herself. "Is that the ring your mother wore?" She points to a ring on Mary Grace's finger.

"Yes, it is."

"The golden ring?"

Mary Grace nods.

And the storm is upon them. Fat raindrops splash against the windows, thunder slams, the windowpanes shudder. The winds spin, turning in ever tighter circles, at one point seeming to focus entirely on the apple tree, whirling around it, leaving the tree trunk and branches coated with ancient black sand—crushed onyx, obsidian, druzy. As quickly as the storm was upon them, it is over.

Paul arrives soon after. "Quite the storm," he says. "The streets are covered with branches, lines are down."

"Quite," says Mary Grace, distracted. She is once again looking at the birds for clues. They appear to be flying around the house, circling.

"Just wanted to make sure you two were all right. We lost power, so I closed for the night. How is it that your lights are on?" Paul asks.

"I don't know," Mary Grace says, going back into the kitchen, busying herself with dinner.

"I met the funniest fella today. A Chinese man came to town, said he'd been here before and that he knew Pop."

"Hmmm," Mary Grace says, winking at Ruby.

And then she remembers the widow across the street. "Can you two knock on her shelter door, let her know the weather is over for now and see if she'd like to join us for dinner?"

Ruby and Paul dutifully go across the street and knock on the shelter.

The widow won't come out. "They say more is coming soon," she says. "Things don't happen just once."

"Would you like us to bring you a plate of supper?" Paul asks.

"Oh," she says, "thank you, that would be nice."

At the Holiday Inn downtown, the two Chinese men ask about dinner. "We have been looking forward to something special. We are craving the McDonald's. Is there one near here? Do they have a Happy Meal? It comes with a prize inside like a fortune cookie? Have you ever had one?"

Ruby calls her mother from the phone in Mary Grace's kitchen.

"Hi, Mom," she says.

"Hi, Ruby," her mom says.

"Grandma wants me to invite you for dinner."

"That sounds nice, but I still have a headache. Are you okay?"

"I'm fine," Ruby says. "Grandma told me something interesting."

"What did she tell you?"

"We're Chinese."

"You're Chinese," her mother says.

"So are you," Ruby says.

"Please, Ruby, don't start."

"What, Mama? I'm just telling you what Grandma told me."

"Can you put her on the phone?"

Ruby looks at Mary Grace, who is standing right there listening. Mary Grace shakes her head.

"She can't come to the phone right now," Ruby says. "She's very busy."

Ten minutes later Ruby's mom arrives wearing her cranial ice helmet, looking like an angry linebacker. "I don't know what you're up to, but I'm not liking it," she says to her mother. "You are confusing Ruby."

"Ruby is not confused," her mother says.

"Well, then I must be."

"Perhaps, but it's not your fault," her mother says, going into the kitchen for the supper plates. "Can you and Ruby set the table?"

"I'm not hungry," Eliza says, "I'm nauseated. Why is this orange box on the table?"

"That's the box I came in," Ruby says.

"No, it's not," Eliza says.

There is an old baby doll, like the baby Jesus, in the clementine crate on the dining room table.

"Well, it's like the box I came in," Ruby says. "We were playing Trip from China."

"Why is it I can't even just have a headache and lie down for two hours without the whole world slipping out of control?" Eliza asks.

"Maybe you want more control than is possible?" Paul says.

"There's something I need to tell you," Mary Grace says when they're all in their places.

"Are you thinking the end is coming soon?" Eliza asks, worried.

"It's inevitable," Paul says.

"Ruby, go in the other room and watch television," her mother says.

Ruby doesn't budge.

"I have some information," Mary Grace says.

"What kind of information? Like top-secret information? Like someone from the government is going to come knocking on the door?" Paul asks.

"I was born out of wedlock," she says. "My father was Chinese."

"Your father was killed in the war," Eliza says, correcting her.

"It was a lie," Mary Grace says.

"Why didn't you tell us before?" Paul asks.

"I'm telling you now," she says.

"If you'd told us earlier, we could have known you better," Eliza says.

"You knew me well enough."

"Did Dad know?" Paul asks.

"I can't remember," Mary Grace says honestly. "He knew something, I'm just not sure what. I was going to tell him more, but after the gadget he was afraid of things, and it seemed best not to say too much."

"Am I right in remembering that sometimes the doorbell would ring and strangers would be standing on the doorstep bringing boxes and crates?" Paul asks.

"Yes."

"They'd just arrive with no warning?"

"That's correct."

"And you'd take the things they brought?"

"Yes, it started in the late 1940s, when this was still my mother's house. And then, after she passed, we continued to accept what came—that's simply the way it was."

"They just arrived?"

"Yes."

"Men would come and no one asked why?"

"It wasn't about the men, it was about what they carried—big boxes, small boxes, suitcases."

"Did you ever look inside the boxes?" Paul asks.

"No," she says unequivocally. "My mother used to say, 'Someday someone will claim them,' and I assumed that she knew what she was talking about. The boxes were ours to hold, not to open."

"We still have the boxes," Paul says.

"That's right," Mary Grace says.

"And what about the Unit? How does all this fit with the Unit?"

"You're conflating the Unit with the news from China," Eliza says.

"Am I? They worked on the trigger at the factory. They built the trigger of the first atomic bomb—the gadget."

"The Unit and the gadget are entirely different," Mary Grace clarifies. "The Unit came after the gadget. It was a civilian effort, no military interference. As far as the government is concerned, they probably don't know those things ever got built—to them it's folklore, like visitors from outer space." She pauses for a moment. "When the men would come with the boxes, they would talk with your father. Sometimes your father would take them downstairs and show them what he was working on. They talked about the bonds between countries, things they had in common—not everyone wanted to blow us all to kingdom come."

"The bomb was dropped on Japan not China," Eliza says. "China wasn't part of it."

"China and Japan are next-door neighbors," Paul says, as though that clarifies things.

"I believe the Unit is still in the basement," Mary Grace says. "All around the world, men and women built them. It's meant to work like a magnet, gathering things."

Ruby asks, "When did your mama die?

Mary Grace turns to the little girl. "August of 1974. She had a stroke the day after President Nixon resigned. She lost her faith."

"And am I right in remembering we also used to get boxes of fruit every month? Oranges, grapefruit, citrus?" Paul asks.

"That's right," Mary Grace says. "Our regular mailman would bring those, every month a box of fruit."

"Who sent them?" Eliza asks.

"Someone in Florida. December 1974, that was the last box we got," Mary Grace says, suddenly tired.

Paul takes more lamb onto his plate. "I want to be sure I've got this right. You're saying that you're part Chinese?"

"Yes, and you are, too," Mary Grace says. She is suddenly a little agitated, flighty, unable to eat. It's much more difficult to explain than she anticipated.

"Buy firecrackers, eat lychee nuts?" Paul says.

"It means only what you want it to mean," Mary Grace says.

"I think we should open the boxes," Paul says.

The doorbell rings.

"I'm scared," Ruby says.

"Nothing to be afraid of," Mary Grace says, grateful for the interruption. She opens the front door, and there is a Chinese man holding a large basket of fruit.

"I am returning the kidneys," he says.

Paul comes up behind his mother. "The kindness," he says, translating for Walter. "Come in, come in. It's Walter, the man who had car trouble earlier."

Walter makes a little bow, and Mary Grace takes the fruit basket from him.

"In China I am Yao Walter, but here I am Walter Granger, all at once like the name Campbell's Soup. My grandfather was digger at the bone cave with Walter Granger of Middletown Springs, Vermont. He had no children of his own, and so they name me after him. No one in my village has ever been named Walter. I hope I am not too late," Walter says.

"Not at all," Mary Grace says. "We're just having dinner." Eliza gets another plate.

Ruby pats the empty seat next to her. "Sit here," she says. And he does.

Paul passes the lamb.

"I am vegetarian," he says, passing it to Eliza.

"So am I," Ruby says, not knowing what vegetarian means but knowing she and Walter have something in common. "We have homemade mint jelly," Ruby says, passing it to him.

Walter puts some jelly on his plate. "Have you got any peanut butter?"

Excited, Ruby runs back into the kitchen and returns with the peanut butter and bread.

During dinner Walter tells stories of his adventures as a delivery-man, carrying things back and forth from China, crisscross apple-sauce all around the world.

After dinner Walter asks for a tour of the house. He tells them how excited he is to be there and that he wants to see "under everything."

While Paul shows him around, Ruby and Eliza bring a plate of supper to the widow, who is still refusing to come out of the shelter. "Let's wait and see what tomorrow brings," she says as she pulls the hatch shut and locks it from the inside.

"Good night!" Ruby and Eliza call from her backyard. "Sleep tight!"

In the basement Paul shows Walter all the things that his father built. "My father always had a soldering iron in his hand. We built radios, fixed toasters, lamps, always working at something. But these here, these were something he said had a lot of potential. They were something he hoped would be perfected."

"That all he say?" Walter asks. "He leave any instructions?"

Paul shakes his head. "To be perfectly honest with you, Walter, my father talked about a lot of things, and I was never really sure what he was getting at. He took the bomb pretty hard. He quit the factory and started saying things about how it's no longer a government for the people by the people but that it's one guy with his finger on the trigger and so on."

Walter nods like this is all very familiar stuff. "We have similar at my home," Walter says. "My father built a machine for us. He calls it a wishing machine."

"You mean washing machine?"

"Wishing machine," Walter says slowly, carefully enunciating.

"My father called it the Unit," Paul says. "Do you know what it's supposed to do?"

"It's a magnet," Walter says. "When they are all turned on, it pulls us closer together."

Paul and Walter turn the units on—each has a red light, like the flame of a match, like a beacon glowing. Nothing happens.

"Maybe they no good anymore," Walter says. "Maybe like magic genie lantern, the wishing wear off?"

"I don't know," Paul says. "Maybe it takes a while, maybe it takes a lot of units working together to make something happen. I'll bring them upstairs, and we'll try again tomorrow."

"Ah," Walter says, slapping himself on the forehead for effect. "I always forget, here today is yesterday in China."

Mary Grace invites Walter to stay the night, and given the oddity of the day, Paul decides he'll stay, too, and then Ruby, not wanting to miss a sleepover, insists that she and Eliza stay as well.

"It's been a long time since I've had a full house," Mary Grace says happily.

After everyone has gone to bed, Mary Grace goes into the kitchen. Walter finds her there, making tea. "I can't sleep," she says.

"Me three," Walter says. "It is a very exciting time." He takes something from inside his coat. "I wanted to wait until there was privacy. I have mail for you—really for your mother, but at a certain point in time, when the mother is no more, you become your mother. I am sorry to be so late—it was lost in transit." He hands her a letter written in Chinese.

"Read it to me," Mary Grace says, pouring two cups of tea.

"It is complicated," Walter says. "My reading in Chinese is not so good. Do people in English have learning disabilities? In China trouble reading is very big problem, too many characters. Anyway, your father writes to say that in America he is like a forgotten ghost—no more Chinese. He went home to China, but when he got there, he was no more Chinese in China either. His mother wants him to stay, she finds him a wife, but the night before the wedding he runs away. He runs, he walks, he swims back to America. He arrives as traveling salesman—selling knickerknackers floor to floor. He can never go home again. He met your mother in Florida. He loves her very much. He wishes he could marry her. In the letter he mentions the kindness—that is why I come today, to return the kindness and to deliver the mail."

Walter excuses himself from the table and opens the front door. A loud, hot wind blows through the house, lifting the letter out of Mary Grace's hand. She grabs it in midair, folds it, and tucks it into her apron pocket. Walter returns carrying a box wrapped in very old paper, tied with string so worn that it is crumbling.

"This is a box he want to send to your mother."

"I am ready for something new," Mary Grace says, opening the box. Inside is a wedding dress, almost a hundred years old, long red silk in perfect condition. "It is time for a fresh skin," Mary Grace says, holding the dress to her heart.

"Time for bed," Walter says, raising his teacup. "Tomorrow more will come."


The next morning Peter, the half-dollar cowboy from the day before, pulls up at nine with a giant box of doughnut holes—"fortifications."

Walter is on the front lawn doing his tai chi. "I don't mean to interrupt, but I have to shake your hand," Peter says to Walter. "You have loomed large in my consciousness. I'm not here just by accident. I am the beautiful boy, the bastard son of Pierre Teilhard de Chardin, descendant of Voltaire. My mother knew Mr. Roger Giroux; she knew Mr. and Mrs. Stanley Hyman of Bennington, Vermont. She knew everybody who was anybody. In fact, I have some of Shirley Jackson's ashes in the back of the car—a gift from

Chuck Palahniuk, who was given them by a Jackson/Hyman daughter. I grew up on Park Avenue and in Poughkeepsie and have been waiting for this moment my whole life. I feel as though I have known all of you forever. This is it!" he shouts. "This is the Omega Point!" He kisses Walter square on the lips. "Everything that rises must converge!" he exclaims.

Ruby looks out the front window and announces, "I just saw two men kissing."

"I'll put a pot of coffee on," Mary Grace says.

Paul opens the front door, ushering Peter and Walter into the house. "We have to be careful," he says. "Don't want people getting the wrong idea."

"Would you like a doughnut hole?" Peter asks.

"What flavor?" Paul asks.

"Assorted," Peter says, opening the box.

Paul plucks out a chocolate glazed for himself.

Walter goes for jelly and seems surprised when he bites into it. "Fun," he says. "The boys outside will like this." He opens the front door and calls out to Yin and Yang, the gymnasts who appeared at dawn and have been warming up on the front lawn, doing backflips and cartwheels.

"Fun food, catch," Walter says, tossing doughnut holes to Yin and Yang, who catch them in their mouths. "Yin and Yang are Siamese twins separated just after birth," Walter says proudly. "They do good now, read each other's mind."

"Do you know them from before?" Mary Grace asks. She spotted them earlier when she opened the front door in her robe to get the morning newspaper.

"Mother, may I?" they asked.

"Yes, you may," she said.

And they began to perform a ritual dance on the lawn while singing a Chinese version of "Singin' in the Rain."

"Of course I know them," Walter says. "They are part of the job, they are the heavies."

"Well, then invite them in," Mary Grace says.

Walter opens the door again, and as Yin and Yang cartwheel through the front door, Yin, Yang, and Walter all take off their black coats and turn them inside out, revealing the white undersides, like lab coats. From their pockets they take out old pieces of paper that look like parts of a puzzle or a map and put them on the kitchen table, where Walter works with a roll of Scotch Magic Tape, putting it all together. The map turns out to be a list of boxes with the contents annotated in Chinese code—which takes Walter a while to decipher. He keeps getting frustrated and ripping up his work, throwing it on the floor and stomping on it. Ruby sits next to him and very calmly asks, "Can I work with you?" And together they solve the problem.

"Walter, buddy," Paul says, "I don't mean to interrupt you while you're working, but what is this all adding up to—the units, the wishing machines, the boxes?"

Walter holds up his palm, asking Paul to wait. As soon as the code is cracked, the puzzle pieces all fit together and Walter gives the results to Yin and Yang, the Chinese strongmen who quickly move through the house gathering all the boxes, suitcases, trunks that arrived over the years, preparing to unpack.

Meanwhile, Ruby delivers a box of Cheerios across the street to the widow's secret hideout. "Ollie, ollie, oxen free," she says, knocking on the door. "Come out, come out, wherever you are. If there ever was a time, this is the time. The moment is now."

"Okay, I come clean," Walter says, gesturing that Paul, Eliza, and Mary Grace should take their places at the kitchen table. "I offer you a belief history lesson."

"I think you mean brief," Paul says.

Walter goes on. "In 1920 and 1930s, the bones of *Sinanthropus pekinensis*, *Homo erectus pekinensis*, were discovered on Dragon Bone Hill by a group of anthropologists," he says, struggling to pronounce the words. "Among the scientists were Mr. Walter Granger of Vermont and Mr. Pierre Teilhard de Chardin, geopaleontologist and Jesuit priest from France. Do you follow?"

"I hear you," Paul says. "But I'm not sure I follow."

"The bones of primitive man were discovered in China a long time ago," Mary Grace says, translating for her children.

Ruby has returned and is sitting on her mother's lap. "Did you discover them, Grandma?" she asks.

"No," Mary Grace says, "I didn't go to China until you were born."

Walter corrects, "Good guess. Your grandfather's family was involved, and in China family is very important."

Everyone nods.

"In 1937 Japan invaded China," Walter continues.

"I told you there was a link," Paul says to Eliza.

"People worried what might happen to the bones, and so the bones were packed and were about to be shipped to America when Japan attacked Pearl Harbor. In the upset the bones vanished. Some say they sank on a ship, some say they were taken by train, no one person knew what had happened, and no one has seen them since. But little by little, like undercover operation, the bones were making their way to America—to North Adams, Massachusetts, the safest place in the world."

"Why our house?" Paul wants to know.

"It is not about your house, it is because you are Chinese,

descendant of the Citrus Wizard Lue Gim Gong," Walter says, as though it is obvious. "You were Chinese, but nobody knew, and therefore nobody could suspect. Nobody would think to look here. The boxes came over very long time to be discreet, but now it is time for them to be revealed. These are bones of Peking Man. We, the people of China, thank you for holding our history."

"And what about him?" Paul asks, pointing to Peter, who has finished writing his speech and is now frantically working both Mary Grace's landline and his own cell phone.

"He is our PR *macher*, the bastard son of Pierre Teilhard de Chardin, the anthropologist priest. 'Omega Point' was his father's term to describe maximum complexity and consciousness toward which we are hurling."

And with that, Peter slams down the telephone and announces, "I've got NBC, CNN, CBS, the local affiliates, and more coming soon."

"This is it," Walter says. "Our moment is now."

Yin and Yang cover the dining room table with beautiful red cloths they magically extract from inside their pant legs, and Walter begins to lay out the exhibit—keeping the basket of fruit he'd brought yesterday in the center. The bones are not that of a single skeleton but bits and pieces, fragments of men and women who lived three hundred thousand to five hundred thousand years ago. There are skullcaps, braincases, teeth, jawbones, and stone tools. With each piece is a note written long ago in Chinese, containing information on where and when it was found.

Peter peeks out the front window. "News spreads fast," he says as satellite trucks start pulling up. The widow comes out of the storm shelter and walks across the street, wondering what the fuss is about—she thinks it is all about her.

"Isn't anyone entitled to a private life anymore?" she asks Ruby.

Peter works the front door like a bouncer, a carnival barker, a docent at the homemade Museum of Early Man. "Come one, come all, step right up and see what's inside. This is history in the making, the missing returned, the secret revealed, the story of man's evolution made whole."

At noon, when factory whistles and volunteer-fire-department sirens and giant city clocks around the world sound their bells marking the middle of the day, all the units, the wishing machines, the peacemakers, the whatchamacallits are turned on. Giant rainbows begin to crisscross the sky in a show of light, sound, and magnetism. In this house and that house, in every village and town, appliances, cars, computers, iPhones, and BlackBerrys feel the tug. They slip off the wall and edge slightly forward, coming together, leaning in, ready for more.

Mary Grace is upstairs dressing. She slips into her mother's wedding dress and is transformed from New England matriarch, Norman Rockwell grandmother, to a sagacious Chinese beauty. She takes the bright red lipstick that was among her mother's effects and paints a Cupid's bow onto her mouth. Twirling a long red ribbon, Ruby dances, leading her grandmother down the stairs and out the back door, a most modern maid of honor. Mary Grace silently descends and goes to her apple tree. She slips off her golden ring and hands it to Ruby, who puts it on a dandelion chain around her neck. Mary Grace stands under the tree, arms open, extended, waiting until she catches the light. She rises.

Sensing that something is happening, Paul and Eliza ask, "Where is she?" and are ushered out the back door as Mary Grace is being lifted.

"How did she get there?" the widow from across the street asks, seeing her friend floating feet off the ground.

"I can assure you she didn't climb," Eliza says. "She can't even get up a stepladder."

"It's something about the weather," the widow says, "force of nature, carried by the wind."

"She was lifted," someone says.

"Odd," someone else says.

"Not really," the widow says. "It was a long time coming."

"Mama, are you all right?" Eliza calls out.

"I'm fine," Mary Grace says. She is, after all, a woman of great faith. The feeling for her is one of elongation, stretching. If she pulls back, it is uncomfortable, and she wonders why she is resisting, why she is trying to stay on the ground.

"Mama, no!" Eliza calls out.

"Don't worry," Ruby says, comforting her mother. "You're not alone. You have me."

As Mary Grace rises up, it begins to snow. Heavy, thick flakes, more like shavings or the debris of something that exploded far away, begin to fall to the ground. The flakes melt onto whatever they touch, coating it with something like wax, fixing it in time and space.

Without a word Mary Grace rises further still, surrendering, ascending until she is out of sight—gone.

# She Got Away

When her sister, Abigail, called her at college and said, "You need to come home," Cheryl asked, "Is this for real?"

"Yes," Abigail said.

"Can I talk to Mom?"

"No."

"Is it Mom?"

"I don't know," Abigail said.

"What does that mean, you don't know? It sounds like you're not telling."

"I really don't," Abigail said. "You know how Mom always puts herself in the middle of things." Abigail paused. "And bring good clothes."

"You're scaring me," Cheryl said. "Should I be scared? No one in L.A. wears good clothes unless . . ."

"I don't know," Abigail said again. "Just come home."

Abigail had done this before. The summer Cheryl was thirteen, Abigail made her come home from sleepaway camp. Their parents had gone to Europe; Abigail stayed behind. She was seventeen and supposed to be in summer school.

It was six months after their younger brother, Billy, had died while they were visiting their grandparents in Arizona. Billy told the grandparents that a poisonous snake had bitten him. "Put a cold washcloth on it," they said, and then he was dead.

"I need you to come home," Abigail had said.

"Did the plane crash?" Cheryl asked.

"What plane?"

"The plane Mom and Dad were on?"

"No," she said.

"I thought maybe it did, because you told camp it was an emergency. The camp director came and got me out of the lake."

"Sorry," she said, "I thought I told them you could call me back."

"You told them you'd hold on." Cheryl was standing on the porch of the camp office in a dripping-wet bathing suit. She was talking on a phone with a long yellow curly cord that had been passed through the open window. She used the drops from her wet suit to spell her initials on the wooden porch.

"Where are you?" Cheryl asked.

"I don't know," Abigail said. "I'm lost."

"What do you see around you?"

"Eye shadow," she said.

"Are you in your room?" Cheryl asked.

"Come home," Abigail said.

"I'm in the camp play and the talent show," Cheryl said. "This week there's a bunk cookout, an overnight adventure, and it's my turn to be the baker's assistant. Plus, I'm in the bugle corps—I play reveille."

"Don't make me beg," Abigail said.

When they were young, Abigail was a fairy. She wore white wings everywhere she went. She didn't like to answer questions, didn't like to be pinned down.

Their mother joked that she drank too much coffee when she was pregnant with Abigail. "It wasn't the coffee. It was the pills, diet pills," their father said.

"The doctor gave them to me," their mother said.

"What kind of doctor wants a pregnant woman to lose weight?" their father asked.

"A Beverly Hills doctor."

Cheryl packed her footlocker and said good-bye to her bunkmates.

When she got home, there was a huge sign, drawn in red lipstick on a white sheet, hanging between the telephone poles: WELCOME HOME, BABY SISTER.

And Abigail was very thin.

"Have you stopped eating?" It probably shouldn't have been the first thing Cheryl asked, but it was.

"I've been picking at things. There wasn't much left."

They went outside and looked at the "edible" garden where the swing set used to be—their parents had planted it to encourage Abigail to take an active role in her own nutrition. Most of the plants were dead.

"You have to water it," Cheryl said.

Abigail shrugged. "I have trouble with things that are so needy."

They sat up in Billy's bedroom and talked about how weird it was that no one talked about anything. Abigail was the keeper of the feelings; she hung on to everything. Their mother used to say, "You wear your feelings like jewelry."

When they were young, Abigail was afraid of floating away. She was so worried she might simply vanish that she literally wanted to be tethered to another person.

First they used some old laundry line, then climbing rope and carabiners, until they discovered the small weights that you use to keep helium balloons down. Abigail kept them in her pockets—a big help.

And for a while she was better; she married—Burton Wills, her plastic surgeon—but she also kept her room at home, not like an office but like how it was when she was a kid. Burton didn't seem to mind.

For Cheryl this time, coming home from school in Minneapolis feels even more difficult. On the way from the airport to the house, the car passes a field of oil pumps in the middle of nowhere, milking the earth, which already looked decimated, barely able to feed scrub and the occasional sagebrush. All of it feels entirely different, alien.

"How did you pick Minneapolis?" Cheryl's friends from high school had asked. "We never heard of it before."

"I wanted to go to the most normal place I could find. It's where Charles M. Schulz grew up."

As soon as she arrives at the house, Cheryl walks right through it. She passes through the living room and steps outside; the pool is an inky black wishing well—no toys, only a floating sensor. The view is limitless, all of Los Angeles spread out below. She takes off her shoes and dips her toes in—hot. The heat is like a physical lozenge, a sedative. There is no edge—she has no body, there are no boundaries; she, the water, and the air all are one.

She used to stay out there at night, lingering in the darkness. Her father would come and get her out of the pool. "It's a wonder you don't just shrivel up," he'd say. The pool felt safe, she could hide there—invisible. She takes her feet out of the water and goes back into the house. Her wet footprints evaporate behind her, vanishing as she walks.

"Where are you?" she texts her sister.

"In traffic," Abigail texts back.

The accountant who lives next door comes out onto his deck. His hair is longer, and he now has breasts. He waves. She waves back.

"Where's Esmeralda?"

"She's driving the car."

Twenty minutes later she hears the car pull up. The engine turns off and suddenly she's afraid, flushed with the feeling that this is the before—the end of the familiar. She hears the front door open and close. She stays put, or it's more like she can't move; she's immobile on the lounge chair by the pool.

Abigail comes out onto the patio, so thin that she actually looks flat. Her arms and legs are white like copy paper. The only things normal about her are her feet, jutting out in sandals with red nail polish that catches the light like safety reflectors.

"Should we go inside?" Abigail asks.

"Here is good," Cheryl says, still paralyzed.

"We need to talk."

Esmeralda brings glasses of water with lemon and a plate of carrot and celery sticks.

"Is it that bad?" Cheryl asks, looking at Esmeralda for confirmation.

Esmeralda makes a face; she doesn't want to be the one to say so, but yes.

Esmeralda has been with them since before Billy was born. She was the baby nurse, the nanny, and then the housekeeper, and now Esmeralda does everything for them, because apparently they can't do it for themselves, or maybe it's just been so long that they've forgotten how.

Abigail drinks. Cheryl eats. Amid the hyperconsciousness about food, the threat of starvation, she overeats, having not one or two sticks but the entire plate.

"Is it Dad?" she asks.

"It's Mom and Dad," Abigail says.

"Are they getting a divorce?"

"No."

"I don't understand."

"It was Dad, and then it was Mom."

"Can you just tell me what happened?"

"Dad was at work. He had an incident."

"Like an occurrence?"

"An episode."

"Like a crime show?"

"Like a problem," she said.

"When did this happen?"

"Last Wednesday?"

"And why did no one call me?"

"We wanted to see what happened. We hoped there would be a turnaround. There was nothing you could have done."

Esmeralda gives her a hug. "I'm sorry."

"I could have prayed," Cheryl says softly to herself. She prays every day, something she's never told anyone. "So where's Mom?"

"She's at Cedars, too."

"Did you tell her I was coming home?"

"I told her," Abigail says. Her voice sounds odd.

"What?"

"Mom was at the salon. She had cucumbers on her eyes, was eating almonds—you know how she does. . . ."

"Fifteen almonds a day."

"And you know how she has so much filler and Botox and everything."

Cheryl nods. "Yes. And she doesn't even like the way it makes her look. She just does it because that's what people here do."

Abigail, who has also had all the filler and Botox, nods back. She doesn't smile or frown, because she can't. "Well, somehow a peanut got in. She blew up, and no one noticed because her lips are already so puffy. They didn't get bigger on the outside—she puffed up inside."

"And?"

"She's not 'at' Cedars, she's 'in' Cedars."

"In the same room?"

She shakes her head. "They're heavily sedated and on ventilators."

"Will they wake up?"

"No one knows. She was seriously oxygen-deprived."

"This is like a nightmare."

"That's why I called you."

"It's like the nightmare where I'm trying to tell everyone that something is wrong and no one can hear me. It's like a zombie apocalypse," Cheryl says. Abigail puts her arms around her. They are so thin and ropy that it's like being encircled by Twizzlers.

"I called Walter," Abigail says.

"My Walter?"

Walter is her best friend from childhood, pre-childhood—infancy. "I thought he might be helpful. He said he'd come over later. Shall we go to the hospital?" Abigail asks.

"Should we bring her a plant?" Cheryl asks. "Mom always liked African violets."

Cheryl marches into the house, takes the African violet off the windowsill in the kitchen, clutching it for comfort.

Their father is in the Neurointensive Care Unit. He has what looks like a turkey thermometer stuck deep into his head.

"Is that like a pop-up timer?" Cheryl asks.

"It tells us the pressure in his head," the nurse says.

"Is it permanent?"

"You'll have to speak with the doctor," the nurse says, exiting the room.

"He looks terrible," Cheryl says. "He would never wear a shirt that color."

"You mean the hospital gown?"

"Can we put on his regular clothes?" Cheryl asks. "Do we need permission?"

"Like we could make him any worse?" Abigail says. She tugs on the front of her father's gown, trying to pull it off him. "He's heavy."

"We could try to lift him," Cheryl says. "Or how about we just put a shirt on top?"

The clothes he was wearing when they brought him in are in a big plastic bag in the closet. Abigail lays the shirt on him and pulls up the sheets, tucking him in. Cheryl takes his shoes to the bottom of the bed and puts them on the ends of his feet, hanging off his toes.

"Better?" Abigail asks.

"He looks awful."

"Maybe it's the medication," Abigail says.

"Maybe it's what's left of him, maybe it's all there is. This is not good," Cheryl says, shaking her head no, no, no, as if the repeated motion will set things free. "Not good at all. Can we see Mom? I need to see Mom."

They take the elevator to nine.

"It's me," Cheryl says, squeezing the mother's hand. "Are you in there, Mom?"

"Hard to tell," the nurse's aide says.

"Burton thinks Mom looks good, very relaxed."

"She's unconscious."

Esmeralda rubs the mother's feet. "She always liked me to rub her feet."

Cheryl kisses her mother on the forehead. Her skin is taut, smooth, no wrinkles. "I love you, Mom. Happy Administrative Assistants' Day."

"Is it really Administrative Assistants' Day?" Abigail asks.

"It said so on my calendar."

"Mom loves a special day."

Cheryl puts the African violet on the ledge, in the sun.

"I know you find it offensive, but I have to eat," Cheryl tells Abigail as they're waiting for the valet to come with the car.

"How about a smoothie—they don't really smell."

They drive to a juice bar. Abigail orders just kale, parsley, and cucumber. Esmeralda gets mixed-berry açai. Cheryl orders the Kitchen Sink, and while she's waiting, she eats some raw vegan cookies. "Do you have soup?" she asks.

"Cheryl, it's a hundred and one degrees outside. There is no soup," Abigail snaps.

As soon as they get back to the house, Cheryl is drenched in aloneness, the cologne of empty, the odor of nothing. Mid-afternoon, she has a pizza delivered—she meets the guy outside, eats the whole thing standing on the other side of the fence, and throws the box away out by the curb in the neighbor's re-cycling bin.

Later she finds Abigail in her room, sitting on the floor, ruler in one hand, scissors in the other, cutting the pile on her green shag rug like it's blades of grass, one thread at a time. "It should only be an inch and a half—these are two inches." She shakes her head. Cheryl sits on the floor next to her sister. "I won't be okay if they die. That's always been the issue—how alone I feel. I married Burton because he doesn't intrude on my loneliness, but at the same time I'm never actually alone."

"I know," Cheryl says.

"I'm trying to be the big sister, the one in charge, but it doesn't come naturally."

"You're doing a great job. What's the plan for later?"

"Later when?" Abigail asks.

"Tonight, tomorrow, and all the days after?" she says.

"Burton would be fine with me just staying here," Abigail says, cutting the shag a little more quickly.

Cheryl realizes that if Abigail stays, even for one night, it will create a whole new problem: Abigail will move back home, and Cheryl will be stuck living there with her—forever.

"That's okay," Cheryl says. "I'm fine to be on my own. Nothing is going to happen to me. All the bad stuff has already happened."

"Is Walter coming over? Did he text you?" Abigail asks.

"Yes."

"And?"

"He asked, 'How bad is it?' 'Bad,' I said. 'Big bad?' he asked. 'Supersized,' I said."

Esmeralda is ready to go. "I have to make dinner for my family. I'm sorry. I'll bring you leftovers tomorrow, empanadas." Cheryl sends Abigail with her, giving her a hug, then wishing she hadn't.

Abigail is like a human Post-it; there's nothing to her—no dimension.

When they leave, Cheryl locks herself in the bathroom—she feels the need for a safe room. She needs to be held, comforted, and in the absence of humans the space between the tub and the towel rack will do.

She sits on the floor, not crying, maybe not breathing either. She sits on the floor telling herself to let the tile hold her, let the grout be the cement that keeps her whole. She digs her nails into the rubbery vein of caulking along the side of the tub, takes a deep breath, and instead of an exhalation out comes a bellowing, puking wail. She sobs hysterically until her phone makes a loud *ping*. The ping acts like an OFF switch; the flood stops as suddenly as it started. She abruptly ceases crying and pulls the phone from her pocket. A text from Burton: "Abigail arrived home—do you happen to know, did she eat anything today?"

"She had a smoothie," she types back, wiping mucus from her face.

"Where are you?" Walter texts a little while later.

"I'm hiding," Cheryl writes.

"Where?"

And because she doesn't want to say, "Between the tub and the towels," she gets up, pulls on a swimsuit and a wrap, unlocks the sliding glass doors, goes out to the pool, and sits.

"In the backyard," she types.

Walter comes in through the pool gate.

"You remembered the code," she says.

"One-two-three-four. Some things never change."

"Until they do," she says. There's a pause. "You look good—muscly."

"Eating meat again."

"It's really good to see you."

They grew up together, each other's witness and confidant.

They go into the house. "Should I try to distract you?" Walter asks, digging around the game closet. He takes out the game Operation. She uses the electrified tweezers to extract the wishbone—her favorite part.

"Is this helping?" Walter asks.

"It's certainly matching how strange I feel," she says.

When the game is over, she goes into her parents' bedroom, moves from object to object, touching her mother's things—moisturizers, custom-compounded sun creams made by the dermatologist, tanning sprays.

Walter comes out of the bathroom wearing her father's robe, his arms filled with pill bottles. "Did you know your dad was on all this stuff?"

"I don't think he took all of it all the time," she says.

They play a game of dress-up, of tag, of jumping on the bed, of calling out an event and then diving into the parents' closets to get ready for it.

"Lunch at the club!" Walter calls out.

"Awards ceremony!" Cheryl says.

"Sylvia!" Walter says while wearing the father's tuxedo.

"Ben!" she replies in her mother's ball gown. "Where did we go wrong?" she asks.

"We got what we wanted," he says.

"It's like a kinky psychodrama," she says.

"What time period are we in—before or after?" he asks.

"Let's start with before," she says.

They play until they run out of costumes, until they can't think of what else to say except things that are too painful to say, and then they lie down side by side on the parents' bed, dressed for golf. Walter takes Cheryl's hand—they sleep.

Cheryl wakes up at 3:00 a.m. and goes out to look at the moon. Even when it's a hundred during the day, the city gets cold at night; it's like a wine cooler—somewhere between fifty and fifty-five degrees. The darkness is chalky black; the city below looks smaller, more consolidated than during the day. Through the night she sees a lava lamp glowing in the neighbor's house. She goes back for a blanket, and in her room she finds a book that she loved as a kid, takes it outside along with a flashlight and the blanket, and sits by the pool reading, pretending she is in another time.

She remembers reading stories about children playing outside at night, catching fireflies in mayonnaise jars. She found them comforting—until she realized there was no such thing as a mayonnaise jar in their house and there were no fireflies in Los Angeles.

Across the top of the hill, a thin white plume begins to rise—first like steam creating a cloud of its own, and then it starts to blossom, filling out the night sky like a balloon on a long, narrow string, blooming like a mushroom cloud. Are they smoke signals or special effects?


There are visitors at the hospital.

Carlton, the father's ex–best friend, is the first. "You know that I gave your father his start," he says.

"I know," Cheryl says; this is what Carlton always says.

"I'm the one who encouraged him to go into the law. He wanted to be an actor, and I told him, 'Forget it. You're good-looking, but you've got no talent.' It was me who made it happen. I brought him clients before he had any. As far as I'm concerned, I sent you kids to school, I paid for your mother's face-lifts, and see that bag his pee is going into? I probably paid for that, too. And what does he do for me? Nothing."

"Carlton," Cheryl says, "is there something we could do that would make you feel better, that would show you how much my father valued your friendship?"

"You see that ring he's wearing, the kind of showy one with the emerald? As much as I don't like jewelry on a man, I always admired that ring."

"It's yours," Cheryl says.

"Do I take it now?"

"Sure," Cheryl says. She has no idea why she's giving this jerk her father's ring, but she's not going to back out now. Carlton picks up her father's hand. "Be careful of the IV," Cheryl says.

"It's swollen," Carlton says, holding her father's hand in his own.

"Yes, he's retaining fluid."

Carlton tries to take the ring off, to spin it from the finger. The ring's not budging. He tries again, yanking the father sufficiently that an alarm bell goes off and the game of tug-of-war has to be suspended until the nurse comes in and resets the machines. The nurse gives Carlton a tube of Surgilube; he greases the finger with a grotesque pumping motion that prompts Cheryl to look away.

"Got it," Carlton announces, exiting with his shiny prize.

"I wish I had better news for you," Abigail says when the agitated movie-star client arrives with his assistant.

"I don't believe it for a minute," the movie star says, while they're standing in the hall. "Some people will go to any length not to have to tell me to my face that it's over. If he wants to dump me, he should just say so." His voice is loud, recognizable—people stare. "I may be a big baby, but it's not like I can't take it."

"Come in," Cheryl says, ushering him into her father's room—and out of view.

"Holy shit," the movie star says when he sees their father. He takes out his fountain pen, the one he likes to use for autographs, and stabs her father in the bottom of his foot. The nib of the pen stays in the flesh when he pulls out, and beyond that nothing happens, except ink leaks onto the floor. There is no grimace, no jerking of the leg.

Cheryl pushes the button in the wall. "Nurse, can we have some wipes for a cleanup?"

"I guess I needed closure," the movie star says, plucking the nib like a thorn out of the bottom of her father's foot and departing.

At home Dr. Felt, the mother's shrink, calls repeatedly. He calls and hangs up and then calls again like a stalker. He leaves a series of messages of escalating intensity. "Are you on vacation?" "I can't help but take it personally. Is there something you forgot to tell me?" "Have you no respect for our process?" And finally, "If you don't call me, I'm going to have to release your time—do you know how many people want Monday, Wednesday, and Friday at ten a.m.? That's prime time, baby." There's a long pause, then, "And you know what? You're really selfish. Only a selfish person would behave this way. You're a bitch, a real bitch."

"Do you want me to call him back?" Walter asks when Cheryl plays him the messages.

She thinks of the one time she went to see Dr. Felt, whom she always suspected was having an affair with her mother. "Do you want a boyfriend?" Dr. Felt had asked her. "Yes," she'd said. "Then you need to lose ten pounds," he said.

"I want to be the one who tells him," she says to Walter as she's dialing. "Hello, Dr. Felt, it's Cheryl." There's a pause; he has no idea who she is. "Sylvia's daughter."

"Oh," Dr. Felt says, clearly surprised.

She proceeds to tell him what happened to both her mother and her father, and when she's finished, all Dr. Felt says is, "I'll need some kind of official confirmation."

She's stunned. "Like what?"

"A report from the hospital would suffice. It's quite the story you're telling me. In order to believe it, I'll need to see some paperwork."

She snorts—involuntarily.

"I'll say good-bye now . . . Cheryl," Dr. Felt says, pausing before saying her name, like there's something about it that's bitter on his tongue.


The hospital schedules a family meeting. The doctor, whose name is embroidered on his long white coat, begins, "The problem with modern medicine is we're able to keep people alive who in any other country would have died within hours of the event. Sometimes we're lucky, but more often we end up here." He pauses. "In the land of difficult decisions."

"I've been doing a neurological-stimulation program," Abigail says. "Twice a day for fifteen minutes, I tell my father jokes, read the letter from the White House, and for my mother I wave her favorite coffee beans under her nose. . . ."

"Your parents are not asleep," the doctor says.

"What's the best-case scenario?" Cheryl asks, cutting to the chase.

"That depends on what you're looking for," the doctor says. "Some families hope the patient lives for a very long time, even if it's like a potted plant. And others hope the end comes quickly, peacefully."

"If it were your parent, what would you wish for?" Cheryl asks.

"I would wish I didn't have to make a choice," the doctor says.

Abigail is angry. "I think they're lying," she says. "That's what they say to keep you here. They want you to beg them to keep your loved ones. It's all about getting the business."

"I didn't get that feeling," Cheryl says, and her voice cracks.

"You should get them out of there," Walter says.

"Where would we take them—on vacation?" Cheryl asks. She is not-so-secretly angry that Walter is leaving tomorrow for a family trip to Croatia.

"Home," Walter says.

The thought had never occurred to her.

"You need to get them out before something worse happens," he says.

"Worse like what?"

"Flesh-eating bacteria, MRSA, gangrene. Before they start cutting off pieces of them."

"Walter is right," Abigail says. "They need to be home."

That night before he leaves, Walter pulls out his wallet.

"I don't need your money," Cheryl says.

He hands her a photograph of her brother, Billy. "It's his class picture from second grade," Walter says. "He gave it to me, and I carry it like a talisman, a reminder to trust myself and not let others negate my experience."

"I love you, you asshole," she says, pressing the photo to her heart and hugging him.

"I'll see you soon," Walter says.

It takes a lot of negotiation—lawyers, sign-offs—to get Sylvia and Ben out of the hospital.

"No backsies," one of the hospital administrators says. "If you take them home, you agree to assume full responsibility. If something goes wrong, you can't bring them back to us."

"We understand," Cheryl says.

The furniture is moved to the edges of the living room. The carpets are rolled up. Using blue painter's tape, Cheryl and Abigail mark off two large rectangles on the floor, indicating where the hospital beds will go. They unfurl a padded fluorescent-orange safety mat. "It's antimicrobial," the man from the hospital-supply company says.

The beds arrive, and the night before their parents come home, Cheryl and Abigail sleep there, pretending it's a special kind of spa. In the morning a crew brings the heavy equipment, ventilators, IV pumps, stacks of sheets, diapers, an enormous assembly of goods. "Mom would be pleased," Abigail says. "She loves high production values."

The mother and father come home in a convoy of special intensive-care ambulances. The nurse comes with them and does the unpacking, the fine-tuning.

It's like having a new baby or a pet; there's a lot of anxiety, the girls wanting to be sure they get it right. Cheryl pushes her father's Barcalounger into the living room and parks it between the hospital beds, so the nurse can put her feet up.

The smell of the food one of the nurses brings for lunch upsets Abigail, who first looks pale and then begins to froth, bubbles of saliva beading on her lips. She retches. "Can you say something, please?" she begs Cheryl.

Cheryl goes into the kitchen. "Excuse me. . . ." The nurse looks up from her lunch, as if to say, If your request is going to interrupt my meal—that's gonna be a problem.

"Would it be okay if you ate outside?"

"Pardon? Is there a medical reason I should eat outside? Our contract says that we are allowed to bring in our own food and be provided with equipment to heat or refrigerate it. Is there a medical reason—like, do you have an allergy?"

"My sister is sensitive to food odors."

"That's not a medical reason," the nurse says, taking another bite of whatever is in her bowl.

"It's very hard for her to be around food," Cheryl says.

"So?"

"Mental illnesses are medical conditions," Cheryl says.

"Fine, tell her to get a note from the doctor, and I'll show it to my supervisor."

Later Abigail, exhausted, resists going home.

"I promise you," Cheryl says. "Nothing will happen while you're gone."

"You won't leave them alone, will you?"

"I'll be right here."

Early the next morning, Burton shows up; he finds Cheryl outside by the pool.

"Where's Abigail?"

"She's home." There's a long pause. "She didn't wake up this morning."

"She'll be over later?" Cheryl asks.

"Her body gave out. Her heart stopped."

"What does that mean?"

"It means she's gone. Abigail died."

Cheryl is overcome with the strangest sensation of rising up, levitating, a kind of liberation that feels entirely unfamiliar. She doesn't understand it. Why is this her reaction? Has she been so terrified about what might happen to Abigail that the absence of fear, the absence of the weight, is causing her to float away? And is this it? Is this the kind of floating that Abigail was afraid of? Or was that something else?

She looks around—nothing is out of place. Abigail is dead, but still the coffee automatically made itself, the newspapers were delivered, the morning nurse arrived and fed and changed her parents. She got away, she thinks.

"What do you think killed her?" Cheryl asks.

"Malnutrition and a weakening of the heart," Burton says. "The last few weeks were especially difficult."

"She was terrified about being left alone," Cheryl says. There is a long silence.

"What would she have wanted?" Burton asks.

"I don't think she'd like to be in a coffin," Cheryl says. "She would think a coffin made her look fat. She would like to be made as small as possible, to fit inside a pill bottle." She turns to Burton. "Will there be a funeral? And what about the after bit? I don't think we can do it here at the house, in front of them?"

The funeral is small. Abigail is buried next to their brother in a row of plots the parents bought when Billy died. "They bought more than they needed—in the hopes the family would expand," the funeral director tells Cheryl and Burton.

They stand in their black clothes with their sunglasses on against the bleached sky, the backdrop of the city behind them. Burton, Cheryl, and Esmeralda. It's the first time they've left the parents home alone with only a nurse.

On the way home, they stop at the one restaurant Abigail

loved—Tu Es Moi—and celebrate her life in foams. They have a flight of foams—fifteen of them, each one under ten calories, everything from Thanksgiving Dinner to Salted-Caramel Pastrami.

When they get back to the house, Cheryl opens her father's safe, counts out six months' pay, and gives it to Esmeralda. "You need a vacation," she says. "Tell me where you want to go, and I'll transfer the miles from my father's account."

"It is too much to say good-bye to everybody all at once," Esmeralda says, and begins to cry.

"I know," Cheryl says, comforting her. "But this isn't good-bye, it's just a chance for us to gather ourselves and make sense of things. The fact is, I need to be alone for a little bit."

Esmeralda nods tearfully. "You're all grown up."

The funeral is followed by a Facebook shivah—Cheryl posts a message about Abigail's death, and then the rabbi who married them adds a post, and Cheryl and Burton follow it each evening for seven days by posting a remembrance at sundown. Old friends add memories of their own. And after seven days, Cheryl and Burton write a thank-you note to everyone and post more photos.

Now that it is just Cheryl and her parents, Cheryl spends more time talking to the nurses; she learns things about her parents, details about their skin, their smells, their habits. They may not be able to communicate, but there are things the body enjoys. The night nurse tells her that her father likes a little pot smoke blown in his face. "His blood pressure goes down, his digestion is better." Cheryl nods. The nurse blows a little smoke in her face, and she breathes deeply. He does it again. "I've also got edibles if you want some," he says.

On Thursday at 3:00 p.m., when the morning nurse has to leave for her shift in the ER and the three-to-midnight nurse is stuck in traffic coming from Orange County, Cheryl isn't worried.

"Not a problem," she says. "It's okay. I can be alone with my parents for an hour. Just go."

The morning nurse leaves, grateful. Cheryl, a little nervous, sits between her parents and then after a few minutes goes outside. She is out by the pool when the power goes off. It takes her a few seconds to realize what's happened. There's a peculiar absence of noise. Silence holds the air. The pool pump has stopped, the compressor for the air conditioner is hushed. Cheryl hurries inside; the clock on the microwave is dark, the television screen is flat black. There are high-pitched alarms, squeals like helium balloons coming from the living room. Her first impulse is to call Abigail, and then she remembers there is no more Abigail. She switches the alarms off, turns to her parents, and says, "I'm not sure you noticed, but the power went out. We've been having a heat wave, so it's probably a rolling blackout. There are backup batteries. You're currently at ninety-five percent. All is good. I'm just going to step outside for a minute and see if I can learn more."

Cheryl goes out the front door, wanting to confirm that the blackout is not theirs alone. A man in a white hazmat suit is wandering down the middle of the street, swinging what looks like an incense box in front of him, back and forth like a priest at Christmas. "Has anyone seen my queen?" he cries. "My queen has flown away!" She realizes it's the neighbor. "Stay inside!" he shouts. "The swarm is loose!" She hears the air buzzing and quickly closes the door.

She sends Burton a text, but it bounces back. She calls the nurse stuck in traffic from her cell phone, but the call doesn't go through. She walks from room to room looking for a landline. In Abigail's closet she finds a powder-blue Princess phone. It feels lighter than she remembers a phone feeling. She turns it over—the bottom is covered with duct tape. She peels it off; the insides of the phone have been removed. Four loose joints fall out. She can't reach Walter.

The house gets warmer and starts to smell of urine and shit. Cheryl opens the glass doors. There are birds outside, the sounds of dogs barking, children playing in a pool, a woman talking in the distance.

Meanwhile, the red and green lights blink and the machines continue to breathe for her mom and dad. The IV bags keep dripping. And her parents, Sylvia and Ben, remain unchanged, their bladders emptying into the plastic containers at the ends of the beds. Cheryl keeps thinking she should do something, but there is nothing to be done.

An hour later, as the backup batteries begin to fade, Cheryl gets the favorite book from her childhood, sits in the Barcalounger between her parents, and begins to read aloud. When she is done, she takes her father's right hand and her mother's left and draws them to her, holding them close, on her chest, over her heart, praying, waiting.

# Acknowledgments

Collections of stories happen over time—in this case a very long time and so there are many to thank.

The artists and those who inspired the stories in order of appearance: Eric Fischl, Sarah Jones, Halimah Marcus, Electric Literature, Gretta Johnson, Ghada Amer, Larry Gagosian, Koen van den Broek, Dan Miller, Exhibit-E, Bill Owens, Petah Coyne, Mass Moca, Hannah Tinti, One Story.

Andrea Schulz, Paul Slovak, and Emily Neuberger at Viking; Sigrid Rausing and Bella Lacey at Granta; Andrew Wylie, Sarah Chalfant, Charles Buchan, and Jin Auh at the Wylie Agency.

To the people and places who make writing possible: Jeanette Winterson, Sandi and Debbi Toksvig, Helena Kennedy—for making sure it got done. Andre Balazs, Phil Pavel, Priscilla Washam, the Chateau Marmont and the Mercer Hotel, and Sigrid Rausing again for providing me with a home when I literally had none.

Elaina Richardson, Candace Wait, and the Corporation of Yaddo. The Lewis Center for the Arts at Princeton University. My very patient and wise advisers Faith Gay, Mark H. Glick, and Stephen Breimer.

Marie Sanford, Juliet Homes, Jon Homes, and my beloved mother, Phyllis Homes, for always being there.

And the very good friends, whose hearts have supported me: Steven Harris and Lucien Rees-Roberts, Ann Tenenbaum, Rosanne Cash, Deborah Berke, Laurie Anderson, Anne Carson, Robert Currie, Jim Cass, Lynne Tillman, Leon Falk, Ali Tenenbaum Phyllis Housen, Matthew Weiner, Hyatt Bass, Jane Fine, Phil Klay, RL Goldberg, Amy Hempel, Jill Ciment, Amy Gross, and Claudia Slacik. And when one realizes how deep the threads of these stories go: Amy Godine, Rabbis Linda Motzkin and Jonathan Rubenstein at Temple Sinai in Saratoga Springs, Margot Tenenbaum, Rabbi Andy Bachman, Amy Zimmerman, and Rabbi Angela Warnick Buchdahl in NYC—because sometimes you need to check in with an authority figure.

## THE SAFETY OF OBJECTS

This extraordinary first collection of stories by A. M. Homes confronts the real and the surreal on even terms to create a disturbing and sometimes hilarious vision of the American dream.

"Wonderfully skewed stories . . . Sharp, funny, and playful." –Amy Hempel, *Los Angeles Times*

## THE MISTRESS'S DAUGHTER

A *New York Times* **Bestseller**

Daring, heartbreaking, and startlingly funny, this is Homes's ruthlessly honest account of what happened when, thirty years after she was given up for adoption, her birth parents came looking for her.

"An unflinching, smart, and intensely compelling book." –Maureen Corrigan, *Fresh Air*

## THIS BOOK WILL SAVE YOUR LIFE

Set in Los Angeles, this vivid, uplifting, and revealing novel tells of a selfish, idle, and lonely man's reconnection with the world around him.

"An absolute masterpiece . . . Homes writes ecstatically, and like no one else." –*The Philadelphia Inquirer*